MALAFORMED
REALITIES

VOLUME NINE

THOMAS M. MALAFARINA

HELLBENDER
BOOKS

an imprint of Sunbury Press, Inc.
Mechanicsburg, PA USA

an imprint of Sunbury Press, Inc.
Mechanicsburg, PA USA

For information about special discounts for bulk purchases, please contact Sunbury Press Orders Dept. at (855) 338-8359 or orders@sunburypress.com.

To request one of our authors for speaking engagements or book signings, please contact Sunbury Press Publicity Dept. at publicity@sunburypress.com.

FIRST HELLBENDER BOOKS EDITION: January 2025

Set in Adobe Garamond Pro | Interior design by Crystal Devine | Cover design by Lawrence Knorr | Edited by Lawrence Knorr.

Publisher's Cataloging-in-Publication Data
Names: Malafarina, Thomas M., author.
Title: Malaformed realities volume 9 / Thomas M. Malafarina.
Description: First trade paperback edition. | Mechanicsburg, PA : Hellbender Books, 2025.
Summary: Thomas Malafarina strikes again with 20 spine-tingling tales of horror.
Identifiers: ISBN 979-8-88819-270-2 (softcover).
Subjects: FICTION / Horror | FICTION / Short Stories (single author).

Designed in the USA
0 1 1 2 3 5 8 13 21 34 55

For the Love of Books!

As with all my books,
I dedicate this book to my
incredible and lovely wife, JoAnne.
She is my everything and
without her, I could not be me.

CONTENTS

Introduction ... 1

Gone ... 3
38 Caliber ... 10
Nepenthes Rajah (A Norliss Tapes Story) ... 26
Smudge Pot ... 36
Space Girl ... 46
Leather Apron ... 62
Mausoleum ... 70
Subhumans ... 82
Because ... Just Because ... 93
The Leaper ... 100
Scrambled Eggs ... 108
The Thing About Barbie ... 115
Lincoln Prescott ... 120
Tail Gunner Joe ... 133
Sweet Jane ... 143
Soul Soup ... 154
Bullet Points ... 160
The Box ... 165
Iron Beard, Scourge of Dead Man's Pass ... 180
The Traveler ... 196

INTRODUCTION

Welcome to the ninth edition of my short story collection series, so accurately called Malaformed Realities. As of the completion of this book, *Volumes 1* through *8* are in publication and available from Sunbury Press. *Volume 10* is currently underway. In fact, *Volumes 11, 12, 13,* and *14* are already in process.

That's the thing about creativity. The stories and ideas keep coming, and there is nothing people like me can do but put the stories down on paper and eventually send them out there for you fine and dedicated readers to enjoy. This edition has quite a mixed bag of stories and subject matters, from horror to Sci-Fi to fantasy to just plain weird.

From time to time, different publishers contact me, asking me to submit stories to whatever anthologies they happen to be publishing. Sometimes, the requests are for general horror stories; other times, the requests might be for a specific topic or concept. Occasionally, I get requests for sci-fi, fantasy, and even humorous stories. Always up for a new challenge, I try to provide what they need. Sometimes, the projects come to fruition; other times, they fizzle out and never happen. Either way, I would like to share those stories with my readers through these anthologies.

And then there are my muses that seem to get great pleasure bombarding me with ideas, usually so many that I scarcely have time to put them all down. When one of these antagonistic imaginary sprites hits me with one of their thoughts, and it's something I think might be worth writing, I find a place for it on my "to-do" list. It's quite common for me to start working on a story or book and then leave it to work on something else for a while. Later, when that particular pixy starts yelling at me to get back to it, I'll pick it back up and write some more. I don't like forcing a story to be finished; I prefer it to flow freely and as naturally as possible. I have said in many interviews that I try never to plan a story but to let it happen. I like being as surprised with the direction a story takes as much as the reader will be. Writing a story should be like watching a movie for the first time; I have no idea what will happen next. That's just how I roll.

So, as you read these stories and ask yourself, "I wonder why he wrote this one," you'll realize the various possible inspirations for its creation. I hope you find this collection of my short stories as interesting and enjoyable as you have found the others.

THOMAS M. MALAFARINA
January 2025

GONE

The streets were deserted. Then again, they were always empty these days, as were the houses, apartments, office buildings, and stores. Everything was abandoned because all the people were gone. Charles had no idea what had happened to them or why everyone had disappeared. Nor did he have any idea where they all might have gone. All he knew was that he was alone, and as far as he could tell, he was the only person alive on Earth.

It was all so strange the way everyone had disappeared. It didn't happen all at once. One day, it seemed to Charles that the streets were less crowded with people and traffic. Then, a few days later, the crowd seemed to thin more. Eventually, after a month or so, Charles couldn't find a single human alive anywhere.

For a time, he wondered if the long-prophesied rapture had finally occurred when all the faithful were to be lifted up into Heaven. That theory had a few holes in it, however. For example, if the people had been taken, wouldn't their clothing still be here? Charles was certain there would be no need for Earthly coverings in Heaven. He had once read a book based on this rapture idea; all clothing, jewelry, eyewear, and such were supposed to remain here after the chosen were lifted up.

And speaking of the chosen, Charles was sure that only those chosen by God would be taken in the rapture, and the others deemed not worthy would remain behind. Yet everyone was gone but him, which made no sense at all. Charles knew he might not be Heaven's first choice for a one-way rapture ticket, but he didn't believe he was bad enough to be left behind. Not to mention being the only person on Earth not taken. Charles knew plenty of folks much worse than himself. He had defended many of them.

Charles Harrington was a defense attorney and a well-paid attorney as well. That is to say, he had been until everyone disappeared. Now, he had no idea what his profession was. Being a successful lawyer is difficult when your current and potential clients have vanished. Charles supposed now he was nothing more than a glorified hermit of sorts.

He no longer bothered to live in his high-priced luxury apartment. Charles felt the empty building was spooky, with no one else around. Also, with no one to operate the electric, water, and sewage treatment facilities, Charles had no idea how long the utilities would remain active. He supposed there would be no power for lights, elevators, air conditioning, cooking, or refrigeration at some time. So, he figured he had better get ahead of the curve and start learning to fend for himself.

He had no idea why the lights were still on, why the toilets were flushing, and why buildings seemed to still have heating and air conditioning. Logic dictated that sooner or later, this had to end. Since the city where he resided was in northern Florida, and the climate was not too severe, Charles could live comfortably in the community park. Most of the time, he slept out in the open, under the stars. When it rained or got too hot or chilly, Charles had a makeshift shelter under an overpass by a local river. He realized if things were still normal, some people might consider his current lifestyle a fall from grace for such a well-known and respected attorney. However, things were far from normal, and there were no people to judge him any longer.

If there wasn't a rapture, then where did everyone go? For the past several months, Charles struggled to come up with an explanation for what had happened to everyone. However, his efforts produced minimal results.

Another aspect of this situation made absolutely no sense to him. He couldn't figure out why everything in the supply chain seemed to function as if nothing had happened. Fresh fruits, vegetables, meats, dairy products, and other perishable foods should be spoiling on the shelves. How could there be a continuous resupplying of new goods if no people were around to do the work?

Before people started disappearing, Charles remembered he had gone into a bodega in the park and bought a quart of milk. The sell-by date on that container was May 15th. It was now the end of July, and he went into the same bodega and looked at the milk, expecting it to be outdated and spoiled. However, it had an August 12th sell-by date. But that was impossible. If there were no people to milk the cows, process the milk, package it, distribute it, and then sell it, how could it be fresh?

The same was true of many other packaged foods and drinks. Charles picked up a loaf of bread that morning, and it, too, had a mid-August sell-by date. Yet Charles knew everyone had disappeared from the planet more than three months earlier. He often watched the bodega closely to hopefully see who or what might be resupplying them but never saw anyone.

For whatever unknown reason, Charles had everything he ever needed right within the safe confines of the park. As grateful as he was for that strange and unfamiliar fact, Charles realized he was something of a prisoner in the park.

This was another thing that Charles found disturbing and unexplainable about this strange set of circumstances. He encountered a weird humming sound whenever he tried to leave the city park area. It was a deep throbbing sound that surrounded the park like an invisible force field. At one time, the street that produced this sound would have been busy with traffic, and the park would have teemed with people. Now, there was no one, and that humming sound and the strange invisible barrier were in place of the traffic.

On two occasions, Charles had tried to walk away from the park toward the abandoned street encircling the grounds. As he attempted to step off the curb into the street, he was thrown backward with such force that he landed on his backside in the grass, not understanding what had forced him there. Luckily, there were plenty of small stores and food stands scattered around the park, or Charles never would have been able to survive.

Although he wracked his brain for weeks imagining everything, including space aliens, Charles could never come up with a plausible reason for why everyone had gone. He understood that he would likely never get his questions answered, and he would have to accept this was his life from now on. Charles found himself talking aloud to himself quite a bit these days. It wasn't something he ever did before, but he felt it helped with the loneliness of isolation, and he hoped it might keep him from going insane.

* * *

"Who the Hell is that loony?" Police officer Pete Jenkins said. He was new to the precinct and had been paired up with a veteran street cop, Joe O'Donnell, who was showing him the beat. They were presently strolling through the city park, and Pete had just seen a strange, disheveled old man standing near a group of people talking to himself. The people were doing their best to steer clear of the obviously disturbed man.

Joe said, "That guy? Oh, that's just Crazy Charlie. He's a homeless guy who lives in a tent under the 5th Street overpass. He's harmless."

"What's his deal? Who's he talking to? It's kinda spooky."

"Not to worry, Pete. He's just talking to himself; he does it all the time. Although that might seem weird, it isn't as strange as the story behind the reason he is why he is that way."

"Story? What's story is that, Joe."

"The truth of it is, Crazy Charlie can't see any of us. He believes he's alone in the world, and the rest of us don't exist."

"That's really weird, Joe. You mean to say he can't see that woman standing right next to him?"

"Nope. He can't see or hear her."

"You gotta be kidding me, Joe."

"Nope, I'm being completely serious. As far as Charlie is concerned, we don't exist."

"But there are hundreds of people around, adults and kids, all making tons of noise. What about all the traffic? You mean to tell me he doesn't see any of that that either?"

"Hard as it is to believe, Pete, none of that exists in Charlie's mind. As far as he's concerned, he's alone."

"But how does he keep from walking out in front of a car or truck? It's really busy out on the street. If he steps out onto the street, he'll get smooshed."

"Charlie never leaves the grass or the walkways in the park. In fact, he never leaves the park at all."

"Never?"

"Not as far as I know. I remember a few months back, Charlie went to step off the curb right in front of a bus. I grabbed him by his shirt, pulled him back, and he landed on his butt in the grass. Since then, he seems to prefer to stay in the park."

"So why is he here? How'd he end up a homeless dude?"

"Who knows for sure with these street people? They all got mental issues, the bunch of them. I did hear a story about old Crazy Charlie, though. I did a bit of research back at the station and found some interesting stuff about him."

"Really, Joe? Do tell. Do tell."

"Well, old Charlie over there used to be a big-time defense attorney."

"No kidding? That rumpled and filthy old coot?"

"Yep. And that much is true 'cause I looked it up. The dude used to make mega bucks, had a penthouse apartment, and drove a high-end Mercedes-Benz sedan and everything."

"Wow, how the mighty have fallen. So what happened to him, Joe?"

"Apparently, he was driving around this very park right out there on that road," Joe said, pointing at the busy roadway. "A little kid, no more than three, ran out in front of him, and Charlie couldn't help but hit him. I read the accident report; there was nothing Charlie could've done to keep from killing the kid."

"Whoa, that sucks," Pete said with a sigh.

"Well, after that, old Charlie went into a downward mental spiral until he eventually went royally nuts. His wife left him, and he lost everything in the divorce because he just didn't care anymore. From what I heard around town, Charlie gradually withdrew from the world and people in general. He got to the point where now he believes everyone else in the world is gone and he's alone. I guess his brain did this as a what-do-ya-call-it, some kinda survival thing. Whatever the case, he has no idea any of us are here."

"What happens if you try to talk to him?"

"He doesn't hear you, Pete. Or if his ears do hear, his brain won't allow him to know it. It's hard to figure out. The bottom line is that Charlie lives in the park and has become a sort of accepted fixture among the vendors and bodega owners. He stops by their businesses occasionally and might take a pint of milk, a can of soda, or small stuff like that, and they just let him do it."

"Shouldn't we bust him for stealing?"

"Nah! Nobody will press charges, and what the Hell would we do with him anyway? It's obvious that he's nuttier than a fruitcake, but he's harmless. Besides, with the city shutting down all their cracker factories, wack-a-doodles are wandering around homeless all around the town, and most of them are ten times crazier and more dangerous than Charlie will ever be."

"So we do nothing?"

"We do nothing. One of these days, we'll probably get a call that poor old Charlie was found dead in a bush somewhere, and then we'll send his carcass to the morgue."

"Sad man, really sad."

"Yep, Pete. Just one more sad story among thousands in this sad city."

* * *

Charles walked over and sat on a vacant bench; then again, all the benches were empty now that he was alone in the world and everyone was gone.

38 CALIBER

"I say a murder is abstract. You pull the trigger, and after that, you do not understand anything that happens."
—JEAN-PAUL SARTRE

"Murder is like potato chips: you can't stop with just one."
—STEPHEN KING

"Murder is an inherently evil act, no matter what the circumstances, no matter how convincing the rationalizations."
—BENTLEY LITTLE

/ 1 /

The knock on the kitchen screen door came unexpectedly that dark, cold October night in 1965. Anthony never imagined having a visitor so late in the evening. It was well past midnight, and he and his young wife, Elizabeth, were already sleeping. She was eight months pregnant with their first child and seemed exhausted most of the time. Anthony had done his best to adapt to her schedule as well.

Sleepily, Anthony turned on the overhead light, shuffled to the kitchen door, and, in the glow of his back porch light, saw his elderly father standing there, looking like he bore the weight of the world on his shoulders. Gino De'Angelino was an Italian immigrant who came to the US in 1935, leaving his friends and family far behind, to find work in Pennsylvania.

Gino had married a local woman of German descent, who had given him five sons and four daughters before dying in childbirth with the youngest, Mary, who was the only sibling still living with her father in the family homestead. The others had grown up and married yet still lived in or just outside the nearby town.

"Pop?" Anthony asked, "What are you doin' here at this hour? Are you ok, Pop?"

In broken English, Gino said, "I donna know, Anthony. I gotta a bigga problem. I needa youa to helpa me."

"Of course, I'll help you with anything, Pop. Come in and sit down. Tell me what's wrong." As Gino walked past his son, Anthony noticed his father was carrying something wrapped in a brown leather cloth.

Gino set the item on the kitchen table, where it made a dull thud, indicating something of some substantial weight was inside. Gino slowly began unwrapping the leather cover, revealing a shiny revolver.

"What's that?" Anthony asked, not certain he wanted to actually learn the answer.

"It's a 38. A pistola. Ita belonga to youa brother, Carlo. Datsa da problem." Gino said regrettably.

"Of course, that's the problem, Pop. Carlo's always the problem. What did he do this time."

"He doa somtina really stupida, Anthony. He shoota Vito Vanetti's boy."

Anthony asked in disbelief, "Santo Vanetti? Are you saying Carlo shot Santo Vanetti? Where the Hell did Carlo get a gun, Pop?"

"I donna know, Anthony. But hea gota one, disa one."

"Is he . . . Is Santo dead, Pop?"

"Yesa, Anthony. Santo's dead. Day wasa fighta over somea woman or someatina like that, and Carlo shoota hima dead."

"Why would he do such a thing? Carlo is troublesome and has a temper, but I know him. He would never shoot someone, Pop."

Gino said, "Hea say, hea don't knowa why he shoota Santo. Hea donna remember anything. Carlo donna evena remember where hea gotta da guna. Hea say there wasa somea voice ina his head. Ita wasa like someone elsea pulla da trigger."

Anthony didn't believe the story Carlo had told for a minute. His brother was obviously lying to their father, not being willing to accept responsibility for the murder he had committed. That was typical of Carlo, always trying to blame someone or something for his own failings.

"With that gun, Pop," Anthony said as he pointed to the weapon. It was no longer a question. Then Anthony asked, "Why is that gun here, Pop? Why do you have it?"

Gino hesitated for a moment, then said, "Noa body see Carlo shoota Santo. Noa body know. I needa you toa makea disa gun disappear."

"Me? Why me, Pop? I can't be involved in this. I have a job, a wife, and a baby on the way. I'm not like my brothers. I don't get in trouble like they do. I don't want to get in trouble either. This isn't good, Pop."

"I knowa, Anthony. But I needa you toa do disa for me. The cops are gonna suspecta Carlo. Daya will eventually coma by my house to aska me about Carlo. I can't have the gunna inna case day wanna searcha."

"But you figure since the cops know I'm not like my brothers and have a normal life, that I won't know anything about the shooting. Is that right, Pop?"

"Datsa watta I tink."

"Pop . . . I . . . I can't do this. What if they come here asking me questions? What if they search my house and find this gun? I can't go to jail, Pop!"

"Daya wonta come. You hida the gun. Pleasea, Anthony. Doa dis fora you Poppa."

Anthony knew he had no choice. This was for family; it was all about blood. He looked over at the gun lying on the leather cloth on the kitchen table. He shook his head in frustration and said, "Ok, Pop. But this is between you and me. Don't tell Carlo or anybody that I'm doing this. It has to be our secret. You just tell him you got rid of the gun, ok?"

"Yesa. Anda tanka, you, Anthony. Youa a gooda boy to doa this for the family."

But Anthony didn't feel so good. He didn't feel good at all.

/ 2 /

After his father left, Anthony carried the wrapped 38 down into his cellar and back to an unfinished area with a small dirt crawl space no more than a foot and a half high. Using his hands, Anthony dug a small pocket deep enough to hide the gun. He suddenly realized he wanted to get a closer look at the weapon. Anthony had never held a gun in his life and had absolutely no idea how to use one. But he was curious.

He set the wrapped gun on his wooden work bench and carefully peeled back the leather layers, exposing the gun. Anthony was surprised to find the weapon was not as large as he thought it would be. It was silver and shiny with a black handle and had serrations, which he supposed were for gripping.

Anthony picked up the gun carefully, holding it by the grip and pointing it away from him. He felt a sensation of warmth in his hand, which slowly spread up his arm and seemed to emanate from the gun. He looked down at the gleaming weapon and thought, "My brother killed a man with this gun only a few hours ago. He took a young man's life, and now I'm holding that murder weapon in my hand."

"Yes, you most certainly are," a deep, sinister voice agreed.

Anthony turned around, looking for the source of that voice, but found himself alone in the cellar. Then he again heard the unfamiliar voice say, "Your brother killed a man tonight with this gun, and he found it was surprisingly easy, Anthony."

Anthony realized the voice he thought he was hearing was not coming through his ears but was somehow appearing in his mind.

The voice said, "It's your turn now, Anthony."

"My turn? My turn for what?" he said to the empty cellar.

"Well, that's easy, my friend. It's your turn to murder."

Anthony was stunned. Where had that voice come from? Why would it suggest he do such a horrible and unspeakable thing? Then he realized the voice in his head was coming from the gun he held in his hand.

"You can do it, Anthony. You need to track down your brother, Carlo, and blow his worthless brains out. I'll help you."

Anthony realized he was beginning to agree with the voice. Carlo had been nothing but trouble for years, and as horrible it was to say, if Carlo were killed, it would probably do the world a service. All Anthony had to do was take this gun, go to Carlo's apartment, and shoot him. It really was that simple. He had the gun; it was loaded, and all he had to do was point and shoot.

Then suddenly, Anthony snapped to his senses, wondering what in the world he had been thinking. Carlo may be troublesome, but he was Anthony's brother. There was no way he could murder his brother. In fact, he had no idea why he would ever be thinking such a thing. Then he recalled the warmth in his right hand and the voice that had appeared in his head. Anthony dropped the gun onto the leather cloth, and immediately, the sensation left his arm, and the voice vanished from his mind.

"What the Hell was that?" Anthony said to himself as he shook his head to clear his mind. He could no longer recall the thoughts he had but understood something was very wrong with the gun, something he couldn't explain, but something he sensed was evil. No wonder Carlo had shot Santo. Anthony knew Carlo was not as smart or strong as he was. He realized he would have to get rid of the gun first thing the next day, not just to hide evidence of what Carlo had done but to prevent the evil thing from causing any other harm.

Anthony rewrapped the gun and dropped it into the hole he had dug. Then he covered it with dirt, and after sprinkling loose stones on top, he stepped back to check out his work and was satisfied that even someone looking closely at the area wouldn't notice anything suspicious. Even though he would be getting rid of the gun the following day, he didn't want Elizabeth to accidentally stumble onto the thing, not that she ever came down into the cellar very often.

He went back into the kitchen and was washing the dirt from his hands when he heard someone coming up behind him. He knew without turning around that it was Elizabeth. Anthony had never lied to his wife before but knew he would have to do so this evening for no other reason than to keep her unaware of what had just happened, for her own protection.

"Did I hear your Pop talking to you? Is anything wrong?" She asked.

Anthony said, "Yeah, that was Pop, but nothing's wrong. At least nothing new."

"Leave me guess, Carlo?"

"Yeah, Carlo," Anthony replied.

"What did he do this time, Anthony? Rob a bank? Shoot somebody?"

Anthony was momentarily taken aback by the unfortunate accuracy of Elizabeth's statement. Then he regained his composure and said, "Um, no. It was nothing like that. Pop was just frustrated by Carlo getting into fights all the time. He stopped by to ask me to talk to him. You know, advice from his older brother."

"Do you honestly think Carlo will listen to you, Anthony?"

"Probably not; he never has before. But I promised Pop I would try, so that's what I'll do, probably tomorrow."

Elizabeth hugged Anthony and said, "You're a good big brother and a good son, Anthony. I only hope he listens to you this time."

"I do, too," Anthony said, wishing he had been less of a good son and brother this time, "So, let's see if we can get back to sleep. We both need our rest."

The couple returned to bed, and as Anthony suspected, Elizabeth fell asleep in no time. He, however, was a different story. Anthony was awake for hours trying to come to terms with what Carlo had done, what his father had asked of Anthony, and most importantly, what had almost happened to him in the cellar. As soon as he agreed to hide that 38, he became part of the mess, but he had no idea how bad things were. He was starting to believe he had imagined those frightening feelings he had sensed in the cellar. After all, the thing was just a gun, wasn't it?

Anthony was initially angry with Carlo for causing the problem and his father for asking him to help cover up such a horrible crime. But now, if what he thought he had sensed was real? Anthony understood how and why Carlo could have done what he had done. Still, Anthony was partially angry with himself for agreeing to help get rid of the gun and risking his future and everything he held dear. Knowing what he now sensed about the 38, Anthony devised a plan to get rid of the accursed thing as he lay in his bed, staring up at the ceiling. He felt confident his plan would work. Then again, it had to work; his future depended on it.

/ 3 /

The next day was a Sunday, which meant if Anthony wanted to ditch the gun permanently, this would be his best chance. He had already told Elizabeth he was going to talk to Carlo and would actually do that as soon as he completed his plan to get rid of the gun. Earlier that morning, while Elizabeth slept, Anthony retrieved the 38 from its hiding place in his cellar and wiped it clean of fingerprints using a cloth. He was careful not to let it touch the flesh of his hands. Several times while cleaning the gun, Anthony felt warmth start to spread into his hand, and he had to set the gun back down until the feeling went away. Anthony rewrapped the weapon and put it under the front seat of his car.

After breakfast, Anthony drove to one of the enormous abandoned strip mine pits that pock-marked the county. These massive holes in the earth were all that remained of the once prosperous strip coal mining industry. Locals had, for whatever reason, turned the gigantic pits into their personal garbage dumps. Anything from kitchen trash to small alliances to complete wrecked cars could be found at the bottom of these pits. What better place to make the weapon disappear forever?

The entire process took only him a few minutes. Anthony got out of his car with the leather-wrapped gun tucked under his coat. As a safety precaution, he wore gloves to handle the package. Anthony quickly walked into the pit until he found an area strewn with trash and several abandoned cars. Puddles of water and garbage sludge about a foot deep were scattered around the area.

Anthony picked a car with no tires, doors, or windows and a gaping hole in the driver's side floor, assuming exposure to the elements could only serve to help render the weapon useless. He dropped the 38 and its leather cover into the hole in the floor, happy to see it sink out of sight into the water-filled pocket below. Content that the gun would rust and eventually deteriorate in its watery grave, Anthony turned and walked back up the hill, out of the pit, and drove away.

Unfortunately, he hadn't taken the time to examine the other abandoned vehicles, or he might have seen the hobo sleeping in one of the cars nearby. That man had heard Anthony coming down the hill. The bum watched him from his hidden place inside one of the other cars. He noticed the package Anthony had put into the hole and decided to check it out when the coast was clear.

/ 4 /

Bob Larkin was what you might call a man who was down on his luck. Actually, that description would be too mild. Bob's life was in shambles, to put it bluntly. So much had changed in his world over the previous year. He had lost his job and then lost his home. Shortly after, his wife took what little remained of their meager savings, left him, and filed for divorce. Soon, the drinking started, and not long afterward, Bob found himself living on the street, drunk more often than not and begging for food and money.

As far as Bob was concerned, life had dealt him one raw deal after another, and he had given up. His residence was now a shell of a car at the bottom of an abandoned strip mine. It might not be the Hilton or, for that matter, Motel 6, but it did provide him with a modicum of shelter and gave him privacy, away from everyone and everything that seemed determined to cause him grief.

But something had happened that morning, and Bob had a feeling that whatever the stranger had put into that nearby car might be something he could use to change his luck. Bob might not be the sharpest bulb in the water, as he was fond of saying, but he was smart enough to recognize when someone was trying to stash something they didn't want anyone else to find. He wondered what might be in that leather wrap he saw the man dropping into the hole under that car. Bob imagined a sealed plastic bag full of money that the stranger was trying to hide. Maybe he had knocked over a gas station or liquor store and had to hide the money until things cooled off.

If that were the case, the stranger had just made the worst mistake of his life because Bob would relieve him of his burden. As he exited his car/home and trudged over to the other car, Bob was already fantasizing about how he would spend the stash of money. First, he would check into a local hotel and take a much-needed shower. Then, he would order room service or local take-out delivery and eat one of the best meals he had ever had in the past year. After a good night's sleep and maybe an excellent breakfast, Bob would get himself some new clothes as his current wardrobe was in tatters. Robert J. Larkin was about to go from "Hobo Bob" to "High-living Robert" overnight, which suited him just fine.

As he approached the vehicle, Bob looked around to ensure the stranger didn't double back to recheck his stash. Comfortable that he was alone, Bob bent down and reached into the hole in the floor. He felt the sudden cold of the water that filled the hole, and then his fingers grabbed what he was now sure was a leather-wrapped bag of money. At first, Bob was momentarily disappointed when he lifted the stash from the water and felt its weight. It wasn't a stash of cash; he was certain of that. But now, his mind began to wander again, and he imagined a brick of gold or perhaps a box full of jewelry.

Tucking the leather-wrapped parcel under his arm, Bob scurried back to his car so he could open the mystery package undisturbed. He was still concerned that if the item truly was valuable, the stranger might return to check on it. As he unwrapped the outer layers of the leather, Bob was disappointed at first when he saw the 38 resting beneath. Then he picked up the gun and felt a strange warmth begin to travel from his hand, up his arm, and eventually throughout his body. It felt good, and Bob began to feel strong for the first time in weeks.

"Hello, Bob," a voice said as it suddenly appeared in his head.

Unlike Anthony, Bob was not frightened or concerned. He was too busy feeling an inner strength surge through his body, which felt fantastic. Bob thought, "Hello, whoever you are. I feel amazing."

"It's no wonder you feel amazing, Bob, because you are amazing. Unfortunately, the rest of the world is full of idiots who have no idea how great you are."

"That's right," Bob said to no one.

"Nor do they appreciate how powerful you are."

"Me? Powerful?"

"Yes, Bob, my friend. You are the most powerful man in the world. Can't you feel the power flowing through your body?"

"I . . . I . . . yes, I can feel it," Bob cried.

"As long as you hold that gun in your hand, you will have great power, and no one can stop you."

"But, what can I do? I'm a homeless bum living in an abandoned car at the bottom of a strip mine."

"Not for long, Bob, my friend. Soon, you will be living on top of the world."

"But, how? I don't understand," Bob asked. For the first time, Bob was starting to question his sanity. Who the Hell was talking to him, or was he just imagining everything? But then he remembered the warmth and power he felt flowing through his body. He might be imagining the strange voice, but he was not imagining that feeling of strength.

"Your life is about to change, Bob, my friend. You are on your way to Easy Street. Just listen to what I have to say, follow my instructions, and you can leave this disgusting life behind."

Bob said nothing. He just nodded his head in understanding.

/ 5 /

Charley Murphy stood behind the counter of his service station that Monday morning after opening for business promptly at 9:00 am as he had done every day for the past twenty-five years. He was looking forward to starting this work week because he and his wife were taking a long-awaited vacation the following week. Charlie had arranged for his assistant, Jim, to run the station while he was gone. This was not something that Charlie had considered doing lightly, as he was extremely careful when it came to his business. He hadn't spent all those years building a base of satisfied customers to have that relationship ruined by someone who didn't share his passion.

However, Jim was a different story as he was a good employee and was interested in eventually buying the business from Charlie when he decided to retire. In fact, Charlie and Jim had been working with local lending institutions to help Jim build his credit rating and establish a relationship with those lenders so that when Charlie decided to retire, Jim would find the financial backing he needed. As far as Charlie was concerned, as soon Jim was ready to buy and had the money to do so, the business would be his, and Charlie could ride off into the sunset a happy man. He often fantasized that his dream retirement awaited just a few years away.

Charlie heard the familiar jingle of the customer alert bell hanging over his front door. At first, he thought it might be Jim coming in early since Jim usually showed up an hour or so after Charlie opened for business. But it wasn't Jim. Charlie looked up to see a disheveled-looking man in ragged clothing standing in front of the counter. The man had an overpowering stench of an unwashed body surrounding him like a vile cloud of revulsion. Always considerate of his customers' feelings, Charlie managed to maintain politeness despite the pall of stink surrounding the man.

"Good morning, Sir. How can I help you?" Charlie said, somewhat reluctantly.

The voice in Bob's head said, "Point the gun at him and tell him to give you his money."

Bob hesitated momentarily, appearing unsure of himself, then lifted the 38 and pointed it at Charlie's chest. "Give me all the money in your cash register."

Charlie was confused at first by what was happening and said, "Excuse me?"

"I said give me all the money in your cash register."

"Sir, it's Monday morning, and it's only 9:00. We've had no customers yet. There's almost no money in the cash register except for what little I have in there for change."

The voice told Bob, "Tell the idiot to open the register and take whatever he has."

"Open the register. I'll take whatever you have," Bob shouted.

Then Charlie recognized the disheveled man for the first time as Bob Larkin. He didn't know Bob well but had seen him around town. Charlie had no idea that Bob had sunk so low as to become the pitiful creature he saw standing before him.

Charlie decided to try to reason with him, "Look, I recognize you now. You're Bob Larkin. I haven't seen you in a while, but I can tell you've fallen on some hard times. If you'll just put the gun away, I'll be happy to give you a few bucks to help you out, Bob. But just stop pointing the thing at me. I can see your hands are trembling, and I really don't want you accidentally shooting me."

The voice told Bob, "He knows who you are. He'll call the cops the moment you leave. Kill him now, Bob. Kill him, or your life will be over."

Without thinking further, Bob pulled the trigger and shot Charlie through the heart. Charlie flew back against a rack containing supplies and fell to the floor. There would be no vacation for Charlie and his missus the following week and no retirement in his now-abbreviated future.

"Get the money. Get it now."

Bob tried to open the cash register only to discover it was still locked. Apparently, Charlie hadn't opened it yet that morning.

"I can't get it open," Bob shouted to the empty room. Then the realization of what he had just done hit him, and Bob cried, "Oh my God! I just killed a man! What have I done?"

The voice said, "You just showed that loser behind the counter what a real and powerful man you are. He looked at you like you were dirt under his shoe, but you showed him you are no one to be looked down upon."

Bob panicked and then shoved the gun into his pocket, and as soon as he did, the warm feeling and strength left his body. He ran out the door and down the street, stumbling, sobbing, and mumbling to himself, his mind broken. The service station was located near the outskirts of town and surrounded by a pine tree forest. Bob ran into the forest and stumbled from tree to tree until he eventually collapsed under the canopy of a large hulking pine.

His head began to clear. He looked around and saw that he was sitting in a forest of pine trees, but he had no idea how he had gotten there or why he was there. The last thing he remembered was waking up that morning and picking up the gun he had found the previous day. Then he vaguely remembered doing something bad but couldn't recall what it was. Bob noticed something was in his pocket that made a bulge. It was the gun he had found the previous day. He realized there was something wrong with that gun. Somehow, it had been responsible for the memory lapses he was experiencing.

Bob recalled picking up the gun for the first time and feel-ing warmth and strength surging through his body. Then there had been . . . what? There had been a voice. That was when his memories stopped. Then, he had awoken that morning and picked up the gun again. That was the last thing he could clearly remember, but he still felt something was wrong. He had vague flashes of images. There was something about a gas station and . . . and . . . nothing.

All Bob knew for certain was no matter how bad he had felt the previous day, there was something about that gun that made him feel even worse. He decided to get rid of the thing immediately. Bob reached into his pocket and grabbed the handle with two fingers. As he pulled the gun free, he immediately began to feel heat enter his fingertips. He heard a voice try to appear in his mind, but before it could speak, Bob threw the gun out into the woods, where he heard it thump on the ground somewhere far away.

Bob stood up and slowly walked out of the forest, heading back toward the strip mine pit he called home. As he walked, he noticed a commotion in the distance at the corner gas station. There were police cars, an ambulance, and many people standing around, some crying.

"I wonder what that's all about?" Bob said as he headed home to his car.

/ 6 /

Sammy Thompson and Franky Maloney were two kids who loved hanging out in the forest of pine trees. Every day of their summer vacation, the two boys would meet at the edge of what they called "The Pines" and spend most of the day climbing trees, relaxing on beds of pine needles, and sometimes sliding down those beds on sheets of cardboard. It was a hidden paradise and an escape from the summer heat under the canopy of shade.

The two fourteen-year-olds had been best friends for as long as either of them could recall and were as close as brothers, perhaps closer. Franky was the larger and more athletic of the two, but Sammy was the smarter. As one might expect, Franky excelled in all things athletic, while Sammy was the academic wizard. Instead of these differences driving the two apart, they complemented each other. When Franky needed help with his studies, Sammy was there to lend a hand, and when Sammy was being bullied by one of the many class psychopaths, Franky was there to lend a fist . . . or two.

The boys were walking in the forest the afternoon following the robbery at the gas station, discussing the event as it was the second bit of excitement to hit the area. A day earlier, police had discovered the body of Santo Vanetti, shot to death and left next to a dumpster behind one of the area's less-desirable bars. Then, that morning, Charlie, the guy who owned the service station, was shot to death as well. Before heading off to work, both of their parents told them to stay in the house and not to open the door for anyone. However, boys will be boys, as they say, and these boys snuck out and found their way to their favorite hangout.

"So, what do you think is going on around here, Franky?" Sammy asked.

"Beats me, Sammy, old boy. All I know is folks seem to be dropping like flies. First, that Santo dude gets offed, then Old Charlie at the gas station. It's weird, man, just weird."

Sammy said, "My Dad said that Santo dude was bad news. He said he was always drunk and getting into fights and stuff like that. I heard he also liked to screw around with married women and women with boyfriends."

"Well, that's one sure way to find yourself turned to dead meat," Franky said, laughing.

"Maybe so, Franky, but what about Charlie? He was just a nice old guy who never bothered anyone. As far as I know, he was married and never messed around."

Franky said, "Probably true. I suspect it was two different people. I figure Santo was done for by some jealous husband, and Charlie was shot by some drug-crazy maniac looking to rob him."

"What the heck is happening to our little town, Franky? Crap like this never happened before."

"My Pop always says the world is changing, and we are living in troubled times."

"He's right about that, Franky."

The boys walked over to their usual spot under one of the larger trees to sit down for a while. As they did, Sammy landed on something hard under the pine needles.

"Ow, my butt!" Sammy said.

"What happened?"

Sammy reached underneath his backside and said, "I don't know. I think I sat on a sharp rock or something. My butt hurts."

"Well, Sammy, old boy, I ain't about to kiss it and make it better," Franky said, laughing.

"Sometimes you are so gross, Franky."

"So, what the heck is it, Sammy, a rock or what?"

Sammy dug under the pine needles, and his hand touched something metallic. As soon as it did, Sammy felt warmth in his hand spreading up his arm and all around his body.

Franky noticed a strange, distant expression forming on his friend's face and knew something was wrong. He was about to ask Sammy if he was all right when the boy lifted a 38 pistol and blew Franky's brains all over the forest.

"Excellent work, Sammy. I knew you could do it," a voice said inside the young boy's head." Now we have to head home and kill your mother and your brothers and sisters. Can you do that, Sammy?

"Yes, I can do that," the boy said in a trance-like voice.

Sammy walked out of the forest, his clothing stippled with blow-back blood from killing his best friend and started walking home, the gun dangling from his right hand. He knew what he had to do, and he was going to do it.

/ 7 /

Joe Talmage knew he shouldn't be driving. It was early afternoon, and he was already half in the bag. He had a history of drinking and driving issues. He had previously lost his license and had no business driving sober or not. If the cops happened to pull him over in his current state, he would be on his way to jail before he had a chance to sober up. As a result of his current state, Joe didn't see the young boy walking like a zombie, step off the curb, and right into his path. Before he could react, Joe struck Sammy and sent him flying through the air.

Realizing what he had done, Joe got out of his car and noticed the boy's low-rise sneakers were still on the street, although the boy had been knocked out of them and traveling more than 10 feet through the air. Joe didn't know if the boy was still alive or dead, but either way, it didn't matter. He had no choice but to get out of there as quickly as possible. Joe looked around to see if there were any witnesses to his mistake and was pleased to see no one was around on the seldom-traveled street. That was when he saw something silver gleaming in the roadway, the sun reflecting off its shiny surface.

Joe bent down to examine the object and realized it was a gun. He picked it up, turned to go back to his car, and felt a warm strength coursing through his body. Then he heard a voice in his head.

"Hey there, Joe. Wow, you really are something, aren't you? You just made your first kill, even without my help. But I've got good news for you, Joe, old boy. You'll have many more kills under your belt very soon."

"Yes, I'll have many more kills very soon," Joe said in a monotone voice as he returned to his car, turned on the ignition, never letting go of the gun, and sped away.

NEPENTHES RAJAH

A Norliss Tapes Story

Author's Note: In September of 2022, my friends at Screaming Eye Press told me they would publish a series of new stories based on the premise of the 1973 made-for-television horror film The Norliss Tapes. *The movie was directed by Dan Curtis, written by William F. Nolan, and starred Roy Thinnes and Angie Dickinson. Having been distantly acquainted with William F. Nolan, I agreed to write a story as a tribute to him and his accomplishments. William is best known for writing the 1976 Sci-fi film* Logan's Run. *Below is my contribution to the project.*

Sanford T. Evans stared at the box on his desk, which had arrived earlier that day. The publisher didn't need to open it as he was certain what awaited inside. This was not just because of the name crudely scribbled in the upper left corner in place of the return address label. This wasn't his first rodeo, as he was fond of saying. He had received similar packages over the past several months, and none of them brought him anything but discomfort.

"Where the Hell are you, David?" Evans asked the empty office, thinking about his missing friend and writer, David Norliss.

Norliss had vanished earlier that year, 1973, and had left behind a series of cassette tapes that were verbal documentation of a book he was writing. The recordings were a chronological record of supposed supernatural events, including a reanimated dead man, corpses drained of all their blood, and a demon named Sargoth, a sculpture made with blood-infused clay brought to life by sorcery.

David Norliss had vanished from the world, and since then, Evans had received the mysterious packages. Each one contained a detailed recorded description of supernatural events Norless had encountered. Although most people believed Norliss was dead, Evans was sure his friend was still alive. This was not just because the name scrawled in the return address area was in Norliss's handwriting but because of a deep feeling Evans had in his gut.

Loyal to a fault, Evans walked over to his office door, closed it, pulled down the Venetian blinds separating him from his office staff, fired up a Lucky Strike, loaded the tape labeled 1, and pressed the play button. Looking at the date on the cassette label, Evans realized this recording had been made more than a year earlier than the one he had listened to after David's disappearance. He heard the voice of his missing author begin his dissertation.

* * *

This is David Norliss. Today is January 15, and it's 8:14 pm. I have a tale to tell that you will likely find hard, if not impossible, to believe. It is a story of botanical science gone horribly wrong. Had the tale ended differently, it would have changed the world as we know it forever.

I suppose it's best if I start at the beginning. On the morning of January 1, New Year's Day, I received a telephone call from a man identifying himself as Professor Jameson Sinclair. He claimed to be a professor of botany at Stanburgh University. He said he had made a discovery that would revolutionize plant growth, enhance farming, and eventually end world hunger. To say the least, I was intrigued. I agreed to make the three-hour drive north to meet Sinclair at his Stanburgh laboratory early the following day.

I began my trek northward shortly after 2 pm. Along the way, I wondered what sort of discovery the good Professor might have made. I had made a few calls the day before to verify that Sinclair was actually who he said he was. I encounter a lot of crackpots in my investigations into the occult and paranormal, to say the least. I needed to ensure Sinclair wasn't leading me on a wild goose chase. I couldn't afford to waste money on gas, not at thirty-seven cents a gallon. Times were tight. Then again, in my line of work, times are always tight.

Sinclair checked out. He had a doctorate in botany and taught several different horticultural science classes at the college where he was a tenured professor. The Professor had a reputation for being some-what strange and eccentric, but the man seemed legit other than a few quirks. So, I decided to meet with him and see what he had to show me. I arrived at the college around 5:30 pm, and after checking in at the visitors' center, I was given directions to his lab.

An elderly man in a white lab coat stood waiting when I arrived outside the lab as the sun began setting. Although I had no idea what Professor Sinclair looked like, I instantly recognized the stereotypical scientist with his bald head and a fringe of wild white hair sticking out in every direction. His Coke-bottle-thick glasses hung near the end of his nose while his eyes sparkled with intelligence and perpetual curiosity behind them.

"Mr. Norliss, I presume," Sinclair asked.

"Yes, Professor. But please, call me David," I said.

He replied, "Very well, David. Follow me."

Apparently, the only one of us to be addressed informally would be me since Sinclair didn't invite me to call him by his first name. Then, again, Professor suited him better than Jamison, Jamie, Jim, or perhaps Jimbo. For example, I wouldn't have felt comfortable walking up to him and saying, "Yo! Hey Jimbo, how they hangin'?" if you know what I mean.

I followed Professor Sinclair through two glass doors, past an unoccupied reception desk, and then down a long, dimly lit corridor. I realized it was likely that he and I were the only ones in the building that late in the day. As we approached a windowless steel door with a heavy-duty lock, I noticed something off to the right. It was a large, raised, soil-filled area crammed with various strange and interesting tropical plants. One plant, in particular, caught my attention.

The plant was large and looked like a Venus fly trap mated with a pelican and a toilet bowl. It was white and pink and had a wide opening at the top of a deep bowl, large enough for a small animal to crawl inside. It was filled with some sort of liquid. A natural lid was attached to the edge at 90 degrees to the bowl's rim like a hinge. As soon as I saw it, I imagined a curious rat or other small creature crawling up to take a drink.

"What is that plant?" I asked Sinclair.

"Oh, that? Well, that's a very interesting plant indeed. It's known as the Giant Montane Pitcher plant or Nepenthes rajah from the mountains of Borneo. It's the largest carnivorous plant known to exist in the world."

"Carnivorous? Really?"

"Oh yes, David. As you can see by its size, it's large enough to trap and consume animals as big as rats, although recent research suggests it doesn't do so very often. It will trap and eat small insects and such."

I was intrigued, "Wow, that's very interesting."

Sinclair continued, "It is. But what's even more interesting is that recent studies suggest that there is something it prefers to eating meat, and that's feces."

"You mean poop?"

"Yes. Specifically, the droppings of the mountain tree shrew. Scientists believe the plant has evolved to this shape for this special purpose. Like the Venus fly trap, the plant's nectar attracts bugs who fall into the liquid, where they drown, and the plant ingests them. But when there aren't enough bugs around to eat, the Pitcher plant is content to become a toilet for shrews. The juice it produces attracts the tree shrews, which use its bowl much the same way we use our toilets. As I'm sure you've noticed, the rim and the pitcher resemble one."

"But won't the plant capture and eat the shrew while it's, you know, doing its business?"

"Originally, it was thought that the plant's size and shape meant it would do so, but now we think differently. I suppose if a small animal were to fall into the liquid and drown, it would be consumed just as the plant does with insects. The bowls of the largest plants can hold up to two liters of liquid."

I suggested, "Good thing this plant isn't two or three times its size. It might be like that plant creature in that movie, Little Shop of Horrors." Then, I noticed the Professor looking strangely at me. I assumed it was because he was unfamiliar with the 1960s Roger Corman film, but I later learned that look represented something much more sinister.

He mumbled, "Well . . . um . . . yes, I suppose. Enough chit-chat; let's go into the lab. I have something I want to show you." He unlocked and opened the steel door.

I followed the Professor through the doorway, being sure to give myself a wide birth of the meat-eating plant. It wasn't that I didn't believe the Professor, nor is it to suggest this particular plant was large enough to do me any damage, but I've never been one to take unnecessary chances.

When we got inside the poorly lit lab, all sorts of internal alarms went off inside my brain. I started to question the logic of my coming there based on a phone call to meet with some potentially crackpot brainiac I didn't know from Adam. Perhaps it was because of the darkness, or maybe it was caused by the huge, silhouetted images I saw lurking in the shadows to my left and right. Whatever the reason, I was getting the heebie-jeebies big time.

I asked, "Ok, Professor. How about you show me this revolutionary advancement in farming, you discovered? You know, the one that will end world hunger."

From the darkness, I heard the Professor say, "Mock me if you must, David. However, I should point out that you weren't the first, and I'm certain you won't be the last."

Before I could respond, Sinclair walked over to an electric panel and flipped up the main breaker. It made that familiar clunking sound they all make. Suddenly, the front part of the room was awash with bright light, and as my eyes adjusted, I saw things come into focus that I would never have believed possible.

I saw a pumpkin patch overflowing with fresh, ripe pumpkins to my right. That might not seem special, but each pumpkin was as big as a Volkswagen van. You know, like hippies drove a few years ago. I couldn't believe my eyes. Then I looked to my left and saw corn stalks over forty feet tall, each with more than six ears of corn on each limb. And each ear was about five feet long and two feet around. I was stunned to the point of being struck dumb.

Sinclair said, "I'm sure you realize, David, most corn stalks only yield one, possibly two years of corn, but as you can plainly see, my stalks yield many more. Not to mention the incredible size."

I was too stunned to respond. The Professor said, "Walk with me, David. I have so much more to show you." We walked further into the darkness of the lab, and all along our travels were wooden poles with switches attached. Sinclair made a point of being theatrical as he turned on each bank of lights.

I saw more giant plants, trees, and tons of incredibly gargantuan fruits and vegetables in each section: pea pods as big as canoes, grapes the size of baseballs, and apples that looked like bowling balls.

Finally, after regaining my composure, I asked the Professor, "This is all so incredible. I've never seen anything like it in my life. But I have to ask, why did you call me? Why not call the TV station or some science magazines? You know, someone who can give your discovery worldwide recognition?"

He hung his head and said, "I can't do that now. You see, I have signed a non-disclosure agreement forbidding me to tell anyone but a few high-level government officials about my discovery. If I ever went to the media with this, it would destroy my reputation, and I'd never be able to continue my work here or anywhere, assuming I was not thrown into prison."

I was confused, "But Professor. You're showing me. Isn't that a breach of your contract?"

"Yes, I suppose in a way it is," he said. "But you're an independent paranormal researcher with no ties to any media service."

He still didn't make sense to me. I asked, "But what's to stop me from going to press myself?"

"Nothing, I suppose. But without proof, who would ever believe you? That's why I made sure you didn't bring your camera."

"So, why show me at all, Professor?" I asked.

He hesitated, then said, "Earlier today, the University insisted I give the same tour you are seeing to a group of government officials. I thought they would be as amazed as you were. However, their reaction was not what I had expected. They refused to see my research's great benefit for mankind. They called my work an abomination of science. They said they would return to Washington and recommend cutting all my funding, destroying my plants, and seizing my notes. That's why you are here, to witness my work. So that if anything happens to it or me, at least someone will know."

I said, "But that makes no sense whatsoever. Why wouldn't these officials want to encourage you to continue? What motivation would they have for not wanting to end world hunger?"

"Money and greed. Those are always the motivators. A world filled with well-fed, comfortable citizens is a content world, not a hungry world. It is a world where more people would be free to pursue interests, becoming a well-informed, well-educated population. To control them, those who wield power must maintain a large portion of the world in hunger, ignorance, and poverty. These officials know about such things and saw my work as a threat to their power."

"So, what will you do, Professor."

He hesitated, "I've already done all I can do for now to deal with these individuals. I will continue my work until someone else tries to stop me."

Sinclair had a strange gleam in his eyes when he talked about dealing with the officials, one I didn't care too much for. Then, I noticed a large set of double doors on the back wall of the giant room. I asked, "Professor, where do those doors lead?"

"Oh, that. That's just a utility closet. Nothing special. You have no need to look in there."

Then I heard a telephone ring loudly, the sound coming from the opposite side of the room.

The Professor said, "That's the phone in my office. I'd better get that. It might be important. Why don't you look around some more and enjoy my beautiful plants while I take care of that call."

Things would have turned out much differently had I just listened to what Sinclair suggested, but doing what I'm told is not how I operate. I was suddenly very curious about those double doors and the supposed utility closet behind them. I believed the Professor was lying to me about that. Don't ask me to explain why; it was just a gut feeling

I had. I looked back toward Sinclair's office and saw him still busy talking animatedly on his desk phone through the open doorway. He appeared to be in a heated discussion with someone.

I walked casually over to the doors and turned the knob on the right door. It was unlocked. I opened the door wide enough to sneak through and closed it quietly behind me. The room was pitch dark. I felt for a light switch but couldn't seem to find one. There was a strange smell in the air. It was something earthy yet sweet, like decaying vegetation with a hint of something else, some underlying foul stench.

Like everyone else I know, I'm a smoker, and I always carry a cigarette lighter with me, so I figured the lighter would provide me with enough light to at least see something. I clicked it on and waved the flame around the room. From what I could tell, it wasn't any utility closet but was another large room similar to the lab I had just left, about a third of the size, although the ceiling appeared just as high. I couldn't see much in the darkness around me, but I thought I noticed movement in the shadows, slow, creeping motion, and thought I heard a low, deep guttural moaning or growling sound.

To my surprise, as I held the lighter toward the floor, I saw an overturned table and a mountain of papers scattered around. Then I saw a pile of clothing consisting of several business suits, one of which was a military dress uniform adorned with many medals. The clothing was riddled with bullet holes and large deep-crimson blood patches. I suddenly realized how the good Professor had dealt with his visitors. My gut clenched, and I thought I might be sick for a moment. But then I wondered what he had done with the bodies. This guy was no spring chicken, and the odds of him getting rid of several dead bodies were not very good. I had visions of a mad botanist chopping up corpses into tiny pieces for fertilizer. But that, too, would be more work than an elderly academic could handle. Then, the room was suddenly filled with a blinding light.

I saw the Professor standing in the doorway, with both doors open wide. He held a pistol in his hand and pointed it right at me.

"Oh, David, David. I told you to ignore this room, but you didn't listen. You have no idea how sorry I am to find you here."

"What the Hell happened in here, Professor? What did you do?"

He looked down at the scattered papers and bloodstained clothing and said, "I did what I had to do. As you can see, there was a bit of a struggle, and my papers were scattered all over the place. Those officials were going to shut down my project. I couldn't let that happen, David. My work is important to the betterment of humankind, but all these people cared about was maintaining their wealth and power. I couldn't let that happen."

I asked, "But the bodies. What did you do with the bodies?"

He said, "Turn around and see for yourself, David. Behold the new and improved Nepenthes rajah!"

I slowly turned around and saw what Sinclair wanted me to see. It was a much larger version of the plant I had seen outside the laboratory, perhaps ten times as large. And this plant wasn't standing motionless, waiting for some small animal to crap in its bowl. This thing was moving around like it had a mind of its own. The lid and the bowl formed a type of mouth, and this creature had somehow become equipped with many rows of shark-like teeth. It also had dozens of vine-like tentacles that were moving slowly toward me. I now knew why the Professor had reacted to my Little Shop Of Horrors comment. What he had here was much worse than anything the film depicted.

"You were wondering what I did with the bodies, David. I did the only thing I could do: feed them to my very special project. You weren't supposed to see this. You were supposed to be the one who would witness my other achievements. But now it seems you will have to join the others and become food for my baby."

I didn't take the time to think; I just turned back and charged the Professor. I managed to knock the gun out of his hand, but not before it discharged and shot him in the leg. Blood spurted from the wound, and Sinclair slumped to the ground. Before I realized what was happening, several long green tentacles wrapped around the Professor's torso and began pulling him upward toward the gaping maw of the carnivorous monster plant. I started to back away from the screaming Professor as he was pulled inside the dripping mouth of the beast. Then I smelled smoke.

I realized I must have neglected to close the lid on my lighter and had dropped it in the struggle. The mountain of papers had become a blazing inferno. The flames had lept onto dried leaves and debris at the base of the monstrous plant and rapidly found their way along its vines. To my shock, the plant began screaming like a wounded animal with a high-pitched, keening cry. I turned and fled the room into the main laboratory, then through the lobby and onto the street. As I stood gasping for air by the side of my car, I turned and was shocked to see the flames had spread throughout the laboratory, and the entire facility was engulfed in fire.

Everything in the lab was destroyed by fire: every plant, every note, and any proof of the Professor's experiments. This recording is the only documentation of what I saw that night, and of course, no other verification exists. It will be up to you to decide whether you believe me. David Norliss . . . out.

* * *

Stanford Evans pressed the stop button on the tape machine and sat staring at it for a few minutes. Once again, he wondered what had happened to his friend, David Norliss. Was David still alive, and if so, where was he? How long would Evans continue to receive these recordings of strange events, and what bizarre happenings could he expect to hear about on future recordings? So many unanswered questions. Evans turned and left the office, switching off the light as he headed home.

SMUDGE POT

"It's hard to believe you're gone, Frankie." The thin old man said as he sat on the edge of his worn and tattered sofa, wearing a dirty yellowed wife-beater tee shirt and faded plaid boxers. His head hung down, and his hands dangled between his legs. The ashes from his half-smoked cigarette fell to the thread-bare carpet to join the ashes from the last five cigarettes he had lit but never got around to smoking. An empty pint bottle of rot-gut bottom-shelf whiskey lay on its side on the carpet, its last remnants of that less-than-desirable brew turning the tan carpet brown.

Frank Warwick and George Newton had been friends for as long as either could remember. They grew up together in the small Pennsylvania town and lived there their entire lives, and now Frank had died there after a long and painful illness. The actual cause of his death was lung cancer, but no one in town ever used the term cancer. They preferred to say that George was "sick" instead as if to suggest saying the word cancer aloud and acknowledging its existence would cause it to spread throughout the town like a plague. Sometimes, small towns could breed small, superstitious minds.

Earlier that day, Frank had been laid to rest next to his parents, his infant son, Charles, a few other relatives, and hundreds of former town folks he had never known in the Protestant cemetery at the edge of town. Despite the town's small size, it did manage to have two cemeteries, one for Catholics and one for Protestants. The Protestant cemetery was also home to former Catholics who had left the church, excommunicated, or committed suicide and were refused burial on sanctified Catholic soil. The Protestants didn't seem to mind taking in the outcasts, so it became an accepted practice somewhere along the line.

Frank was neither a Catholic, a former Catholic, nor a suicide victim unless you're willing to consider a 55-year three-pack-a-day habit of smoking unfiltered Camels suicide, which many people might. Truth be told, he wasn't much of a churchgoer either. He was technically on the membership rolls at the Presbyterian church on North 9th Street but hadn't seen the inside of the place since he and the former Sally O'Toole had tied the knot there some 49 years earlier. He had been waked from the church earlier that morning. His wife, now a widow, had attended church services on special occasions throughout the years and maintained their membership.

During their years together, the two had only produced one child, poor Charles Edward Warwick, who died of crib death while only a few months old. After that, neither Frank nor Sally desired to have other children. They managed to keep their marriage together throughout the years after their loss and live what most would consider a normal life, but Frank was never quite the same after baby Charles passed away. They owned a nicely maintained row home on Market Street and, by all appearances, were a typical small-town couple. Frank had always had a good job at a local factory and retired a year or so earlier with a comfortable pension.

However, Frank's best friend, George Newton, was an entirely different story. He never married, rarely dated, or was never seen around town in the company of women. Some rumors suggested that George had been involved with several married women throughout the years, but there was no evidence to support those accusations. The truth was, George liked his almost hermit-like reclusive existence of solitude in his rundown house on the poor side of town.

No one ever told George how he should live or dress. He ate and drank what he wanted when he wanted and smoked as few or as many cigarettes as he chose. That all suited him just fine. His house was not much more than what might be considered a decrepit shotgun shack in a part of town that most local residents felt would be better served by wrecking balls and bulldozers. George never held a regular job to speak of and had no visible means of support, Yet he always managed to do the minimum required to pay his taxes and maintain ownership of the property.

Yet despite their radical differences as adults, Frank and George maintained their life-long friendship. Although Sally was not a fan of George's situation and might have secretly harbored fears that Frank was envious of his friend's free-wheeling lifestyle, she never tried to come between the two. During the past six months, she was glad she allowed the friendship to continue as George had been very good at helping out during her husband's long illness. Because of how upset George had been at Frank's funeral, Sally assumed that George would be hitting the bottle fairly heavily that day, and she was right.

The next morning, George awoke in an extremely uncomfortable position, lying face down, half on and half off his tattered sofa. His back, legs, and arms ached almost as badly as his throbbing skull. Through blurry eyes, he saw his last cigarette had fortunately burned out without setting the alcohol-soaked carpet on fire.

"Oh boy, Frankie. I coulda' been comin' to join you in the hereafter last night, but I s'pose it ain't my time yet," George said aloud through a nervous chuckle, realizing how his drunken carelessness could have resulted in his being burned to death. "Thank goodness somebody's watching over me. Maybe it's you, Frank. If so, then thanks for the save, my old friend."

George got off the sofa and, after waiting for blood to flow back into his pins-and-needles legs, stumbled to the bathroom with the hopes of brushing the whiskey-saturated night out of his teeth and taking a much-needed shower might make him appear at least somewhat presentable. It had been a long time since he showered two days in a row, and George had no intention of making a habit of such things. But Sally had asked him to stop by, and he had reluctantly agreed to do so. The fact was, George had no more love for Sally than she had for him.

Shortly after noon, George stood on the front porch, ringing the doorbell at the home of his once best friend, Frank Warwick. George had done this many times before, but it seemed strange to be doing so with his friend just one day on the wrong side of the dirt. George supposed that no matter what Sally might want from him, he would have to agree with him out of respect and, yes, love for his dead friend.

Sally opened the front door, and George stood staring at the woman, unsure what to say. He cast his eyes downward and said, "You asked me to stop by, Sally, so here I am. If it ain't a good time, I can come back."

Sally looked the disheveled man up and down, then said, "Now is fine, George. Please come inside."

George shuffled into the parlor, feeling like he would rather be anywhere else in the world than there. Sally motioned for him to take a seat on a wooden chair near the front window. She sat across from him on what looked like a very expensive sofa. George supposed the last thing she would want was for him to put his sorry butt on her fine upholstery.

Sally was a retired school teacher, and the stern gaze she was casting his way made him have momentary flashbacks to the same looks he used to get from his teachers back in school. It made him feel like squirming in his seat as he had done in those old days.

She said, "Well, George, I suppose it's no secret that I don't care very much for you."

"Nope. I s'pose not." He said, still not making eye contact with her.

"Be that as it may, my Frank thought the world of you. I have no idea why, but I accepted it as a bit of unpleasantness I had to deal with to keep my Frank happy. But Frank's gone now, and although I appreciate the support and help you provided during his illness, well, that's all over now."

"I understand," George said timidly.

"That's good to hear, George. Because after I give you something Frank left for you, I'll expect you to leave here and never return. As far as I'm concerned, you and I are never to see each other again. Am I clear?"

George was beginning to get a bit perturbed. Sally may not have cared for him, that was true, but that didn't give her the right to be so rude. God knows George only tolerated her overbearing personality for the sake of his friendship with Frankie. Never setting foot inside this house with that abrasive sow suited him just fine.

He stood up and said, "Well then, if that's the way you feel, maybe I should just be going now."

Sally shook her head insistently and said, "Not yet, George. Not until I give you the box from Frank."

George reluctantly said, "Fine. Give me the box, and I'll be on my way. I don't make a habit of staying where I ain't wanted."

Sally stood and headed for the doorway to the adjacent room. A minute later, she returned carrying a cardboard box about a foot and a half square, which looked a bit heavy. As angry as he was with the woman, George didn't rush to take it from her and ease her burden.

"So, do you want this or not?" Sally demanded.

George finally approached her and took the box. He asked, "Do you know what's inside?"

Sally shook her head and said, "Absolutely not! Frank packed this up back when he could still get around, sealed the box, and told me to give it to you after he passed. It hasn't been open since he taped it shut."

"Ain't you even a little bit curious about what might be in here?"

"No, I most certainly am not!" Sally said, perhaps a bit more disrespectfully than was expected. "What's in there is between you and Frank. I'm not now and have never been part of whatever it was you two had going on. I wouldn't care if the box was full of money. All I care about is closing this chapter of my life and moving on to the next. And you will not be part of that story, George. So just take your stupid box and be gone."

George could tell by the weight of the box there was probably no cash inside. He also didn't know whether to believe Sally didn't look inside, no matter what she claimed. She might want to ensure her husband didn't give away anything of value to her. After all, she was getting ready for the next "chapter" of her life. Still, the box did look as if it hadn't been tampered with.

What Sally didn't know was that George was well aware she had already started that so-called "new chapter" several months ago while her husband lay helplessly dying in bed. George had heard stories and whispers around town. He had even followed Sally once to a hot-sheet motel on his side of the tracks, where she met another man. She might come off all prim and proper and all high and mighty, but George knew the truth about her. She was nothing but trash. George never told Frank what he had learned. The last thing a dying man needed to hear was that his wife was stepping out on him, and George was too good a friend to hurt Frank in that way.

George carried the mysterious box back to his house, where he sat it on his kitchen table and sliced through the tape with a box cutter. He pulled open the flaps and saw the box contained only one thing. It was wrapped in heavy black plastic. George cut through the plastic and noticed an unusual smell that suddenly reminded him of something from his childhood, but he couldn't recall its origin. He peeled back the plastic and found Styrofoam and newspaper.

He carefully removed the paper from the top and immediately recognized what it was. He reached into the box, pulled out some of the Styrofoam, then lifted a heavy metal ball and set it on the table. The thing had originally been painted black, but age and exposure to the elements made it a faded dark gray with plenty of rust. It had a flat spot on the bottom to keep it from rolling, and on top, it had a cylindrical cap with two elliptical openings on each side. The words "Dietz Company Highway Torch - Made In The USA" were embossed around the outside.

George said aloud, "I remember these things now. I believe they're called smudge pots or something like that. We used to call them fireballs," George recalled how back in the early 1960s, when he and Frank were mischievous seven-year-olds, smudge pots were used to mark road construction areas and hazards around town. Workers would, for example, put a white wooden saw horse over a hole in the road and then hang one of those round balls from a wire dangling precariously below the crossbar of the horse. The workers then filled the balls with Kerosene and lit the wick at the top in the elliptical openings, and the things would give warning light for hours.

But it also provided a great opportunity for curious young boys to have unimpeded access to that great sought-after gift of fire. Whenever the borough was doing repairs in Frank and George's neighborhood, it meant nights of all sorts of pyro-maniacal activities. They would simply place a stick or rolled-up paper into the flame, and seconds later, they would be off to the races.

George couldn't recall when these torches began to disappear and were replaced by battery-powered flashing lights, but he knew they were no longer in use. There was no way a society that practically bubble-wrapped its children would allow such a thing to exist. Now that he thought about it, George realized how fortunate he and Frank were not to have set themselves afire playing so haphazardly around such a dangerous device.

He supposed he'd have to add this memory to all the other things he and his generation somehow managed to live through. For example, mothers who smoked and drank during pregnancy, not to mention cribs and playpens, were essentially death traps. Let's not forget lead paint, asbestos, and the ever-deadly lawn darts. The playgrounds in his town had metal and wooded swings, slides, and merry-go-rounds with no safe or soft places to land. George realized how lucky he had been to make it out of childhood alive with all his limbs.

Then his reminiscing was cut short when he saw several sheets of paper stapled together and folded, sitting in the bottom of the box. George picked up the papers, unfolded them, and immediately recognized his late friend's handwriting.

The note read, "Hey George, old buddy, old pal, Frankie here. If you're reading this, I'm dead and rotten, but hopefully not forgotten. I suppose I shouldn't joke, but hey, why stop now, right? How do you like the present I left for you? Remember the fun we had with these things? We're lucky we didn't burn the town down. I stole this thing back when we were like nine or ten. I hid it in my Dad's garage and eventually moved it when I got my own place. Luckily, Pop never found it, or he would have tanned my hide.

"I never told anyone about it, not even you. I didn't want to risk being sent to a reformed school. Seriously, I got to ask: did anyone ever really go to reform school? Or was that some mythical place the adults came up with to scare us and keep us potential criminal types in line? Whatever. The bottom line is this, George. You're alive, and I ain't. So I need you to do something for me.

"You see, Sally thought she was pulling a fast one on your old pal Frankie, but she was wrong. I know she was going out and doing the beast with two backs with half the guys in town while I was back home struggling to stay alive. That's seriously cold, George, even for her. Can you imagine such a thing? Of course, you can. Who am I kidding? You probably knew about it but didn't want to upset me in my failing condition. You're that kind of pal, and that's why I love ya, you lug. You may never have been able to hold down a job or maintain what people call a normal life, but you're no dummy, Georgie. In fact, you're smarter than most folks I know. You just operate on a different frequency than most folks. Anyway, thanks for trying to look out for your old dying buddy.

"But now that I'm gone and rapidly becoming a maggot motel, I have to ask you a favor. Believe me, Georgie, I know this is going to be a big ask, but I'm going to ask anyway. If you decide not to do it, no sweat. What the Hell can I do about it anyway? I'm eventual fertilizer now. I'm pretty sure I won't be able to come back to haunt you or anything. That's all a bunch of crap. But before I ask, I should tell you to burn this note after you read it for your own protection. I'm dead, so nobody can hurt me, but if you do what I'm about to ask, you won't want anyone finding this note. Unless you want to spend the rest of your golden years as a love pin cushion for a dozen bubbas up at the state prison. And I know your gate don't swing that way, my friend.

"Well, here goes. George, my lifelong friend, I want you to fill this Smudge Pot with Kerosene and light it one last time. Then I would like you to use it to burn dear Sally alive, preferably while she is in the company of one of her men. Yeah, a two-fer would be icing on the cake of marital justice. Yeah, I know I'm asking a lot, but I'm too sick, too weak, and, to be honest, too big a coward to do it myself. And now, as you're aware, I'm also too dead. So, I guess that's everything. Again, no pressure, Pal. Either you will or you won't. It's your call, Georgie. I suppose I'll see you on the other side, assuming there is another side. Frankie."

George read the note again to ensure he had read it correctly the first time. Then he read it a third time. He walked out into his back-yard, put the note on the bare ground, and burned it, just like Frankie had suggested. Then he returned to the house and brought out the box the smudge pot had come in. George put the Styrofoam pieces and the plastic wrapping into a large trash bag. Tomorrow, he would take it across town and leave it to be picked up as someone else's trash. Then he burned the box and the newspapers.

A few days later, George took Kerosene, which he had stored in a gallon jug in his backyard shed, and transferred it to glass bottles. He got two full bottles with enough left over to fill the smudge pot. He made Molotov cocktails with the two bottles. George knew the smudge pot couldn't be used in the exact way Frankie had wanted him to use it, but it could assist in the final outcome. The idea of the pot was more symbolic than functional anyway. The smudge pot represented something from the two friends' shared past, and George figured any way it might be used would be good enough.

George followed Sally one night to the same rundown, fleabag motel as he had done before. However, this time, he had something else in mind. He waited until he believed the couple had finished the deed and were sleeping. Then he approached the room with the flaming smudge pot and the two Molotov cocktails. He lifted and threw the smudge pot as hard as possible through the motel window, then immediately tossed in the two flaming bottles.

He smiled as he heard the two lovers screaming in pain. One of the burning bodies lept screaming through the broken window, landing hard on the concrete pavement. At first, George was unsure which of the two it was as flaming Kerosene covered the person's entire body like napalm. Then he noticed the long, blond hair rapidly burning away, and he knew it was Sally.

George walked over to the twitching, screaming body in time to see her look up into his face with dying eyes. He said, "Say hi to my pal Frankie when you see him. Tell him I took care of business and look forward to seeing him soon." Then, the burned woman died.

The next day, George was sitting on his battered, paint-peeled front porch, smoking a big cigar and chugging another bottle of that same cheap whiskey he had previously when a local police car pulled up in front of his shack. The driver's door opened, and the chief of police,

Big Joe Klingman, got out, strolled casually up, and put his foot on the front steps, which were as rickety as the rest of the porch.

"Mornin' Joe," George slurred drunkenly.

"It's past noon, George," Joe replied.

"It is? Well, then noonin' Joe," George said, bursting into fits of laughter at his own stupid joke.

"You know why I'm here, George?"

George replied, "Well, I s'pose I do. Sally?"

"Yep, Sally. And Brad Johnson."

"Is that who that was? I couldn't tell."

"Us either. Thank goodness for dental records," the chief said.

"Yeah, I s'pose so."

"Well, George. It seems I'm going to need you to come along with me now."

"Ah, Hell, Joe. You know I can't do that. I'm sixty-seven years old and still way too pretty for prison," George laughed again.

"Yeah, I s'pose you are at that. Still, George, you know I gotta . . ."

Before the chief could finish his sentence, George pulled out a pistol, placed it under his own chin, and blew the top of his head off, splattering his front window with gore.

When the chief recovered from his stunned shock at the horrible suicide he had just witnessed, He shook his head in disgust, walked back to his cruiser, and did the only thing he could do: he called it in.

SPACE GIRL

Author's note: In early 2023, Twisted Pulp *magazine asked me to write a short story to accompany some space-related pinup photos they would publish. This is the result of that request.*

/ \ /

The high school cafeteria was buzzing with excitement on Monday. The 1956 championship football game between the Johnsonville Spartans and the South Clarion Blue Devils was scheduled for the following Saturday night. The two schools had been rivals for as long as anyone could remember, and the excitement was palpable. Students, faculty, and staff planned to attend a pep rally in the gym after lunch that Friday.

Friday night, a special sock hop was scheduled with Mr. Edwards, the science teacher spinning records on his hi-fi turntable system. He was everyone's favorite because he had albums from all the greats, like Bill Haley and the Comets, The Four Aces, Pat Boone, The Chordettes, and The Platters. The word on the street was Mr. Edwards even had the debut album by a singer from Mississippi named Elvis Presley. His single "Jailhouse Rock" was being played everywhere, and people said he might be bigger than Tennessee Ernie Ford someday.

The sock hop had the potential to be one of the school's finest events of the year. Unfortunately, the rumor was that the old maid,

Miss Wilson, the Social Studies teacher, would be chaperoning. That meant no spiking the punch bowl, and only a few absolute best make-out spots would remain safe from her ancient evil eye.

Almost every table in the cafeteria that day was packed with students chatting and laughing about how incredible it would be if the Spartans won and took the state championship. It would be something that would become Johnsonville legend for decades to come. But not everyone was excited about the upcoming event.

In a secluded corner in the back of the cafeteria, a lone figure dressed in shabby, soiled clothing sat reading the February 1955 issue of EC comics Weird Science-Fantasy #27, with artwork by Wally Wood. The loner's name is Billy Enders, and the comic book was almost a year old and tattered, with most of the ads removed except for the Charles Atlas advertisement entitled "The Insult That Turned a Chump Into A Champ."

It featured the typical 98-pound weakling being shown up at the county fair by a muscle-bound moron who could swing the heavy mallet, ring the bell and win a prize. The weakling's ditsy girlfriend tells him to be a man and then dumps him. Of course, the weakling buys Charles Atlas's dynamic tension course eventually to become an even bigger muscle-bound idiot. Ultimately, he punches the bully in the face and wins back the brain-dead girlfriend. Billy figured the couple would eventually marry and live in a run-down mobile home with a dozen of their muscle-bound, equally stupid children.

Billy didn't like this ad very much. It was different than the one he usually saw called "The Insult That Made a Man Out of Mac." That one was more well-known, and although it was essentially the same theme, it took place at the beach with the muscle-bound bully kicking sand in the weakling's face. The result was the same; Charles Atlas, dynamic tension, big muscles, punch in the face, dopy girlfriend, yadda, yadda, yadda.

The truth was Billy didn't care about the ads anyway or the fact that the magazine was almost a year old. He had no money to buy anything advertised, even if the ads were still there. Billy couldn't even afford the ten cents to buy the comic book he was reading. He had found it on the sidewalk next to a trash can, and although it was torn and soiled, Billy felt like he was holding something sacred.

To say Billy Enders's family was poor was an understatement. It would be considered a substantial economic advancement if Billy's family could move up to the poor side of town. His clothing came from the second-hand store, and he suspected most of the stuff he wore might have been fourth or fifth-hand, like the battered comic book he was reading.

That condition of the comic didn't matter to Billy as long as he could see the action, adventure, and those incredible-looking babes Wally Wood drew. Billy had no idea how Wally Wood got away with publishing the buxom, curvaceous women he depicted in his cartoons, but every teenage boy with raging hormones was grateful for Mr. Woods's skills with pen and ink.

Billy spent many private moments in the bathroom, using his imagination and Wally Wood's drawings. He heard some older boys refer to these illustrations as "whacking material," and he had to admit, he agreed wholeheartedly. Billy especially liked when comics featured incredibly well-proportioned young ladies depicted as space aliens. He often fantasized about meeting a hot-to-trot babe from another world. As far as Billy was concerned, any beautiful space chicks that wanted to have their way with him, well, that was fine with him. In fact, it would be his duty as a red-blooded, healthy American male to accommodate them. He chuckled to himself.

Unfortunately, there were no space girls in real life. Billy figured if there were space girls, they would probably ignore him, just like those popular cheerleaders and snotty rich girls who wouldn't spit on Billy if he were on fire. He was sure his reputation as a social misfit loser was known all over the galaxy. That was just his sort of luck. But little did William J. Enders know that his luck and life were about to change drastically.

/ 2 /

"Is this seat taken? May I join you?" a soft female voice said from across the table.

Billy looked up, appearing at first a bit angry, and was about to tell whoever it was to leave him alone. But what he saw left him a speechless, blithering idiot incapable of forming even the shortest sentence.

He sat mouth agape, eyes bugging out of his skull, staring at a sight he couldn't believe. It was a girl, a young woman, and for some bizarre reason, not only was she speaking to him, but she was asking if she could sit with him.

"W . . . waaa . . . what did you say?" Billy managed to squeak out.

"I asked if anyone was sitting here and, if not, was ok for me to do so."

"You . . . you . . . want to sit . . . with me?" he said again in amazement. The girl was pretty, not movie star gorgeous like Marilyn Monroe or Jane Mansfield, but far more attractive than any girl who had ever paid the slightest attention to him. She had long dark brown hair pulled back in a ponytail, with a wide headband holding everything in place. She wore red lipstick, eye shadow, and a pair of dangling earrings that seemed a bit too modern for 1956 Johnsonville High. As if that wasn't unusual enough, she wore a sleeveless turtle-neck sweater and tight-knit pants, which no girl ever did in his school. Most of the girls wore poodle skirts and Bobbie socks. Around her neck hung a gold chain with a large exotic blue stone. She was a sight to behold, and the vision left Billy's mouth dry.

"Yes, if you don't mind," she replied, "my name is Cindy, Cindy Jones. What's yours?"

Billy struggled to form the words, "Me? Ah . . . I'm Billy, Billy . . . um . . . Enders."

"Well, Billy Umenders, it's nice to meet you." She stood with her hand outstretched, waiting for him to shake it.

"No, sorry. It's just Billy Enders. Not Umenders."

"Yeah, well, I sorta figured that already."

Billy reached out his arm with an obviously sweaty palm in a feeble attempt to shake hands with the lovely girl. When their fingers touched, a strange, almost electric current shot through his skin, traveling up his arm and into his brain, then right down to that magical area between his legs. It wasn't bad, like when he accidentally touched the electric fence at the farm not far from his house, but this was a good feeling, perhaps one of the best feelings he had ever experienced.

He wanted to ask her to sit, but his words were again stuck in his throat. Fortunately, Cindy took the initiative and sat down right next to him. When she did, their knees touched, and Billy could feel those almost electric vibrations even through their clothing. He was afraid he would lose control of himself, like when he was in his early teens and woke up with a mess after a particularly erotic dream. But somehow, he managed to hold on.

"So, Billy. What's all the excitement going on around here?"

Billy struggled to regain control of his senses and said, "That? Oh, I don't know. Some sort of big football game this weekend. A championship thing or something like that."

"Football doesn't interest you, Billy?" She asked.

"Me? No, not at all. I'm not part of that scene, you know? I just sort of go my own way."

"Ah, a lone wolf," she said and winked at him. That wink sent another series of vibrations throughout his body, and Billy felt for the first time that he might actually be falling head-over-heels in love with this strange girl he had just met. Was that even possible? He didn't know or understand what was happening but didn't want it to end.

Billy asked, "Are you new here at school? I don't think I ever saw you around before."

She said, "Well, sort of. I'm here to test the waters and see if this is the right place for me to teach."

Billy was stunned yet again. "Did you say teach? You mean you're not a new student here?"

"Well, aren't you just full of kind compliments, Billy Enders?"

"No, Ma'am. I mean Cindy, I . . . I mean, Miss Jones, Ma'am. I honestly thought you were a new kid. I'm so sorry."

There's no need to be sorry, Billy. I'm flattered. And listen, Billy. You only have to call me Miss Jones in front of the other students and teachers. When we're alone together, you can call me Cindy. By the way, Billy, I can tell already that you and I are going to become very special, very close friends, and we'll be spending a lot of alone time together."

"You do? We will?" Billy asked, both confused yet aroused by the direction the conversation was taking. Then Cindy laid her hand on the top of his leg under the table, her fingers coming dangerously close to his inner thigh and crotch.

He struggled to think of anything to get rid of the pup tent that had formed in his pants but to no avail. Billy suspected he'd be late for his next class, waiting for the trouser monster to disappear, or he would have to walk to class with his books strategically placed to hide his bulge.

More importantly, Billy knew from that moment on that his nocturnal fantasies would have a new leading lady resembling Miss Cindy Jones. Time to say goodbye to Wally Wood's sexy space girls and make room in his dreams for Cindy. He knew it was probably weird and maybe a bit wrong for a school teacher to be so overtly friendly with a student, but he didn't care. Cindy was hotter than the best-looking girls in his school and wanted to become close to him, which was all that mattered.

/ 3 /

"Hey, beautiful. Where have you been all my life?" An oily voice said from across the table.

Billy and Cindy looked up to see Brad Parker, captain of the football team and all-around egotistical moron standing bent over with his palms on the table, flexing his overly-developed muscles and eye-balling Cindy like he was at an all-you-can-eat buffet, and she was apple pie.

Cindy turned to Billy and said, "Well, isn't that special, Billy? This gentleman just asked you a question."

Brad took a step back and insisted, "Woah! Wait a minute, here. I wasn't talking to that greasy little circus geek. I was talking to you, sweet cheeks."

"The name's not Sweet Cheeks; it's Miss Jones, as in Miss Jones, your substitute teacher. I don't know who you are, but hey, I'm not one to judge. If you think Billy is beautiful, that's ok with me. Although, honestly, I don't believe Billy's gate swings in the same direction as yours; he's obviously all man."

As funny as this was, Billy couldn't show any signs that he was enjoying this interaction, or Brad and his jock buddies would destroy him. He suddenly wished she would lay off the insults before Brad decided to pound him just for witnessing the jerk jock being put in his place. Yet she continued the barrage of insults.

"I can see by your letter sweater that you must be some hot-shot football star around here. Am I right?"

Brad recovered enough composure to boast, "That's right, honey. I'm captain of the football team and plan to be the MVP of the championship game this Saturday. That means Most Valuable Player. So yeah, you could say I'm a hot-shot football star."

"I'll just bet you really love getting naked and showering with all those big and burly teammates of yours. I'll bet you stand there waiting for someone to drop the soap. Or do you prefer it when you and your buddies snap towels at each other?"

Brad's face turned red, then a terrifying shade of purple, as his bulging eyes switched from Cindy to Billy. They seemed afire with hatred, and Billy knew he would get the crap beat out of him once Brad got him alone. Billy caught Cindy's eye and slowly shook his head, doing his best silently to tell her she had gone too far and that he was going to pay for it. Cindy simply smiled her angelic smile and winked at him.

Then Cindy reached over and touched Brad's hand. When she did, Brad became as still as a statue, petrified and unable to move. His face bore a look of complete surprise and utter confusion, and he finally wore a vacant stare.

Cindy said in a soft, melodic, and hypnotic voice, "Now you listen to me, Mr. Football hero. My friend, Billy, is completely off-limits to you. Do you understand?"

"Yes, Miss Jones, I understand," he replied in a monotone, distant voice as he stared sightlessly into space.

She said, "If you or any of your friends even consider hurting Billy Enders, you will embarrass yourselves in a manner most degrading. Do I make myself clear?"

"Yes, Miss Jones," he replied.

Cindy pulled her hand away, and after a beat, Brad shook his head involuntarily, clearing the cobwebs from his mind. Then, he recalled how the teacher had insulted him and his teammates by questioning their masculinity. He turned to Billy, again redirecting all his anger at the boy. He might not be able to touch this big-mouth teacher, but he could take his fury and frustration out on her slimy boyfriend.

He pointed his finger at Billy and growled, "I'll be looking for you after school, Enders, and when I do, I'm going to make you pay for what your pretty little girlfriend here said to me. I'm gonna hurt you so . . ."

But Brad couldn't finish his sentence. He stood, with his mouth agape, looking down at the front of his pants, which had suddenly become darker and wet. A strong smell of urine filled the air. The cafeteria was thrust into silence. Several nearby students had heard him shouting at Billy and now saw his shame. Within a few seconds, the whispering grapevine had spread the news around the entire cafeteria at a speed somewhere north of the speed of light. After all, it wasn't every day that the biggest and most popular football hero wet his pants in the cafeteria, at lunch, no less.

Brad stood dumbfounded, then humiliated. A moment later, he turned and fled the cafeteria, fighting back the tears of shame, leaving a trail of golden droplets in his wake.

/ 4 /

"There. That should take care of that," Cindy said as she wiped her hands together as if brushing off dirt.

Billy was shocked and said, "But . . . but how did you . . . what did you do to him?"

"Don't worry about that, Billy. Just know that he won't bother you anymore unless he wants to make a habit of soiling himself in public on a regular basis. So, Billy, how did you like it when he called me your girlfriend? I loved it and thought it was really sexy. How about you?"

Billy's face blushed bright pink when he said, "I liked it. I liked it a lot. But you're a teacher, maybe only a few years older than me, but still a teacher. Ain't there some rule that says you can date a student or something like that?"

"Oh yes, Billy. There most definitely is. So, if you really want me to be your girlfriend, we'll have to play it cool here during the day, and we'll have to sneak around after school. As a teacher, I will be happy to show you many intimate things you probably never imagined. Would you like that, Billy?"

The blue jewel hanging around her neck began to glow brightly when she said that, catching Billy's attention. However, as his eyes turned toward the pendant, he focused on Cindy's breasts. He had never seen anything so firm and round anywhere but in the pages of magazines. To be so close in real life was beyond his wildest dreams.

He replied, "Oh yes, Cindy. I would like that very much."

"Well, Billy. Do you know where the bandstand is back behind the gym?"

"Yes, I know where that is."

"After school, miss the bus, then take a slow walk over to the bandstand and wait by the road running behind it. Do you know where I mean?"

"Yep. I know the place."

She smiled, winked at him, then said, "Excellent, Billy. If you wait there for a few minutes, I'll drive by and pick you up. I'll be driving a brand new red and white Chevy Bel Air. I bought it as a college graduation present for myself. You'll love it. It has a lot of room in the back seat, and I plan on us spending a lot of time back there." She winked at him again, licked her red lips seductively, then got up to leave. As she walked away swinging her round backside, Billy noticed that every boy in the cafeteria was watching that magnificent specimen in action. However, if his luck held out, he would be the only one in the school to see it in the flesh.

Billy couldn't believe his good fortune. It was beyond his comprehension. Not only did he get to meet the girl of his dreams, and she liked him, but she had practically told him they would do "the deed" that night after school. But maybe he had imagined that part. Perhaps his raging testosterone-driven mind had made more out of this than Cindy had meant for him to understand.

After all, he was just some nobody, a shabby kid from the poorer side of the poor side of town with nothing to offer such a gorgeous woman. Yet she had come on to him; he was certain of it. Billy supposed he would have to wait until the end of the day to see what happened. If he stood behind the bandstand and she never showed up, he would know it was the butt of yet another mean joke. It wouldn't be the first time, and it likely wouldn't be the last. But Billy didn't believe it was a joke this time.

/ 5 /

That night after school, Billy did his best to sneak out to the bandstand without anyone seeing him. At least he didn't think anyone had seen him. But he was mistaken. As he waited by the road for Cindy to arrive, he heard boisterous laughter and jeering coming from around the side of the bandstand.

A moment later, Brad Parker and three teammates came strutting across the grass toward him. Billy could tell by their overconfident swagger that they were there for one reason: to beat him to a bloody pulp.

"Hey there, Billy boy," Brad said, "I bet you thought I forgot about you, didn't you? Oh, you should know better than that, you greasy little maggot. I never forget, and I always pay my debts. The way I figure it, I owe a big debt thanks to your smart-mouthed girlfriend. Say, where is the little slut anyway? I was thinking we'd let her watch us messing you up. Then, when we were done with you, we could each take turns showing her what real men have to offer." The group laughed, enjoying making the little wimp squirm.

"But she's a teacher," Billy said.

Brad said, "Ah, that's where you're wrong. She hasn't officially been hired yet. I checked. She's just here to audit some classes and sub for a few, hoping to get a permanent job. But when we make it known that she's banging one of our fine school's students, one who is mentally deficient, she won't be able to get a job cleaning the toilets."

One of the other boys, Jim Sheaf, grabbed his crotch and said, "I got a job for her right here!"

"Yeah, me too," Another boy said, duplicating the crotch-grabbing gesture. "It don't pay much, but the tips are big." They all shared a good laugh at that one.

Then Brad said, "Ah, poor Billy. It looks like your skank whore girlfriend stood you up. Too bad. But that's ok, 'cause we're going to mess you up anyway."

Billy realized he was going to have to try to fight them off or run away. He had no problem running away but knew it would be useless against this mob of shaved apes. He might get in a lick or two if he fought, but that would be moot compared to the beating he would have to endure.

The four muscular troublemakers simultaneously took a step toward Billy, their hands clenched into fists, ready to rain a shower of pain down on the helpless boy. However, as soon as they did, the young men stopped in their tracks, looking down at the dark stains spreading out from the crotch of their pants.

"What the Hell!" Jeff shouted, "I just pissed myself. Hey, you guys did, too. What the Hell is going on?"

"Forget it," Brad said, "Just ignore it, and let's beat this clown."

But when they took another step toward Billy, their stomachs clenched, ached, and gurgled, and then all four attackers simultaneously had explosive running diarrhea in their pants. They fell to the ground, clutching their convulsing stomachs, then began experiencing projectile vomiting.

As Billy watched in amazement, he heard a car horn and turned to see Cindy waiting at the curb. He climbed into the passenger seat, and they drove away.

"It looks like Mr. Touchdown didn't learn his lesson today. Too bad his boys had to suffer right along with him," Cindy said.

"Yeah. But I still don't understand how you did that."

"Not a problem, Billy. I'll tell you all about it soon, but first, we have some urgent business to take care of."

"We do?"

"Yes, we most certainly do." Cindy winked at him and jerked her head toward the back seat.

Billy slowly turned and looked into the rear of the car and saw that the back seat was covered with thick, warm blankets. He realized he hadn't been imagining things after all, and for whatever reason, this gorgeous creature was going to have her way with him. "Well, a man's gotta do what a man's gotta do," he thought.

A short while later, Cindy pulled the car onto a dirt road, drove for a few hundred yards, and then turned off the engine. She looked at

Billy with large, seductive eyes and said, "I want you, Billy. I need you more than you can ever know. I hope you find me attractive and you want me too."

/ 6 /

A few minutes later, the two were in the back seat doing what countless red-blooded American couples had been doing in their back seats at drive-in movie theaters for many years. They didn't call drive-ins passion pits for nothing.

When they were finished, they sat naked, covered with one of the blankets; Cindy asked, "Was that good for you, Billy?"

Billy looked at her with wide eyes and said, "Good? It was way beyond good; it was incredible. I think I'm in love with you, Cindy."

"Oh, Billy. My silly boy. You're not in love; you're in lust. But that's ok too. Because, you see, this was a test to see if you had what we needed, and believe me, you passed with flying colors."

"I don't understand. What do you mean by 'test'? And who do you mean by 'we?' I'm confused."

Cindy sighed and said, "Well, I suppose I'd better come clean about a few things, Billy. You see, I'm not really looking to get a job teaching at your school. In fact, I'm technically not really a teacher, or for that matter, I'm not even a college graduate."

"You're not?" Billy asked with disappointment obvious in his voice, "I mean, I kinda liked the idea of sneaking around with one of my teachers. It made everything seem . . . I don't know . . . dirtier. The idea was sort of . . . exciting."

Cindy looked at Billy with pouting eyes and said, "Does that mean you don't want me anymore?"

Billy was stunned, "Oh no. It doesn't mean that at all. I want you plenty."

Cindy looked under their blanket and said, "It certainly looks like you do."

Later, after another half hour of the Chevy rockin' and rollin', Cindy said, "There's something I need to tell you, Billy. It's something you might have trouble wrapping your head around, but it's very important."

"Ok. Sure, what is it?"

"Well, you know how you enjoy reading those comic books with the space girls running around dressed all sexy, with their boobs practically hanging out?"

Billy found himself blushing again, "Um . . . yeah."

"How would you feel if I told you that I was actually not from Earth but was from another world?"

"You mean like another planet?"

"No, Billy. I mean like another universe, light years from Earth."

Billy looked at Cindy in awe and said, "I suppose I might think that was cool. I might be a bit freaked for a while, but it would still be really cool."

"Then I suppose you'll have to prepare to be freaked because the truth is, I am from another planet in a universe far from Earth."

Billy realized, despite his desire to think otherwise, that he actually believed her. It helped to explain the strange hypnotic thing she did to Brad and his friends. He said, "I don't understand. Why are you here, and why are we here doing this?"

"It's like this, Billy. Our planet is in trouble. All of the males on our planet have died off, either through war, old age, illness, or misfortune. Now, we are unable to reproduce. We searched space to find a race of beings physically close enough to ours and found that Earth had males capable of impregnating us and allowing our race to carry on."

"But why me? Why not some big strapping guy like Brad back there? I'm just a weak, nerdy guy. Why would you want me?"

"Those overly masculine types are just like our previous males. They always end up fighting and killing each other. If we were to bring back those types of men, we would be in this same situation all over again."

"Bring back? Does that mean what I think it means?" Billy asked with concern in his voice.

"Look, Billy. It's not that we would kidnap you or anything. We want you to return to our will with us voluntarily."

"There's that 'we' again," Billy said.

Just then, an identical Chevy Bel Air pulled up behind Cindy's car, turned off its headlights and engine, and Billy heard two car doors open and close. Cindy opened her door and slid out from under the blanket, standing naked in the moonlight. Billy got out as well but kept himself wrapped in the blanket.

Two of the most gorgeous women he had ever seen slowly walked toward him and Cindy. They were clad only in see-through sheer gowns, which left nothing to the imagination. They smiled seductively at Billy, and he was surprised to find he was as smitten with them as he had been with Cindy. Obviously, Cindy knew these women, and Billy realized she had been expecting them.

"Is this Billy?" One of the girls asked.

"Yes, this is him," Cindy replied.

"Did he measure up to the task required?" The second girl asked.

"Oh yes," Cindy said, "And then some. And I should say most energetically."

The first girl smiled and said, "May I test his capabilities now?"

Cindy turned to Billy and said, "Billy, sweetie, would you mind doing what we did in the car with Mindy here? She would like to make sure you meet our requirements."

Billy couldn't believe his ears, "You mean you're ok with Mindy and me . . . you know . . . doing it? You won't be jealous?"

"Oh no, Billy. As I said, we are here on a mission to find males to help repopulate our planet. As much as I like you, I can't let jealousy get in the way of saving our species."

"Well then," Billy said, "Let the festivities continue."

Billy and Mindy climbed into the back seat, and the festivities did, indeed, continue. While they were in the back of the car, Cindy spoke quietly with the other woman who, for this mission, went by the name Lindy.

However, these two women no longer resembled the gorgeous creatures Billy had seen. That was all an illusion they created based on the characters from the noted cartoonist Wally Wood, meant to satisfy the young boy's carnal desires. Had they appeared in their true form to him, not only would he not be able to perform sexually, but he would have likely run away screaming or dropped dead of fright.

These women might only vaguely resemble humans if perhaps seen in silhouette, in that they had the general shape and outline of women, but that's where the resemblance ended. The things standing next to the car, which was currently bouncing rhythmically on its springs, were hideously alien in appearance.

/ 1 /

Their foreheads extend far back along their skulls from large, segmented, insectile eyes, ending in a cluster of long, stringy tentacles hanging down like serpents. The hideous appendages even moved like snakes, as if they had minds of their own. The segmented eyes glowed blue-white in the moonlight and were wide apart, almost positioned near the sides of the creature's heads.

These creatures had no noses to speak of, but each had three nostrils positioned where a nose should be found. When the aliens breathed, these nasal orifices pulsated with each inhalation. The creatures' ears were large and pointed with long, floppy dangling lobes. However, the most frightening facial features were their large, thick-lipped, wide mouths that stretched from one ear to the other and were filled with multiple rows of sharp shark-like teeth.

Although the women were naked, they had no firm breasts like those Billy had believed he had seen. Instead, they possessed a series of eight teats, like those found on some nursing animals. Although their bodies were mostly hairless, the area between their legs was so furry it appeared like a thick thatch of tumbleweed had grown there. Their fingers and toes were four times the length of their human counterparts, had thin, fleshy webbing between them, and sharp claws on the ends.

The alien, who called herself Cindy, looked through the steamed window into the back of her car and saw Billy giving Mindy all he was good for. Mindy's tentacles were glowing bright red and moving hypnotically like Medusa's head full of snakes. She cried out with fake pleasure as her segmented eyes rolled back and her cavernous mouth opened wide to scream.

Lindy looked at Cindy and asked, "So you're sure he has no idea what we actually look like?"

"None at all. You know that. They never do. And if he did, he couldn't perform so admirably." Cindy said in their guttural native language. Then, handing her the comic book Billy had been reading. It showed one of Wally Wood's sexy space girls in an action pose. "Remember, this is what we look like to these humans."

"Ugh! Hideous!" Lindy replied in her deep, harsh, and raspy voice. "And they find this attractive?"

"Yes, I'm afraid so. But what else can you expect from such a primitive species? The point is that Billy is more than willing to come back with us and service our needs."

Lindy asked, "If he only knew what our real needs were. Did you feed him that line about repopulating our species?"

"Oh yes. And he bought it, hook, line, and sinker, as did the other several dozen recruits, I found. How did you and Mindy do?"

"We managed to find more than fifty candidates. They will all be ready when we leave at midnight."

Cindy said, "Excellent. You know, the males on this planet are easily persuaded simply by offering them sex. It's like they stop thinking with their brains and think only with that ridiculous appendage between their legs. Little do they know, if they would only take a few minutes to forget about what they're doing, they might see through our disguises."

Lindy said, "Then they might also realize that we were asexual creatures that self-reproduce and have no need for insemination or sex of any kind."

Cindy smiled with that mouth full of shark teeth, licked her thick lips with a serpentine tongue, and said, "They'll find that out once we travel through the interdimensional portal and come to our world. But then it will be too late. They'll see us as we are, and their interest in sex will instantly disappear. Then, eventually, they'll learn the painful truth. We only want them for food."

LEATHER APRON

Author's Note: In 2023 I was asked to write a story about Jack the Ripper for an upcoming anthology from Screaming Eye Press. Although Ripper stories are almost as abundant as Zombie stories, I was intrigued and decided to take a slightly different approach.

"No doubt, Jack the Ripper excused himself on the grounds that it was human nature."
—A. A. MILNE

"I am obsessed with the whole Victoriana thing, the whole Jack the Ripper London era, the grayness of it, the haunted feeling of it, all ancient and bloody."
—FLORENCE WELCH

"Who do I think Jack the Ripper was? Do you know, I've got no idea who Jack The Ripper was. No idea."
—JACK FLYNN

"Don't cry because it's over, smile because it happened."
—JACK THE RIPPER

"Do we really want Jack the Ripper living 400 years, zipping around the country in his hypercar, unleashing misogynistic nanorobots?"
—Ken Wilber

I always hated that wretched name those so-called newspaper journalists slandered me with: Jack the Ripper. Good Lord, it sounds so crass, so crude, so barbaric. I am no common savage, not some Ripper. I am an artist of the highest degree. Yes, that is how I think of myself, and with good reason. After all, I've created the sort of incredibly detailed fine art that few men could even imagine, let alone hope to accomplish. I am an artist who produces the art of the flesh, and my medium is skin and blood.

That horrible moniker, "Jack the Ripper," was said to have originated in something the press referred to as the "Dear Boss Letter," supposedly written by me and sent to the newspapers. Seriously? The fact that so many people believed that I might actually be the author of that ridiculous piece of drivel is a testament to the ignorance and gullibility of the great unwashed. Because of the sensational and relentless coverage in the newspapers, this absurd fakery was accepted as fact, and practically overnight, the name Jack the Ripper became legendary. Some believe this falsehood was perpetrated by someone seeking fame by pretending to be me. That was too simple an explanation to suit me. On the other hand, I believe those hacks who run the newspapers concocted a scheme, this bogus letter, to capture the public's interest for no other reason than to sell more papers.

The press also occasionally called me the Whitechapel Murderer. Although that name was far less sensational than Jack the Ripper, it was a small-minded attempt at mocking my art. True, I did conduct my business in London's Whitechapel slums starting back in 1888 and continuing from there. Technically, I supposed the public might have considered me a murderer since I have killed and disemboweled many of my patrons. Yes, patrons were how I also chose to think of those women who, in their deaths, have supported me by making the ultimate sacrifice for my creativity. So, I suppose if you looked at my art through the eyes of an impoverished, uneducated member of the lowest classes, my work could inadvertently be mistaken for murder. However, to a more enlightened, educated, and aristocratic individual with a true appreciation of fine art, what I did could not seriously be considered murder. They should have called me the Whitechapel Michaelangelo.

The name some of the journalists called me early on, and one that I preferred was "Leather Apron." Ironically, this was the least popular of all the names they chose for me. Don't get me wrong, I realize that particular choice of names was most likely a reference to a butcher's apron and had been meant to be derogatory, but I choose to look at the name differently. A butcher's apron tends to be made from the cheapest scraps of leather, discarded pieces haphazardly sewn together for functionality and durability, not for fashion. Good quality leather, by contrast, is fine material taken from the hides of strong animals, tanned to perfection, and then hand-tooled by expert artisans. High-quality leather products are sold in only the finest stores, commanding high prices, and are generally bought by the wealthiest of London's elite. To purchase an entire apron of finely crafted leather is surely indicative of someone of the highest social strata. Therefore, I have no problem being considered part of that group; coincidentally, it is where I am most comfortable.

Speaking of social classes, there are many reasons I chose to use prostitutes for my sculptures, the most obvious of which is ease of access. What could be simpler than a woman who would do almost anything, no matter how sexually depraved, for a complete stranger for money? These fallen women lived and practiced their chosen trade in the decrepit slums on the Eastern side of London. Most had no families to miss them; their only friends were their fellow streetwalkers. That is why I chose that area to find my lovely models.

I had a favorite method for creating my flesh sculptures. The coppers called it my "motis operandi." I just thought of it as my creative process at work. The first thing I would do was just to slit their throats from ear to ear, sometimes so severely that I almost decapitated a few young ladies. Sometimes, I would get so involved in the work that my creative side would take charge, and the analytical side of my mind would get pushed to the side. I also took great pleasure in disemboweling my girls and removing their internal organs. Sometimes, I kept certain organs as souvenirs and other times, I fed them to the various hounds that roamed freely in the alleys of Whitechapel.

Scotland Yard speculated that it was logical to presume I might have a degree of anatomical, medical, or surgical knowledge because of the precise manner in which I removed my treasures. I always left that assumption a mystery. There was no point in making the Scottland Yard coppers' job any easier. As I'm sure you know, I had never been caught and preferred to keep things that way.

As I said, I took pleasure in removing certain organs that either interested me at the time or those I determined added something special to the ambiance of my flesh sculptures. If memory serves me, Scotland Yard investigated more than eleven murders in the Whitechapel area between 1888 and 1891. For some reason, likely incompetence, they only credited me with five of the deaths. They referred to these victims as the canonical five because the investigators determined they were all related. These deaths occurred between August and November of 1888. As I rendered their flesh into art, I had no idea what these women's names were, nor did I care. In fact, all these years later, those irrelevant names are still unknown to me. I'm sure I must have read them in the newspapers at some point, but I have opted to forget them.

When I was gaining popularity in the press, I decided to have a bit of fun with a particularly annoying organization called the Whitechapel Vigilance Committee. I sent a letter to the organization's leader, accompanied by a small box containing half of a kidney I had saved from one of my girls. I had written the words "From Hell" at the top of the note as I knew it would most certainly get their attention. It eventually became known in the press as the "From Hell" letter. My favorite part of the letter is where I said I had "fried and ate" the other half of the kidney. Yes, I realize the correct phrase would have been "fried and eaten," but I was doing my best to throw the blighters off my trail by sounding less sophisticated. You're also probably wondering, did I or did I not resort to something as savage and depraved as cannibalism? Sorry, folks. That is a secret I'll take with me to the grave.

Then again, I have no intention of ever going to my grave and believe me, I never will. There was more to that "From Hell" letter than most people realize. You see, people like me, especially those of us who not only have an artistic and creative flair but are also a bit homicidal and manage to avoid capture, tend to stand out and get seen. By that, I don't mean to suggest being noticed by the press or the police, as that is a given. Nor do I refer to having unwanted attention from the public. No, I am talking about being noticed by, shall we say, somewhat darker, hostile, and supernatural forces from beyond the realm of what we consider life.

That dear friends, is the situation in which I surprisingly found myself and why I can write this account for you in the 21st century. It is also why I have been able to create my works of art for so many years since gaining fame in 1888. So how, you might ask, have I accomplished such an incredible, if not impossible, achievement? The answer is in the two-word title of my most famous letter, "From Hell."

I didn't just write that note to terrify people, although it definitely did have that effect. I also wrote it as a bit of a game or perhaps a type of cipher, if you will. Ironically, this code could simply be deciphered by taking those two words at their literal meaning. This letter was essentially written and sent from Hell. A day before I got the idea for the letter, I had made a bargain with someone or something, I suppose you might say. You might be inclined to call it a "deal with the Devil," so to speak, but it was nothing quite so grand as that. It would be more accurate to call it "a deal with a lesser demon acting in Hell's best interest," but I suppose that particular phrase doesn't roll off the tongue quite as comfortably.

During my interactions with said demon, I determined there must be something of a pecking order in Hell, just as here on Earth. I find it rather ironic that even after death, we still have to deal with the issues of social stratification. Then again, perhaps that is a situation reserved for the damned. Still, we all know that dealing with the haves versus the have-nots is something of a Hell in itself. Anyway, the boss man, numero uno, the big cheese, Belzabob himself, apparently never deals with humans, no matter how violent their crimes or how infamous they might be. He has others who handle things like that, or perhaps I should say, like me.

Here's what happened. The day after my final kill of 1888, I had been relaxing in my flat a few blocks from the Whitechapel area. My residence may not have been as upscale as I would have preferred and deserved, but it was significantly more affluent than the impoverished areas where I created my art. I also appreciated the close proximity to my patrons. Anyway, one night, I was resting on my rocker, enjoying a glass of sherry and reading an illustrated book on human vivisection, when, without warning, a hideous creature appeared in my living room engulfed in flames. Needless to say, I was both surprised and equally concerned. My flat was located in a building of wood frame construction, which was obviously not very conducive to open flames. I suppose I should have been terrified since a huge monstrous thing was in my home surrounded by fire, but I was too perturbed to be frightened.

To my surprise, I found myself shouting at the creature, "Hey there, my good man. Yes, you with the pig-like snout, the ram horns, and bulging eyes. I must insist that you do something 'bout those flames before you burn my apartment building to the ground and be quick about it."

Unfortunately, that sounded equally unthreatening to me. The creature neither said a word nor made any move to attack me. It simply stood there staring at me like a scientist examining a bug under a magnifying glass. That was when I realized the flames surrounding the beast were not burning anything anywhere in the flat. They danced on my imported wool rug and up along my drapes, yet nothing caught fire. I realized such a phenomenon was not possible, yet it was occurring right before my eyes.

The huge monster occupied most of the space allotted by my high ceilings. Its shoulders were massive, and the practically naked beast rippled with muscles from head to toe. Its brownish-gray flesh was glistening with a sheen of sweat. It wore a type of leather loin cloth that barely covered its enormous private area. An incredible stench surrounded the creature, a mixture of spoiled fish, sulfur, and decomposing flesh. The monster stood silently, watching me with its large, bloodshot, hooded eyes.

In my anger and fear, I shouted, "What manner of beast are you? And what is it you want of me?"

The hulking behemoth slowly smiled with a grin that appeared more like that of a raving lunatic than a creature with any degree of sanity. That was when I got a good look into its cavernous mouth spilling over with long, dagger-like fangs that appeared capable of tearing the hide off a charging bear. Then the monster spoke in a deep guttural voice that sent chills racing along my spine. It was unlike anything I had ever heard before.

"My name is of no more import than yours, my murderous friend. All that matters is that you are here, I am here, and a bargain will be struck this night."

"A bargain, you say? What sort of bargain."

The creature's hideous smile never left his face, nor did those insane eyes ever stop staring a hole through me.

"We will make a bargain this night, resulting in one of two outcomes. Either you will agree to turn over your mortal soul to me, whereby you will live forever and be free to practice your art forever, or else I will tear your mortal body to shreds, slowly, painfully, piece by piece, and then take your soul and cast it into the fires of Hell where it will be tortured for eternity."

I replied, "Well, that doesn't sound like much of a bargain to me. It sounds more like an ultimatum, one which I have little choice in the outcome."

The demon's expression never changed as he said, "Call it what you will. It is of no consequence to me. What is your decision?"

As you can see, I had very little choice in what direction my future would take. On the one hand, this beast offered me a chance to live forever and continue to create my amazing works of art. Or I could be torn to pieces and sent to Hell and be tortured for eternity. Although it was true that I was born at night, it wasn't the previous night. I chose the first and only logical option.

A few moments later, the creature vanished from my home, and I felt an incredible sense of strength coursing through my body. I walked over to my living room mirror and was shocked to see that although I was not an old man, to begin with, the image in the mirror appeared ten years younger than I had looked previously. I couldn't believe my good fortune.

That was more than 100 years ago. Since that time, I have been able to practice my art all around the globe. And I had never been caught. That is to say, until a few weeks ago. Ironically, I once wrote,

"One day, men will look back and say I gave birth to the twentieth century." I have gone far beyond that, at least for a while.

Sadly, it appears that eventually, everyone's luck runs out, and in the early part of the 21st century, thanks to the influx of cameras and the incredible advances in forensic technology, I was apprehended and, as they say, brought to justice. Ironically, the police had no idea the person they were putting on trial was none other than Jack the Ripper or, as I prefer, Leather Apron.

At first, I wasn't overly upset by my capture. After all, I had a good run, more than a century of practicing my craft and art. Most artists throughout history barely succeed for a few decades. I always suspected that someday I would eventually be caught, tried, and sentenced to death. I had sold my soul to Hell, and since I continued to kill, I assumed when I was eventually executed, I would naturally gain a place of honor in the netherworld.

Unfortunately, that was not to be. You see, I made the mistake of being brought to justice in a state that had abolished the death penalty. As such, I was sentenced to life in prison. Now, I sit in a six-by-eight prison cell and will do so until the day I die, which, as you know, will be . . . well, never.

MAUSOLEUM

The road-weary sedan pulled off the main highway and stopped before the rusted rod iron entrance archway. Across the curved top of the opening, the words ETERNAL REST CEMETERY were formed from what was now a series of broken iron letters. The name seemed to be hanging so precariously in the air that it appeared that it might come crashing to the ground from even the most minuscule external stimuli.

High overhead, the harvest moon glowed brightly in the autumn sky, casting an ethereal glow down upon the abandoned cemetery. In the moonglow, giant oak trees with skeletal limbs and the chilling breeze combined to project a macabre shadow ballet upon the crumbling tombstones below, creating the illusion of dozens of frolicking specters engaged in a ritualistic dance of death. The sound of the wind whipping through the overhead branches was like the long-dead spirits of the damned trying to whisper their songs of sorrow to the living.

A couple exited their car, a young man from the driver's side and a young woman from the passenger side. The driver approached the passenger side of the vehicle, where he joined the woman who was looking up at the arch. They said nothing for a minute or two as they stared across the expanse of ancient tombstones in awe and childlike wonder.

The couple had just experienced a long day, leaving Pennsylvania early that morning and arriving at the Boone County, Indiana airport after numerous plane switching, layovers, and what seemed like countless delays. As if that wasn't trying enough, they had to rent a car and drive North to a secluded, weather-worn estate to meet with their wheelchair-bound client, Mrs. Beatrice Goldstein. Then they traveled west and north again along Rt. 100 until they found their destination on a gravel-side road off Witt Road.

The woman sighed, then said, "Well, Frank, I do believe this is the place."

"Yes, it is Molly; it most certainly is," He agreed. "Now, we had better get to work. Mrs. Goldstein isn't paying us to stand around gawking."

Molly replied, "She won't pay us at all if we don't bring her the proof she wants."

"Agreed. But we will bring her exactly what she asked for because that's who we are, and this is what we do. Then again, I should say this is what you do." He turned, kissed her head gently and perhaps reverently, and then he walked to the back of the car. He popped the trunk and withdrew two black duffel bags. One bore the gold initials F. T. and the other M. T.

The two uninvited visitors pushed open the rusted entry gate, which hung askew next to its equally rusted partner. It creaked loudly beneath the twisted, wobbling, overhead ironwork letters. They both looked upward as if willing the rusted sign to stay in place and not come crashing down on their heads.

A strong cold breeze blew through the trees, causing what few leaves remained on the trembling branches to appear to grip tighter as if struggling futilely against being torn away. Most were unsuccessful, ripped from their moorings, and sailed away in the wind.

This was not the sort of night most typical people would want to be found in such a dismal, desolate place. But Frank and Molly Treadwell were not "most people." In fact, they were far removed from what anyone would consider "typical."

There was the familiar Autumnal scent of decomposing vegetation on the breeze. However, there was also another smell lurking just below the surface. It was something dank and unpleasant, like a rotting animal carcass baking in the sweltering summer sun. But summer had been put to bed weeks earlier.

The curious couple walked along what they believed was the remnant of what was once the main pathway through the cemetery. It was difficult to determine for certain as the trail was thick, with tall grass and weeds growing more than three feet high.

"I wonder when the last time was that anyone cut the grass in this place," Molly asked. "I feel like we should be using a scythe to cut through this mess."

Frank said, "There is no caretaker for this place, Mol. This grass probably grew all summer long. It likely does every summer. Then the winter cold comes and beats it down, burying it under a blanket of white, killing it until fresh grass starts to grow again in the spring. I suppose you could say Mother Nature is the caretaker."

"She isn't doing a very good job, in my opinion. This place just seems so sad," Molly said as she waved her arm around at the broken tombstones, many of which were toppled over. "All these old graves. They were once living people. Their loved ones buried them here, thinking their final resting places would be taken care of forever."

"Well, from what Mrs. Goldstein said, as far as she knows, this place has been abandoned since the mid-sixties. If anyone has buried anyone here since then, chances are that grave digger would have been one of those large, bent-nose gentlemen who wear expensive suits and have questionable wealth from various ill-gotten gains."

"You mean mob types?" She asked.

Frank nodded and said, "Yup. It wouldn't surprise me. I have heard rumors of things like that happening in places like this."

Molly said, "In that case, I think we should remember to stay away from any graves that might appear too fresh."

"Good call, Molly. Speaking of which, are you getting anything yet?" He was speaking of her ability to sense things.

She said, "No, nothing other than the general heebie-jeebies anyone would get in a place like this."

"Yeah, I have those as well."

Frank looked at a rough, hand-drawn map he held, pointed to a small building at the far end of the cemetery, and said, "We need to head over to that building."

"That mausoleum?"

"Yep, the mausoleum."

"How can we be sure it's the right one?" Molly asked.

Frank did his best to hide a sly smile, then said, "Well, there are two reasons. The first is the map Mrs. Goldstein gave us points to that building. And the second reason is . . . take a look around. That's the only mausoleum in the place."

Knowing she had just fallen victim to Frank's sarcastic wit, Molly smiled and replied, "Oh, ok. I get it. Good one, Frank."

"Sorry, Molly. I couldn't help myself."

As the couple approached the mausoleum, they found the rusted gate at the entrance of the structure standing wide open. For a moment, they stood uncertain about their next move. This was supposed to just be a job like a hundred others they had done before, but somehow, it seemed like it had the potential to become much more than that.

Although she couldn't exactly explain why, Molly was somehow drawn to the darkness inside this structure; it was as if the black, mysterious opening was a mouth calling to her in a soft, haunting, hypnotic voice. The building stood alone, away from the main part of the interfaith cemetery, as if suggesting it had no business being located anywhere near the resting place of formerly good religious people. Molly sensed this, and it filled her with a feeling of dread unlike any she had felt before.

As the pair approached the mausoleum entrance, their footfalls echoed on the marble steps and bounced around the cemetery, making them feel like they might not be alone in this place of departed souls. A cold chill ran down Molly's spine, and she shivered involuntarily.

"You ok, Mol?"

"Uh . . . yeah. Yes, I'm fine. At first, I just got a chill. Now I'm starting to pick up something that's strange, even for me."

"Strange how, Molly?"

"Strange as in different, unfamiliar, distant, and very possibly evil. As if that's not bad enough, I kinda feel like we're being watched."

Frank looked around the deserted cemetery and said, "I know what you mean. I feel the same, but I'm sure there's nobody out there. It's probably just the creepy vibe of this place."

On the opposite side of the cemetery, among a cluster of trees, the silhouette of something large and foreboding lurked in silence. It watched the couple from its unseen hiding place, its purpose known only to itself.

The concrete mausoleum was old and weathered, and when the wind blew, its rusted door squealed, then slammed closed, sending even more icy tendrils of shivers down Molly's spine. Frank and Molly Treadwell were co-owners of a paranormal investigation agency. That was what brought them to the unpleasant cemetery on this chilly Indiana October night.

Mrs. Beatrice Westerly Goldstein was a wealthy, eccentric old widow who, upon doing research for her family's genealogy, found a document stating that her two great-grandparents had been laid to rest in a mausoleum in the abandoned Eternal Rest Cemetery back when it was a well-known exclusive resting place for those people of wealth. Mrs. Goldstein had been confined to a wheelchair for many years following an accident, which she never spoke about to anyone, including the Treadwells.

Beatrice's parents, grandparents, and several departed siblings resided in an exclusive mausoleum on the family estate grounds. She told the Treadwells that if her relatives truly were in this rundown, pitiful excuse for a resting place, Beatrice planned to relocate them as soon as possible.

The Treadwells were hired to do what the wheelchair-bound Beatrice Goldstein could not. Their responsibility was supposed to be simple. Enter the mausoleum, look for Mrs. Goldstein's great-grandparents' crypts, and then return with photographic proof of their location. She claimed she wasn't looking for signs of restless spirits or anything of a clairvoyant or paranormal nature. In fact, Molly and Frank had repeatedly tried to explain that others could do the job for much less money, but Beatrice insisted on hiring them based on their reputation as paranormal investigators. Although the couple found this odd, they chalked it up to Mrs. Goldstein's eccentricities. After all, her money was as green as anyone else's.

Molly was the one with the sensitive abilities, and Frank was the businessman, cameraman, and whatever else he needed to be. The pair had become somewhat famous for their paranormal investigations, appearing in national magazines and several talk shows. They had their own weekly podcast with a large following and several major advertisers.

There were, of course, the unbelievers and naysayers who publicly criticized the couple, calling them fakes, charlatans, and purveyors of snake oil. The pair tended to ignore these comments because Molly and Frank knew her abilities were genuine. Most people had difficulty understanding both the skills and the limitations of her gift. It wasn't that she could see the future or predict winning lottery numbers. Molly didn't believe anyone could do that.

However, she was sensitive to feelings and emotions at a level most adults cannot sense. Molly believed all people started life with similar gifts to hers, but as they grew up and were pressured to be molded into what society expected from its adults, most people first suppressed, then eventually lost those abilities. She based this theory on studying young kids who seemed to have similar skills to hers. She didn't know why, as an adult, she could still do what she did, nor was it something she could control or turn on or off at will.

However, putting herself into situations that were potentially paranormal in nature tended to trigger these sensitivities and often would cause her receptors to go into overdrive unexpectedly. No matter how frequently it happened, it always caught Molly off guard. Sometimes, the feelings started like a low humming inside her mind, and then they would gradually increase in strength. Those incidents were what Molly thought of as manageable experiences.

Other times, when she least expected it to occur, something would cause her senses to jump into high gear instantly. She was never prepared for those times. Then again, how could she be? Molly hoped this wouldn't be one of those times. She was currently not feeling much of anything other than that slight bad vibe coming from the mausoleum and that sensation of being watched. She hoped that would be the extent of any interactions she might have that evening. But that was not to be.

With uncertainty, Frank grabbed onto the rusty mausoleum gate. Upon hearing that eerie hinge screaming and revealing a chamber of long-dead, long-forgotten souls, Molly turned on the flashlight and directed the beam on the blackness within. The mausoleum was so dark that it seemed to suck the light from the flashlight the way a black hole in space absorbs everything it encounters.

"We're going to need more light, Frank."

He reached into his duffel and pulled out a strange-looking item that resembled a security spotlight mounted to a box with a handle. The contraption looked quite heavy, which it was, as the rectangular box to which it was mounted contained several rechargeable dry cell batteries. Frank pointed his light into the void, and at last, the place was illuminated bright enough for them to see all the way to the back.

As the beam hit the mausoleum floor, several furry creatures ran toward them to escape the beam. Their red eyes glowed momentarily as they scurried out of the building.

"Rats?" Frank asked.

"Yep. Rats," Molly replied.

"Why the Hell does it always have to be rats? Couldn't it be chipmunks or squirrels or something like that? No, sir, nothing so cute and cuddly for the Treadwells. It's always got to be rats."

"It sort of goes with the territory. I suppose it could be worse, Frank. They could be skunks."

Frank hesitated momentarily, then said, "There is that. Now, let's get what we came here for and get out of Dodge. This place gives me the creeps."

The couple entered the mausoleum and began reading the names engraved on the brass plates mounted to the face of each crypt.

Frank looked down at his hand-drawn map again and said, "Look for either Jacob or Emma Westerly. If we find one, we'll find the other."

"Some of these tags are worn to the point where you can't hope to make out the name," Molly said. Then she suddenly had a feeling, one of her sensations, as she ran a hand along one of the brass plates. She said, "Frank, give me some light on this plate . . . I have a feeling."

"You got it, Babe. Your feelings never let us down."

Frank readjusted the light, and Molly said, "This is it, Frank. It says, 'Jacob Westerly,' and this one next to it says, 'Emma Westerly.' We've found what we came for. See if you can get a good picture."

"Will do, Mol. But as usual, WE didn't find them; YOU did."

"We're a team, Frank. The two musketeers. One for all and all for one."

Frank clicked off several shots with his Nikon Digital camera and was checking them for clarity when Molly said, "Frank, we've got trouble."

He turned to look at Molly and saw her steady herself against the wall of crypts. He knew his wife, and this was not good. "What is it, Molly?"

Molly was panting, trying to catch her breath and not pass out, "I . . . don't know . . . it's something big and something evil."

From a distant blind, the figure watched the couple carefully as they entered the mausoleum. It saw the light spilling from the mausoleum, it saw the rats running away, and it understood that fear. It also hated the light, which was why it only hunted in the dark. Even the moonlight was unpleasant for the creature. Fortunately, clouds had moved in and greatly dimmed its glow.

The watcher knew the couple would soon find whatever they were looking for, and then they would turn out that infernal light, leave the mausoleum, and come right into its waiting hands. It didn't care what they sought, but they were in its mausoleum, in its cemetery, meaning they must pay. Soon, they would encounter something far more horrifying than they could have imagined. Little would the investigators know, the horror that awaited them outside that crumbling building or that it had the potential to consume their very souls and condemn them to an eternity of endless torment in the netherworld of the damned.

But the watcher knew because it was that horror, it was that terror. The unwelcome intruders would never leave this cemetery alive. The watcher would see to that. The huge hulking shadow crossed the cemetery, reaching the mausoleum entrance. It stood on the large marble landing in the shadows, away from the light spilling from the entrance. It could not hear the conversation inside, but that was not a problem. It would take them both when they came out.

"What is it, Molly?" Frank repeated, "Are you ok? I've never seen you like this before."

"Yes . . . I know . . . I've never felt anything this strong . . . this evil before. We have to get out of here right now, Frank." She seemed to be regaining her composure.

Molly bent down, zipped open her duffel, and withdrew a black pistol. She gave Frank a knowing smile, indicating she had recovered and was ready to face whatever awaited them.

"Right there with you," Frank said as he put his camera back in his duffel and withdrew a similar pistol. He picked up his light unit and was about to turn it off.

Molly whispered, "Leave it on and change the setting to as bright as possible, and when we go out the door, shine it to the left. That's where it will be. Then, when I tell you, start shooting. I have a feeling."

"That's good enough for me," Frank said as the couple turned to face whatever awaited them outside.

They simultaneously stepped out the door onto the large flat area at the top of the steps. Frank immediately directed his barrage of light toward the left as Molly had instructed, and the couple were momentarily stunned by the horror they encountered.

A creature, the likes of which Frank had never seen, loomed over them, howling like a wounded animal. Everything that happened next took place in a matter of a few seconds.

The beast stood more than nine feet tall and was impossibly composed of what appeared to be sticks, dirt, grass, dead leaves, and other debris found lying around the cemetery. As the creature howled, it covered what Frank supposed was its face with giant shovel-sized hands. Its arms were massive and bulging with muscles. The thing stank of decomposing Autumnal detritus and that other underlying foul smell of rotting flesh. Frank had no idea what manner of demon this thing might be but knew he had never encountered one before.

Molly knew exactly what this monster was. She had seen it in her vision inside the mausoleum and had read about such creatures in Hebrew Mythology. It was called a golem and was formed of lifeless, natural substances. It was brought to life by ritualistic spells cast by a human creator. Someone had created this monster and left it to roam the abandoned cemetery. Perhaps the golem had killed its creator.

Molly knew a golem was created by issuing a series of Jewish incantations and could be destroyed by saying the words in reverse. Unfortunately, she didn't know those words. But she did have something that might at least stun the monster long enough for them to hopefully escape.

"Now, Frank! Shoot it now!"

Frank and Molly began shooting the beast and didn't stop until their ammunition ran dry. The creature screamed and began to quake all over. Then, it disassembled back into its natural form as it collapsed into a pile of debris. A cloud of sparkling dark gray matter flew from the pile and disappeared out into the darkness of the cemetery.

Molly lifted the tip of the gun to her lips and blew on the plastic red tip cowboy style. She said, "Nice shootin' Tex!"

Frank said, "Is it dead? Did we kill it?"

"I don't think so. I think we only injured it and frightened It away for a bit. A bath in holy water has a way of hurting just about any form of evil there is out there."

"How did you know it would work?"

Molly smiled shyly and admitted, "I didn't. But it was the only game in town. Now, let's get out of here before that thing reforms and decides to give us another go." The couple ran through the cemetery to the safety of their rental car, tossing their gear haphazardly in the back seats and backing out onto the main highway, leaving a cloud of dust in their wake.

In the cluster of trees, the golem was already slowly beginning to reform. It had been badly injured by those interlopers, but eventually, it would become whole again and return to protecting its cemetery as it had done since its creation. Molly was right in assuming it had tried to kill its creator but was not yet strong enough and failed. It had only managed to cripple her as she crawled out of the cemetery, where her driver lifted her into a car and drove away.

On the way to their hotel, Frank said, "Well, that certainly was one for the podcast. That is, assuming we can figure out how to explain what that was all about."

Molly sat quietly, not responding. Frank knew that meant she was deep in thought, rehashing what had just happened.

Frank said, "At least we got the pictures Mrs. Goldstein wanted. Now we can collect our fee."

Molly remained silent as Frank drove on. Even though he knew she wasn't listening, Frank kept talking. He was pumped up on adrenaline and couldn't stop himself. He said, "I wonder about the crew that comes to relocate the two Westerly's. I suppose we'll have to recommend they come in the daytime. That thing didn't seem like light. And what about that thing? What are we going to do about it?"

Molly finally broke her silence and said, "That thing, Frank, it's called a golem. It is something straight out of Hebrew folklore."

It was Frank's turn to listen.

"Such a creature is made by someone issuing a series of incantations in Hebrew. And it can only be killed by saying the words in reverse."

"Ok," Frank said, unsure where this was going.

"Since we took this job, I've been wondering why Mrs. Goldstein was insistent about hiring us for such a simple task."

Frank agreed, "Yeah, me too."

"I think now I know why, Frank. Suppose Mrs. Goldstein knew all along that the Westerlys were in that mausoleum. She is Jewish, and suppose she also knew about such things as golems and mystic incarnations."

"Ok."

"The cemetery was abandoned, and there was no caretaker or security to watch over the place, meaning no one to protect the mausoleum and her relatives."

"Got it."

"So now, suppose an older but still mobile Mrs. Goldstein visits the cemetery and sees its deplorable condition. She becomes overwhelmed, returns home, and begins researching golems further. She finds the incantation, the words that will create the monster. Then she returns to the cemetery late one night, perhaps with a driver, and says the words that bring the golem to life. She commands the golem to protect the cemetery from intruders."

"Do you think the monster considered her an intruder and attacked her?"

"Yes, Frank, that's exactly what I think. But since the golem was newly created, it was probably still weak. I believe Mrs. Goldstein was able to escape with the help of her driver but was crippled in the process."

"So, her driver knows her secret."

Molly said, "Her driver may have known her secret but no longer. Mrs. Goldstein mentioned he was elderly and passed away several years ago. She never replaced him, and as you know, she has become something of a recluse."

"And you think that's why she insisted on hiring us?"

Molly said, "Yes, I do."

"If that's true, why didn't she just give us the magic words to kill the thing, and why have us go up there at night?"

"I believe she didn't want us or anyone to know her secret. She likely assumed that being paranormal investigators, we might already know about golems."

"Lucky for us, you did."

Molly hesitated, "Lucky for us is right. Still, we barely got out of there with our lives. That miserable woman almost got us killed."

Frank asked, "So now what."

"We collect our money and ride off into the sunset."

"Do you think she'll ask us about it, the golem?"

Molly replied, "Nope. She won't say anything, and we won't tell her anything. We'll just show her the pictures, collect our money and leave. As you suggested, we could tell the workers to move the bodies in the daytime, although I suspect they will likely do that anyway, so they should be safe."

"So that's that," Frank said.

"Yes, I suppose it is."

"And the golem?"

Molly said, "It will likely return. Perhaps I'll do some more research, and if we feel ambitious, it could become a project for another day."

Frank shook his head and said, "To be honest, Molly, I hope that day never comes." But in his heart, Frank knew it would.

SUBHUMANS

No one aware of the hideous creatures could begin to accurately determine how the horrid subhumans originated or what level of threat they might eventually pose to mankind. These repulsive monsters defied even the darkest imaginations of the most twisted minds, and their inhuman countenances were scarcely within the realm of understanding. None who encountered them physically ever lived to describe what they saw. However, one fateful night, I became the exception to this rule. I had seen the monsters up close and personal. I smelled their vile stench and felt the pain they could inflict, yet I miraculously lived to tell this tale. I have yet to decide if my survival was fortunate or unfortunate, as that near-death encounter will haunt my nightmares for as long as I live. I don't want to imagine how many more years I will wake up screaming in the dead of night, but I suppose time will tell.

These things, these subhuman creatures, appear to have arisen from the darkest recesses of someone's horrific nightmare. They encompass the grotesque union of the most savage primal monsters imaginable and the equally profanely obscene abominations of the human form. Their ashen, gristly flesh stretches like sinew across their skeletal frames, and their bulging eyes glow from black-encircled sunken orbs deep in their bulbous heads. With a look of complete and unbridled malice combined with obvious insanity, the beasts personify the very essence of evil incarnate.

Their speech, if such gibberish can be considered speech, consists of nothing more than a series of unintelligible, guttural, inhuman croaks, roars, ape-like screams, and clicks. Reports claim witnesses have seen chest beating behaviors and hand gestures suggesting some primitive signing. They also rely heavily on facial expressions, using their pig-like snouts, wide, thick-lipped mouths, and heavy eyebrows to supplement their base-level communication.

These creatures possess incredibly large shovel-like hands and long, gnarled fingers complete with claws, sharp and strong enough to render flesh. If the claws alone are insufficient to tear meat from the bone, the mouths of these beasts overflow with multiple rows of deadly shark-like fangs. Their large feet at the end of their thin but extremely muscular legs are likewise equipped with talon-like hooked claws.

I can personally attest that the overpowering reek of decay surrounding these monsters is enough to gag a maggot. The stench alone could send an icy shiver of terror down the spines of anyone unfortunate enough to cross their path. Then again, as I know far too well, the creatures' vile pall is the least of one's worries when encountering these monsters, as any such unfortunate individual would have much more to be concerned about.

Where these monstrosities originated remains a mystery to those few who know of the creature's existence. Although we, the few believers, are considered lunatic fringe by society, we have joined together and formed an online network of dedicated people who have found a kinship among our mutual concerns. Some of our members believe the beasts may have once been human. It has been theorized that they may have arisen from someplace deep inside the Earth, where they lived for generations among surface dwellers' pollution, waste, and refuse, eventually mutating into their present forms. Some say they may be the descendants of ancient space aliens, who, upon finding themselves stranded on Earth, had no choice but to breed with humans they captured. Others believed that a thin membrane may have existed, separating man's world from the dimension occupied by the horrific beasts. Those people claim this membrane was somehow ruptured, creating a passageway, a portal, and had unleashed these monstrous demons on the Earth.

It has yet to be determined which, if any, of these theories is correct, and to be honest, it probably isn't relevant to the danger these monsters present. They dwell in abandoned places, largely in subterranean lairs, only venturing to the surface in the dark of night and moving in the shadows. I believe this is not out of fear but out of necessity. Their numbers are few compared with mankind, so they must move carefully. Perhaps someday, when there are many more of them . . . but I prefer not to think about that.

All I know is these creatures do exist, and they have no qualms about devouring alive those we consider normal humans. I'm sorry if that seems a bit abrupt or harsh or if it might have upset your sensitivities. It is, unfortunately, the painful truth. I have witnessed this myself. And whether you like it or not, sometimes the truth is a hard pill to swallow, as they say. I have seen what these monsters are capable of and barely escaped with my life. Perhaps I'd better explain further.

My name is Sean "Scoop" Stevens. I'm an investigative reporter for this city's newspaper, the Herald Chronicle. Two important things. First, sadly, no one actually calls me Scoop; I sort of gave myself that nickname, you know, because of working for the newspaper and all. I realize giving myself a nickname is probably as lame as the nickname itself and likely more than a little creepy. And I recognize it defies the entire concept of acquiring a nickname, whereby said moniker is usually bestowed upon one by others, often friends. Sadly, I have few, if any, friends, partly because of my chosen profession and largely because of my personality or lack of which.

Second, I realize it's unusual to find a real print news medium in today's digital world, but somehow, we're still hanging in there, although we are struggling daily to stay afloat. Despite our troubles, or perhaps because of them, I am proud to be another hungry reporter for yet another dying newspaper. This job and the need to help keep my company afloat so I can continue to enjoy my meager salary is what led me to my almost fatal encounter with a cluster of savage subhumans.

The Chronicle had received several reports about sightings of strange-looking creatures appearing at the city's south side, down around the former industrial area known to locals as "Deadtown." At one time, that place had been bustling with manufacturing plants of all kinds, and those buildings were filled with hard-working employees.

Then the 1990s arrived, the work went east, far east, the jobs vanished, the factories closed, and the buildings were left to fall into ruin. For a while, the city's growing numbers of homeless folks called Deadtown home, but soon their numbers dwindled to nothing.

By the way, I've been told recently that we're supposed to stop referring to those displaced individuals as "homeless" and should start calling them "unhoused." It's said to be a less offensive term. What a crock! I've dealt with enough of these people to tell you they don't care one little bit what anyone calls them. You see, sometimes the act of simply struggling to stay alive from one day to the next has a way of occupying all their time and energy. That doesn't leave a whole lot of time for hurt feelings. Unhoused? Hell, it took me until 2018 to stop calling them bums.

Local politicians took credit for ending the homeless, excuse me, unhoused problem, suggesting their social programs helped those folks successfully advance out of the Deadtown squalor and become productive citizens. Right. As it turned out, the truth was not so straightforward, and I suspected I knew why, but I needed to find the proof necessary to verify my assumptions.

For the previous several months, I had been personally receiving anonymous tips about weird creature sightings in and around Deadtown. Many of the reports came from a low-income government-subsidized apartment complex that butted right up against the north end of Deadtown. Several residents reported hearing strange, eerie growling and moaning sounds drifting along the streets up from Deadtown. Some even said they heard shrieks so terrible it was as if the screamer was being tortured or maybe eaten alive.

At first, I paid little attention to the reports since they originated in the projects, reputed to be a low-income, high-crime, drug-infested cesspool of debauchery. But the more I thought about it, the more I became convinced the reports might be legitimate. After all, these residents lived with violent crime daily and couldn't help but become hardened to its terrible sounds. So, I figured if they were concerned about the noises they heard coming from Deadtown, this might actually be something worth investigating. And being the ace investigative reporter I am, it seemed like it was time for Sean Scoop Stevens to be on the job.

I interviewed several residents who had previously contacted the paper and myself, and I learned that most of the screaming they heard occurred between midnight and two in the morning. I asked several residents if they had seen anything or only heard things. Several people said they had only experienced hearing the screams, and they were unable to determine if the cries came from male or female victims or both. However, these were not the typical types of screams these people were used to hearing.

One woman told me, "Look, man. You gotta know what kinda place this is we livin' in here. It's public housing, you know, the projects. I seen all kinds of stuff, man. I seen women getting raped and beat, I seen men punchin' and stabbin' each another. I even seen a dude get shot and kilt right in the street here outside my house. Every week, I hear women crying 'cause their son or husband got beat, kilt, or arrested. Hell, I hear cop sirens all night long, and 5-0 don't do squat. I mean, they might arrest a few people, but it just ain't 'nuff. It's like a damn jungle 'round here. But I'm telling you that the noises what I heard coming from Deadtown ain't nuttin' like I never heard before."

I asked one resident, an obvious junkie named Harold if he had ever seen anything strange during or after he heard the screaming. The guy was pretty strung out, so at the time, I had to take what he told me with the proverbial grain of salt.

"You say yo name be Scoop? What the Hell kinda name be Scoop?" he asked.

I replied, "Well, um, it's sort of my nickname."

"Why they calls yo Scoop, man? Do y'all run around cleanin' up dog crap or sumptin'?"

I was beginning to question my decision to talk to this guy. I said, "Look, that's not important. I just want to know if you've seen anything strange or unusual over there in Deadtown."

He said, "Ok, Pooper Scooper, no need to get yer undies all in a bunch. Yeah, man, I seen stuff, but I ain't 'zactly sure what I seen. You know, sometimes I be doin' what I calls mixin' and matchin', see? I be

smokin' and snortin' and sometimes adding some booze and pills to
the mix fer good measure. Maybe I adds a little bitta crack, you know?
So maybe I ain't sure I be trustin' everything I be seein', you feel me?
But I'm tellin' you, if what I seen walkin' in them shadows over there in
Deadtown bees true, then we is in some kinda big-time trouble 'round
here. 'Cause what I seen ain't nuttin' like you and me. But I bees telling'
youse, brother, if I ever see any of them mutants outside 'a Deadtown,
I swear to Jesus, God, and whoever else you want to add up in here,
I bees filling their sorry asses fulla bullets. You dig where I'm coming
from, my man?"

Harold went on, in his barely coherent way, to give me an incredibly accurate description of the horrid creatures. Of course, at that time,
I had never seen any of the things myself, but as it turned out, Harold's
description was dead on. He had used such surprising detail, much of
which I didn't believe at the time because of his obvious pharmaceuti-
cal abuse reasons. It was only when I saw the monsters with my own
terrified eyes that I understood how accurate his assessment was despite
his drug-induced stupor. Then again, as they say, seeing is believing.

I hadn't bothered to run my plans by my editor since he made it
clear early on that he didn't buy into any of these reports. He ranked
them right up there with little green men, Bigfoot, and Elvis sightings.
This meant that any investigation I carried out would have to be on my
own, off the reservation, as we say in the newspaper business. Actually,
nobody says that. I picked it up off a TV cop show and thought it
sounded good here. Whatever!

Anyway, this was how I found myself heading deep into the heart
of Deadtown one night shortly after midnight. I was dressed in black
from head to toe so I could become one with the shadows. I carried
my cell phone to snap any good shots or videos of any subhumans I
might stumble upon. My goal was to bring back proof so I could be the
first reporter to have something concrete to give my boss. A discovery
like that could mean our little newspaper would be the first to bring
this story to the world. We would report legitimate news with actual,
indisputable proof, not grocery store tabloid sensationalism. I was sure
a story like that would not only turn yours truly into a household name

but would help bring our newspaper back from the brink of extinction. So, with this goal in mind, I walked ever deeper into the bowels of Deadtown. Most people would think this was a stupid decision on my part, and unfortunately, they would have been absolutely correct.

I walked carefully along one of the darkened side streets with the only illumination available coming from the moon, and most of that was blocked by buildings. I tried to keep my back pressed tightly against brick walls to ensure nothing could sneak up behind me. Whenever I came to an open doorway or narrow passage between buildings, I had to listen intently and be on my guard for anyone or anything lurking in that darkness. Fortunately, I managed to make it all the way to the intersection with what was once the main thoroughfare of the place without encountering any trouble. That was when I heard a soft female voice pleading for mercy.

"Please, please don't hurt me. I'll do whatever you want; please just let me go."

This plea was followed by the mumbling of several different deep, unintelligible voices that sounded like a rambling collection of moans, clicks, and grunts to me. Then, a hungry, savage roar came from the collective, and the woman's voice erupted into shrieks of terror and agony. I heard the sounds of ripping, tearing, and chewing as the screams reached a crescendo . . . and then abruptly stopped. However, those other horrible noises continued. If I live to be one thousand, I'll never forget those ungodly sounds: groaning, tearing, biting, and, God help me, chewing.

I peeked around the corner and couldn't believe my eyes. A group of five or six hideous creatures were systematically dismembering the corpse of a young woman while simultaneously flaying the flesh from her body and eating it raw. The monsters were the most heinous things I had ever seen. They were not more than about five feet tall and were rail thin, although their stomachs appeared swollen and distended.

Although slight in stature, the monsters' arms were roped with sinewy muscles, as were their legs. Their heads seemed larger than what one might consider normal, and none of them had any hair. In fact, they didn't seem to have hair anywhere on their bodies. As I mentioned, their hands and feet were disproportionately huge for their bodies, and those claws were made for rendering flesh, which they did quite proficiently.

One of the bulbous-headed beasts sank those talon-like claws into the dead woman's stomach, then ripped out her intestines and feasted on her bloody entrails. The slimy, slick organs steamed in the evening chill and slithered through the creature's massive hands like serpents.

Another beast had its thick lips stuck fast to the dead woman's face, sucking her eyeball from the socket. Then the monster scrapped one of its razor-sharp claws across the corpse's forehead and then down the side of its face. With a ripping sound, the creature peeled the woman's face from her skull. When it had torn back a sufficient amount, the beast gripped a section in its teeth, yanked, and ripped most of the dead woman's flesh from her face. It took all of my willpower not to puke all over myself.

Instead, I remembered my cell phone camera and began recording the horrifying spectacle. I knew it was too late to do anything to help the poor woman, but I could still at least get proof of her terrible murder. It soon became a feeding frenzy that was more savage than even the most deranged Hollywood horror movie director could even begin to imagine. I fought desperately to keep from tossing my cookies. In my struggle, I must have released an involuntary gulp or whimper, one barely audible, even to myself, but one that was heard by the keen, predatory ears of the subhumans.

At the front of the cluster, one of the monsters ceased its flesh feasting, lifted its head, and began sniffing the air with nostrils flaring in its piggy snout. Soon, the others stopped as well and followed suit. They communicated with a series of guttural grunts and clicks, which seemed to get louder and more frenetic by the second. Then, the largest beast, the creature I took to be the alpha, raised his arm and pointed a long, clawed finger in my direction. He issued an ear-piercing roar, and the monsters ran toward me as one with the huge alpha in the lead. A dozen or more of the beasts poured out of the ruins of adjacent buildings in answer to the leader's call to join the now rampaging group. Some of the revolting monsters ran on all fours while others hobbled clumsily on two legs.

For a terrible second, I stood frozen, horrified to the point of paralysis. Then, fortunately, I gained the wear with all to turn and run. But unfortunately, it was much too late. The incredibly horrible monsters moved more quickly than I could have imagined. And although I ran faster than I ever thought possible, I heard one of the creature's ragged breathing far too close behind me.

I had almost reached the edge of the projects and, hopefully, whatever safety they provided, when I felt something grabbing my shoulder with a vise-like grip, I knew I would never be able to escape. As sharp claws dug deep into the flesh on both sides of my shoulder, I felt the warmth of my life's blood running down my back and chest. Although the fiery pain was almost too much to bear, I continued to struggle fruitlessly, no longer making any forward progress. I knew that shortly, the monster's other massive hand would reach around, and its razor-sharp talons would easily rip out my throat. As if that were not bad enough, among the stink surrounding the beast, I could hear the other monsters gaining on me, preparing to join their leader and finish me off. That was when my ears rang with an incredibly loud explosion, and I felt the iron grip on my shoulder loosen and then fall away completely.

"Yo, take that, you scum-suckin' mutant freaks!" A voice shouted from nearby. Soon, I heard other voices shouting, followed by the firing of more weapons. I risked turning around for a quick look and saw the horde of subhuman monsters limping away back into the darkness of Deadtown. One or two of the creatures had been wounded and were being carried by the others as a trail of crimson decorated the moonlit street behind them.

I felt what I saw was not so much a gesture of kindness or an attempt at rescue on the monsters' part as it was an act of survival. I was quite certain that if and when the wounded creatures died, their flesh would likely be rendered to feed the rest of the tribe. I believed for these horrid creatures; food was food. And if the alpha creature was as severely wounded as I suspected he was, he would likely be attacked and killed by whichever beast was next in line to be leader.

"Yeah, baby! Now that's what I be talkin' 'bout! You seen them ugly muthers run? I might be stoned outta my gourd, but I be telling' your right here and now, I ain't never been so zonked that I couldn't shoot me a mutant or two!" A voice shouted from the darkness.

I waited for a moment, then saw someone walking toward me. It was Harold, the junkie I had interviewed earlier. He was followed by several other residents of the projects, some of whom I had also spoken to. They were all packing heat, and the barrels of their guns smoked and steamed in the cold night air.

"Hey there, Pooper Scooper, my man. Glad to see you is in one piece," Harold, my apparent new junkie friend, said.

I was bleeding from my shoulder wound, which burned like fire. I would have to get it treated before God only knew what sort of infection took hold. I was panting like an exhausted dog and barely was able to speak, but I managed to eke out, "Harold, thank you. You saved my life."

Harold replied, "It wasn't just me; this here be my posse. I believe you met Ladasha."

A woman stepped forward whom I had spoken to earlier. Apparently, her name was Ladasha. She said, "I done tolt you that 5-0 don't do Jack Squat for us po' folk 'round here, so wees all takes care of us selfs."

I raised my arm, showing it to the cluster of project folks, and said, "But now they're gonna have to do something. I got this, and this is proof. I have a video of the creatures. I'm a reporter, and they'll have to believe me when the story breaks."

Harold said, "You best look at your hands, Scoopster. You ain't be carrying nuttin'."

That was when I realized that in the desperate attempt to flee for my life, I must have dropped my cell phone. I suppose the stress of nearly dying made me not realize my hand was empty. The cell phone was gone, and there was no way I would ever get it back. I couldn't go back in there, even with the help of Harold's posse. Those creatures would hide in the darkness and then overwhelm us with their numbers. That meant any proof I might have had of the existence of the subhuman creatures was gone as well.

In the days, months, and years that followed my recovery from my nearly fatal attack, I had tried to warn people about what happened to me. I told my tale at the hospital where I went to have my wounds treated, but everyone there looked at me like I was a few sandwiches short of a picnic. I tried to report it to the police, and as you may have guessed, they also thought I might not be rowing with both oars in the water. I tried to convince my editor that the creatures really existed and even went so far as to suggest that we should start doing a series of stories about these subhumans, but you can only imagine his reply. I suppose I was fortunate to keep my job, although, based on how everyone in the office looks at me these days, I don't know for how much longer.

I think about this terrible experience far too often and have no idea how many of these horrible monsters may exist. Nor can I imagine what danger they might eventually pose to mankind. I assume they live in abandoned sections of cities worldwide, hiding in burned-out skeletal remains of buildings, living in the shadows, and hunting for flesh at night.

They prey on the weak, the mentally infirm, the helpless, and the forgotten; those people we see as the refuse of society. But for how long? Sooner or later, their numbers will grow, as will their hunger. Then, they'll have no choice but to change their hunting habits to survive. When that day comes, I suspect those of us who we so arrogantly consider normal members of the human race will make an appearance front and center on their menu. When that day comes, I will get no satisfaction from saying, "I tried to warn you, but you wouldn't listen."

BECAUSE . . . JUST BECAUSE

*Just because you're good at some things doesn't mean
you can't be better at them.*
—Auston Matthews

Just because we can't find a solution, it doesn't mean that there isn't one.
—Andrew Wiles

*Tremendous amounts of talent are lost to our society
just because that talent wears a skirt.*
—Shirley Chisholm

*The notion that human life is sacred just because
it is human life is medieval.*
—Peter Singer

*Just because you are different does not mean that
you have to be rejected.*
—Eartha Kitt

You'll have to forgive me. I'm feeling a bit churlish today. This sort of attitude isn't common for a girl like me, yet here I am, and there it is, so whatever. You're probably wondering how I found out about you. I

got your name from a business associate who said you were an excellent freelance journalist who would listen to my story without needing
to know my name and, more importantly, without judging me. My
contact said you had done so before, and of course, when you hear
what I have to say, you'll know why this is critical.

Also, I had hoped that since I'm a woman and you're a woman, our
gender bond and the struggles of being ambitious women in a man's
world might help you better understand why I do what I do. I'll do my
best to focus here so I can get this all out there. But I must warn you,
I'm like the poster child for A.D.D. I have trouble staying the course,
as they say. I'll beg your forgiveness in advance.

I truly am glad you agreed to stop by. I have a lot to explain about
myself, and it seems like telling you, a total stranger, is my best bet. I'm
not even sure why I've chosen to meet with you. Perhaps confession
really is good for the soul if you happen to believe in such things as
souls. I'm hoping the telling might at least be cathartic for me. If you
listen closely and pay attention, you'll learn things you probably never
expected to hear. So, if you're ready, I'll get on with it. I have a specific
direction I want this explanation to take, but I might get off track
occasionally.

It's like this: sooner or later, it always comes down to the same
question they all ask: every last one of them. I just can't comprehend
why they all say the same thing. So, do you want to know what question it is they all ask?

Well, they all want to know, "Why are you doing this to me?"
That's it. I swear, it's what every one of them asks. I mean, seriously?
Is that really what they should be asking at such a critical juncture in
their lives? Shouldn't they be, I don't know, maybe trying to negotiate
their release or something? But instead, they all end up sounding like
whiney-bawling babies to me.

"Waah, waah, waah. Why are you doing this to me? Waah, waah,
waah," they plead.

To which I often respond, "Waah, waah, waah. Somebody call a
wambulance." Get it? Wambulance? No? Oh well, your loss. At least
I'm still able to crack myself up. And so you know, I'm not rambling

here. There's a method to my madness, as they say. So, pay attention, girl, pay attention.

The thing is, you'll never catch me bawling, whining, and carrying on like a baby the way these men do. As you can see, I'm a petite woman who barely weighs a hundred pounds, soaked in blood. I thought that line was clever and appropriate, didn't you? No? Wow, you certainly are a tough audience.

Anyway, my best friend, Christine, says it's because I got a big honkin' pair of "lady balls." I'm not quite sure what that means, but I do know that I don't scare easily. Maybe that's what she's referring to. The ironic thing is, even though I seem to fear nothing myself, I am quite proficient at knowing how to strike terror into the hearts of others.

You see, I understand how to deal with men, the way they need to be dealt with. I'm certain men would disagree with me, but that's unimportant. This is especially true for any of those men who have disappointed me. Maybe that sounds a little sexist, and perhaps it is. Some might say my methods aren't exactly what society or the law would condone, but they have worked for me over the years, so who am I to question such things?

I don't know if this is important or not, but I suppose this is where I should point out that I'm a 100 percent heterosexual woman, just in case you're wondering. I'm not a lesbian or bisexual and have no sexual attraction to other females. I love the company of men and have had many sexual relationships with men, as often as my busy schedule permits. As I'm sure you've noticed, I'm what men consider quite lovely and have no trouble catching a man's eye.

That being said, if you haven't figured out where this conversation is heading, please allow me to spell it out for you. You see, I have a proclivity for capturing, torturing, killing, and dismembering men who, shall we say, rub me the wrong way. (No sexual double entendre intended.) Over the years, I have successfully gotten away with shortening the lives of several dozen males of virtually every shape, size, age, race, or national origin imaginable. I presume I am quite good at my chosen avocation since I have never been caught.

Throughout all the years that I've been enjoying my hobby, it never ceases to amaze me how such big, burly, macho-type men seem to turn into little baby boys at the first realization of what the future holds for them while in my creative grasp. It's quite peculiar. Let me see if I can explain what I mean.

Here's a scenario for you to think about. Assume you're a big, strong, good-looking, strapping guy just over six feet tall and 180 pounds of solid muscle. When you walk down the street, women notice you, and other men are sure to stay out of your way. You're the big man on campus, the alpha dog, and you have no time for wimpy boys or overly assertive women.

Now, suppose you encounter one such assertive woman, and she really bothers you. Subconsciously, she probably represents a threat to your masculinity. As a result, you waste no time putting that "uppity big-mouth bitch" in her place with a barrage of your best and most clever, searingly juvenile put-downs and crude comments.

Pay attention, now, because here's where things get good. Imagine sometime later; you wake up after being drugged and taken to a place deep underground where no one can possibly hear you scream for help. You've been strapped naked to a splintery wooden chair, and your hands are aching.

As you slowly come out of your stupor, you notice that several of your fingers have already been severed, and through drug-tinged eyes, you see those same missing digits lying on a nearby stainless steel surgical cart in a small pool of blood. You're unsure if you're awake or still asleep and having a horrible nightmare.

Then you feel a burning on your chest and a firey pain in your groin. You reluctantly look downward and through your fog to see dozens of angled razor cuts across your chest, leaking rivulets of blood, which form tributaries leading to a lake of crimson puddling between your legs, where your genitalia used to be.

Seeing that you are finally conscious, I say something pithy like, "Welcome back, big boy. Ready to play?"

You look up and see a beautiful young woman, me, sitting on a stool in front of you with a surgical scalpel in her hand, smiling with a look of hunger like a starving timber wolf. You have no idea where you are or how you got there. But you recognize the woman as the same woman you trash-talked earlier, the one you thought you had put in her place. But now, all you know is that you're helpless, sexless, bleeding, and in agony, and you will likely not be leaving this room alive.

And you mean to tell me the best question you can think to ask is, "Why are you doing this to me?"

Why not offer me money to stop the torture and set you free? That probably wouldn't work since you saw my face and could link me to several people who heard you bad-mouth me. Plus, we both know the only way you're leaving this room is in small pieces.

Maybe you could apologize for being a rude, sexist moron and could beg me for forgiveness. That would be cool and might buy you some time; however, the fact remains it wouldn't keep you from your appointment with my handy chainsaw. Again, unfortunately for you, nothing will change the final outcome of our encounter.

Well, perhaps you could claim to be a VIP and that if you're missing, half the city will be looking for you. You could act all high and mighty and tell me how badly I really screwed up and stepped in it big time. Do you think that might help you? Sorry, Charlie, I think not. But at least you gave it a creative attempt.

I suppose that point is moot since nobody ever tries to come up with anything clever like that. They never think of anything to help them get out alive, futile as such a thing might be. Nope, instead, they all seem to want to know the same thing, "Why are you doing this to me?"

Take, for example, that worthless piece of human dung over there in the other room next to us. He is slowly coming out of his tranquilizer dart-induced nap, and when he comes to, he will not be a happy camper. I have all sorts of fun planned for him. I'm not a betting woman, but if I were, I would lay high odds on the fact that once he's awake sufficiently to realize the extent of his peril, the first thing he'll do will be to ask me, "Why are you doing this to me?"

I'm sure by now you've probably formed your own opinion of me based on what I've told you, but I guarantee your perception is very wrong. First off, I'm not insane; I know that. Then again, how many crazy people actually do know they're bonkers? I prefer to think of myself as a creative genius and a flesh artist, much like the legendary Jack The Ripper.

As you can see, I'm not some wild, feral street person living in a moldy blanket tent beneath an overpass. Nor am I some meth-mouthed, toothless drug friend desperate for her next fix. I'm a well-dressed, educated, upper-middle-class businesswoman. I earn my living as a high-end travel agent, dealing only with the richest members of high society. I know celebrities, rock stars, politicians, movie stars, and the like.

My job allows me the privilege of worldwide travel, which has benefited me greatly in my, shall we say, pastime. Spreading my kills around the globe has helped me to remain undetected for all these years. Unfortunately, the question is still the same, no matter what country I practice my craft in.

For example, do you know what "*Wieso tust du mir das an?*" in German means? No? How about French? Do you know what "*Pourquoi est-ce que tu me fais ça?*" means? Not that either? What if someone asks you, "*Perché stai facendo questo a me?*" in Italian? I'm sure you've figured out where this is going by now. Yep, that's right, they all ask me the same damn question regardless of their languages, "Why are you doing this to me?"

After a while, I accepted that they all would ask me. So, now I try to make a point of answering their stupid questions, no matter how infantile and moronic I may feel it is. I mean, it only seems fair since they're just minutes from death. What can a little honesty hurt? The truth is, between you, me, and that soon-to-be dead guy in the other room, I have no idea why I do what I do. I was raised by two loving parents in an upper-middle-class neighborhood. I went to the best schools, had plenty of socio-economic opportunities, graduated from an Ivy League college, and landed my sweet job.

Yet, nonetheless, here I am. For whatever reason, I still have this need, this passion to kill people in the most horrendous ways. I guess it's more than just who I am; it's what I am. So, I suppose to justify my actions, I tend to put myself in situations that allow some unsuspecting half-witted man to disrespect me. When he does, I have an excuse to do what I love, and he becomes my next project.

So, you see why that ridiculous question, "Why are you doing this to me," is not one I can't truthfully answer with a simple response. It, like life, is complicated. On those occasions when I choose to respond, I simply say, "Why am I doing this? Because. Just because."

Some might think such a response is arrogant, but I don't. So, with that being said, what do you think about my story? Do you think I'm crazy, maybe just a bit touched in the head? Do you agree with my methods or consider them a trifle over the top? What? No comment? Nothing to say?

Oh, that's right, I forgot. You can't say anything with your tongue cut out and your lips sewn together, can you? Oops, my bad. Yeah, I suppose it slipped my mind. That's right, you've been dead for several days. I guess that explains the awful smell and all those buzzing flies. And how about those two nasty-looking holes? I can't recall if I dug your eyeballs out before or after you died. I hope I did it before, as that would have been much more fun. Either way, the maggots dripping from those empty sockets seem to enjoy themselves immensely.

Well, you should consider yourself honored. You may not be my first kill and certainly won't be my last, but you were my first female kill, and that's kind of a special thing. This opens up a whole new world of possibilities for me. Adding females who annoy me to my repertoire will be an interesting change. I wonder if they'll ask me that ridiculous question: why am I doing this to them? You know, like all the men do, like you did. I suppose they will. If they do, the answer will be the same. I'll say, "Because . . . Just because."

THE LEAPER

"The hideous creature rises from the depths of its Hellish blackness once every four years, on February 29th, as it has done for centuries. And for twenty-four hours, it mercilessly kills everyone and everything in its path. It hunts without thought, empathy, or remorse. It kills because that's what it was conjured from the fires of Hell to do and because it needs to feast on the organs of its victims. Like any animal fattening itself for a long winter's hibernation, the creature must feed enough to carry itself through its four years of sleep. That's why those people who know and believe call this horrid monster The Leaper."

"Woah! Wait a minute," Josh told his friend Dean, who was narrating the story by reading it from a sheet of paper he had pulled from his pocket. He was part of a group of young boys sitting around a roaring campfire in the woods just outside town. Josh wore his signature black hooded sweatshirt, which he was seldom seen without. Fortunately for the boys, this last week of February had been unseasonably warm. Although they were appropriately dressed, it was good that no snow had fallen for several weeks.

Josh pushed up his glasses, which seemed to be constantly sliding down his nose, and continued, "That story sounds familiar, like I saw it in a movie or something."

Another boy named Charlie spoke up, "Yeah. Dean, that sounds a lot like that Jeepers Creepers guy from those scary movies. Only you're calling your monster The Leaper."

"Heck, it even sounds the same, Creeper and Leaper," Bobby Johns, another boy, somewhat younger than the others, said as he peeked timidly out from under the brim of his green cap. The cap didn't display the image of any famous sports team, but it showed the logo of his dad's dry-cleaning business, a stylized version of the letter J.

Dean argued, "No. No. No. They aren't anything alike. That Creeper dude shows up like once every 23 years and eats for 23 days or something like that. And he's from outer space or somewhere. The Leaper comes once every four years and only eats for a day. Besides, he's from Hell and comes on Leap Day, so that's why he's called The Leaper."

Charlie said, "I don't know, Dean-o. That story of yours kinda sounds sort of like a cheesy, low-budget rip-off to me."

"First of all. It ain't no rip-off, and unlike that other movie story, The Leaper is real."

"Excuse me?" Charlie interrupted, "Did you just try to tell us that this balonie story you've been tossing at us is real?"

Dean continued, "Yeah. The Leaper is the real deal, man. He came here to our town four years ago, in 2020, back when we were all like 5 or 6; that's why most of us don't know about it. Nobody in town likes to talk about it."

"You're serious, aren't you?" Charlie asked.

"You better believe I am. I also heard that when The Leaper came four years before that, in 2016, he killed like 9 or 10 people in town, not to mention over 30 animals, all during the 24 hours of Leap Day."

Josh said, "Hold on a minute, Bud, I gotta call you out on that. This ain't a very big town, Dean-o. And if this Leaper dude showed up every four years, going back, like you said, a couple hundred years, and killed a boatload of people every time he showed his ugly face, there wouldn't be anyone left in town. Am I right?"

Dean hesitated for a minute as if contemplating Josh's logic and perhaps trying to find a way to get himself out of the corner he seemed to have apparently painted himself into. Then he had an inspiration, "I never said he only killed people who live here. I just said he killed everyone in his path."

Then Dean pointed in a western direction and said, "You guys hear those cars? The interstate runs right past our town, and as you all know, cars are constantly getting off at our exit to stop to get gas and food. We have a ton of restaurants just at the edge of town, all open 24-7. Out there are probably like three truck stops and five gas stations with minimarts. Everybody stops here. Also, many people stop to rest overnight at one of the gazillion hotels outside of town. For a monster like the Leaper, that's like an all-you-can-eat buffet."

Charlie asked, "But get serious, Dean. Even if such a monster could exist, which, by the way, it can't, there's no way somebody in town wouldn't have blown its brains out by now. Everybody in and around town is gun crazy; they all own guns, they hunt, and any one of them would jump at the chance to take a few shots at any monster like that."

"I suspect somebody or other probably did try to kill the thing sometime, Chuckster. It only makes sense. But it wouldn't do no good. This thing is what they call immortal. It was sent here by the Devil himself to do his dirty work. So, there ain't nobody can kill it."

Charlie was visibly frustrated, "First of all, don't call me Chuckster. Second, every monster can be killed. They all have their weaknesses. You just have to know what kills 'em. Ain't that right, Josh?"

Josh hated to be put on the spot, especially when it came to his pal, Dean. But Charlie was right; every movie monster Josh had ever heard of had a weakness that could be used to kill them. The werewolves could be killed with silver bullets, Frankenstein's monster feared fire, and zombies needed a good shot in the brain. Vampires had more weaknesses than most, such as sun, garlic, crosses, holy water, and a wooden steak through the heart. It's a wonder anyone was even scared of vampires. Even though Josh knew what Charie was saying was valid, he didn't want to make his friend, Dean, look bad, especially in front of the gang.

Josh tried to remain impartial and perhaps act as the peacemaker to defuse this escalating confrontation. He said, "Hang on a minute, Charlie. What you're saying is true for all the fictional monsters we know about, but that's just a bunch of junk some writers made up. If they wanted to, they could make up anything. They could say that werewolves could be killed by grated mozzarella cheese. So, I suppose if Dean wants his creature to be indestructible, then I don't see why he can't. After all, it's his story."

Charlie was getting angrier by the minute. He said, "But that's the point here, Josh. Dean is saying it ain't just a story. He's claiming this Leaper monster really exists. Although I don't believe one bit of that, if the Leaper was real, then something could kill it."

Dean said, "Fine! Don't believe it. Either of you. What should I care?"

Bobby spoke up, "Whatever, you guys. Look, it's getting late, and if I don't get my sorry butt home soon, I won't hafta worry about no Leaper, or Creeper or nothin'. My Mom will skin me alive."

"Hang on a second, Bobby. I'll walk home with you," Charlie said as he checked the time on his smartwatch, "I gotta get home too. Besides, I've had about enough of Dean's goofy story. I'm outta here. I'll see you two guys tomorrow." He gave a slight wave as he turned to follow Bobby.

"Well, I suppose the boys have a good point. We should probably be gettin' home as well. What do you think, Dean-o?"

Dean shook his head slowly as he looked with disappointment at his friend. "You know. That wasn't exactly much support you gave me a few minutes ago when Charlie was ragging' on me, Josh, old buddy." Josh couldn't help but notice how Dean said, "old buddy." It was blatantly obvious that his words were dripping with sarcasm.

"I . . . I don't know what you're so upset about, Dean-o," Josh responded, knowing exactly what Dean was angry about. Josh knew his wimpy response to Charlie's argument had been a feeble attempt at dodging any commitment to support Dean and his story.

Dean said, "Look, Josh. I get what you did, and I understand why you did it. You wanted to go along to get alone. It's just . . . I don't know, I guess I expected more from you, is all. You know, 'cause of us being friends. I thought maybe we were better friends than that, but I guess I was wrong."

"No, Dean, you weren't wrong. We are buds. I don't know what I was thinking. I guess I was just being . . . I don't know."

"A dick head?" Dean offered. He couldn't manage to hide his smirk.

Josh smiled and said, "That might be a bit harsh, but ok, I guess I deserved that."

"And a douchebag," Dean added.

"Guilty as charged," Josh agreed.

"And a . . ."

Josh interrupted his friend, "Enough already, Dean-o. No need to kick a man when he's down. Point taken. Now, how about we head home for the night and start fresh tomorrow?"

Dean looked at his friend and said, "You won't see me tomorrow, maybe Friday."

"What's wrong wrong with tomorrow? It's just Thursday, what's the big deal? We get together like every day after supper."

"Let's just say I have no intention of going anywhere until Friday."

"Including school?" Josh said, disbelieving.

"Yep, including school. I already got my Mom to call me off."

"Why's that?"

"In case you didn't notice, Josh, old boy, tomorrow is Thursday, February 29th. That means it's Leap Day. And you know what that means?"

"Seriously, Dean? You're going to let some goofy story control your life?"

Dean said, "I told you before, it ain't just a story. It's true."

Josh was surprised to see that he was getting angry and no longer concerned about what Dean thought. As he pushed up his glasses for what seemed like the millionth time, Josh said, "Fine. If that's the way you want it, then enjoy your day of seclusion while Bobby, me, and Charlie have our daily fun out in the woods tomorrow night. Maybe we'll all tell stories about what a chicken you are and how you hide in your house with the covers pulled up over your head, all because of some lame story."

"Whatever, Josh. You do what you have to do, and I'll do what I have to do. Maybe I'll see you all Friday after school, that is if the Leaper doesn't get you first."

"Leaper, schmeeper, Dean," And with that less-than-effective comeback, Josh headed home in his typical westerly direction while Dean headed to his home in the East.

* * *

Dean stood staring down at his feet as the storm dumped gallons of water, soaking him to the skin. He seemed either to not notice or not care that his clothing hung like sodden bath towels from his slumped, trembling shoulders. The young boy was weeping uncontrollably and with no concern who saw him because anyone watching would agree his sorrow was understandable. He had accidentally stumbled upon the ruined remains of what had once been his best friends, Josh, Charlie, and little Bobby.

He had showed up at their usual meeting place in the woods after dinner on Friday, expecting to find them waiting for them. Dean hadn't seen them at school that day. However, that wasn't unusual as they were in different classes and had different lunch periods. Yet he was surprised he hadn't at least seen them in passing during the day. But upon arriving at their meeting spot, Dean had unfortunately found them waiting for him as they must have been since the previous night. They hadn't heeded his warning. They hadn't believed him, and now it was too late.

Had it not been for their clothing and discarded backpacks, even their own mothers wouldn't have been able to identify what was left of the bodies. Little Bobby's ball cap was splattered with blood. Charlie's smartwatch lay shattered in the mud, and Josh's black hoodie was shredded. Josh's formerly troublesome glasses were smashed and lying bloodstained in the mud. In hysterics, Dean immediately called 911 and tearfully explained where he was and what he had found. The police soon arrived in several cars with lights flashing and sirens blaring.

While he waited for the police to arrive, Dean looked at the remains of what had once been his friends with a clinical detachment that had to be the result of his shocked condition. Each of their heads had been torn from their bodies by some creature of incredible strength, as their neck stumps appeared shredded rather than cleanly cut during the decapitation. The corpses' flesh had been sliced as if by a creature with razor-like claws, and it seemed as if all of the vital organs had been removed from hollow cavities that remained in the bodies. The torsos lay limbless, with those missing arms and legs lying haphazardly on the grass nearby. The flesh on those stumps was as tattered as the neck flesh had been. It was obvious that whatever animal had done this was incredibly strong. It had to be to rip those limbs from the bodies.

When the police arrived, both uniformed patrol men, as well as plainclothes detectives and a forensic team, did what they could to recover evidence, although they knew their job would be an exercise in futility as the torrential rain had washed away most of the evidence they might hope to find. All three boys had been reported missing the previous evening. Unfortunately, their parents were unaware of the boys' secret meeting place in the woods and could not point the police in that direction.

In addition, police resources had been spread thin over the previous twenty-four hours as they dealt with similar murders of more than a dozen other people at the truckstops and hotels out at the edge of town. However, the local authorities hesitated to call these deaths murders and had chosen instead to refer to them as "attacks." This reference was because the authorities were certain some wild animal, like a bear or mountain lion, must have been responsible for the deaths. They were so savage that no one could imagine anything but a beast being responsible.

Dean had been interviewed first by the uniformed police, and then the detectives had their turn questioning him. It was all a matter of protocol, crossing Ts and dotting Is. Everyone present, from the detectives to the beat cops to Dean, knew this was a complete waste of time. They had no doubt that Dean was incapable of being responsible for the carnage. The police were convinced whatever animal had been accountable for the other deaths was guilty of these as well. They assumed the beast likely had been passing through the area and inadvertently stumbled upon its victims. They felt that the animal had probably moved on by now, especially with all the commotion caused by the bright lights and sirens.

The town Mayor was anxious to close this case and had made it clear for investigators to keep a lid on the situation. The last thing his already economically challenged town needed was bad publicity. However, no matter how the Mayor wanted to sweep these events under the rug, the story would get out sooner or later. He, of course, would spin the story of a wild animal at his press conference.

But nothing could change what Dean knew to be true. He knew exactly what sort of monster had done this, just as his friends had sadly discovered moments before they died. There was, however, no joy in his being right. His friends were dead, savagely ripped to bits, their insides devoured, and their remains left in the mud like so much biological refuse.

Dean understood it would be four more years before such a horror would return to his town. When it did, he would hide again. But someday, Dean would be a man. Then, he would find a way to kill the monster and get revenge for his dead friends. Dean swore with all his heart and soul that someday, even if the creature was supposed to be immortal, he would be the one to destroy The Leaper.

SCRAMBLED EGGS

At last, the long, stressful week was over, and Don was hoping for a chance to put his work troubles behind him for a couple of days. That goal might seem achievable in theory or perhaps on a television beer commercial, but in reality, problems couldn't simply be switched off or drowned in the bottom of a beer mug. Don knew because he had tried it on many occasions. Even drinking whiskey or vodka in generous proportions couldn't blind him to the seemingly insurmountable problem of his idiot boss. The previous night's foray into alcoholic stuper had proven that.

Don looked around his low-rent apartment through bleary eyes, trying to make sense of the mess his life had become. His wife was gone for good, as was his house, Lexus, and half of his money. To say she took him to the cleaners was an understatement. It would be more accurate to say on the way to the cleaners; she took him to about thirty proctologists, each of whom did a rectal exam on him with chainmail gloves.

At least he still had a job. Even though the thought of returning to work in two days made Don feel like puking. The reason was his direct supervisor. The nicest thing Don could say about his boss, a loser named Guy Littleton, was that the man was way beyond pathetic. In fact, such an image would be a stretch goal the man should strive to achieve.

They say that everyone eventually gets promoted to their level of incompetence. Guy "Little Done" Littleton had reached his level of ineptitude several promotions earlier. In fact, everyone seemed to know it except Guy himself. His over-inflated narcissistic ego allowed him not only to believe that he was performing flawlessly in his current managerial capacity but could and eventually would excel at positions much higher within his company.

Guy's superiors either didn't know about his shortcomings or didn't care. Maybe they consciously chose to turn a blind eye to his ineptitude. Don had heard stories of how some higher-ups in management, those uncertain of their capabilities, liked to have managers under them who didn't pose a threat. Guy Littleton fit that mold perfectly.

It was Saturday morning, and Don was sitting at his kitchen table, feeling lethargic and more than a bit hungover after another night of excessive drinking followed by restless sleeping. He hadn't even given breakfast a second thought. Instead, he stared out the kitchen window into the early morning darkness, hoping for some revelation to pop into his foggy brain.

He knew he had to find some way to get his mind off his conflict with his idiot boss. Don had given up fantasizing about slowly torturing and then killing the man several weeks earlier. He was sure he could never do such a thing; Don simply didn't believe he was wired that way. So, instead, he tried to focus on not thinking about the man. He soon found such an idea was futile; it was like someone asking you not to think of the color red or the number three. Once you tried not to think of them, that became all you could think of.

Don heard and then felt his stomach growl loudly. At first, he thought it was an accumulation of acid from stress. Or perhaps his stomach was in rebellion against the alcohol he had consumed. Then, just before he reached for an antacid in the powder room medicine cabinet, Don realized he hadn't eaten a thing since breakfast the previous morning.

"It's not a bad stomach, just a hungry stomach," Don said to the empty room. He was relieved to realize his problem was hunger. Not only that, but he knew exactly what he was hungry for. He lifted his right hand with his index finger extended in an "ah ha" moment and said, "Scrambled eggs."

Don hoped making himself one of his favorite meals might prove to be therapeutic. When he made breakfast, it was more than simply preparing food; it was an event, perhaps even an experience. Don knew this cathartic, almost ritualistic act was exactly what he needed.

"It's gonna be a great morning. I can feel it in my bones," Don said. Then he set to work getting ready for the culinary adventure into the world of flavor. That was before he realized it had been weeks since he had made breakfast. He had been under the gun so badly of late that most days, he grabbed a breakfast sandwich at a local fast food drive-through window or a 24-hour mini-mart choke-and-puke food counter.

But not today! This morning, he wouldn't eat swill, pretending to be food, like some pitiful loser. No, Sir. This morning, Don would treat himself to a breakfast fit for a winner, and he would do all he could this weekend to prove he was a winner despite how Guy Littleton tried to make him feel.

Don went to the refrigerator to find what he was looking for. There was an egg carton on the top shelf with two eggs remaining. That was exactly the number of eggs he needed. He checked the expiration date and saw they were a day over the due date. Don decided the date was likely arbitrary or simply due to some bureaucratic legislation. As far as he was concerned, a day over the expiration date was nothing to worry about.

Besides, he had hardly opened his refrigerator in days, so the contents were well protected from outside influences. When Don checked the date on the butter, he saw it was close to expiration, but he could still proceed confidently. Don thought he might like a tall glass of milk with breakfast, but unfortunately, that expiration date ship had sailed more than a week ago. So, he'd have to grab a bottle of Coke from the garage and cool it in a glass with ice cubes.

He decided to forego buttered toast when he discovered a new, "previously-undocumented-by-science" form of green penicillin growing on the four remaining slices. Checking out his freezer, he found a couple of frozen waffles that were only partially covered with frost. He knew he had some strawberry jelly in the refrigerator on the door, which would work for the waffles. Then Don was surprised to find some frozen heat-and-eat sausages that he hoped would round out his breakfast nicely. He decided it might be best not to bother checking the date on those. He figured, why mess with a good thing?

Don grabbed what had been his favorite small frying pan, back when he had more time to cook, and placed it on the front burner of his gas stove. He turned the unit on low, giving the pan time to warm up. He cracked his two eggs into a teacup that he took down from the cabinet and had rinsed, just in case.

He shook in generous amounts of salt and black pepper and stirred the contents thoroughly using a fork. Although Don was not usually a fan of spicy foods, he did like pepper in his scrambled eggs. Seeing the pan was ready, Don sliced about a one-quarter-inch pad of butter off the stick and dropped it into the pan, where it began to sizzle and melt.

Don grabbed the pan's handle and slowly swirled the melting butter until the entire bottom of the pan was covered. Then he poured in his stirred eggs. While the eggs cooked, Don put two frosty frozen waffles in the toaster and microwaved the sausages for two minutes.

He chopped and scrambled the eggs, and just as they were done, he heard the sound of the toaster dinging. Then he heard the microwave oven finish its cycle as well.

"Perfect timing all around," Don said to the empty kitchen as he spread jelly onto his waffles. He scraped the scrambled eggs onto the plate beside the sausages he had taken from the microwave oven.

He walked over to the table and sat down to what he hoped would be one of the most eventful breakfast feasts he had enjoyed in a long time. Don had no idea just how eventful his meal would be. He took a cautious bite of his waffle, expecting to be accosted with a nasty freezer taste, but was pleasantly surprised to find it delicious.

"Apparently, jelly hides a multitude of sins," he mused to himself.

He didn't fair quite as well with the sausage links. They bore the trace elements of freezer burn so much that Don decided he couldn't hope to eat them. He took a healthy swig of his soda to wash away the taste. At least he still had his scrambled eggs.

Don looked down at his plate of eggs, eager to begin, when he noticed something odd. In one area of his plate, the scrambled eggs, combined with the black pepper, formed a shape no more than an inch in size. Don couldn't place the name of what he saw, but it looked like a caricature of a dog from a cartoon he used to watch as a kid. The eye was a dot of pepper, and the tip of the creature's nose was several bits of pepper combined. The rest of the tiny face was formed by the eggs.

Was it Scooby Doo, Huckleberry Hound, or maybe one of those dogs from the Scrooge McDuck cartoon, the Beagle Boys? Don couldn't tell, but he knew it most definitely was some sort of dog image. He blinked his eyes several times, hoping the shape would fade back into being just eggs, but it remained.

He found it strange that, after years of eating scrambled eggs, he never previously noticed a shape like that. It was like looking up at clouds and seeing them morph into familiar forms. Don recalled reading accounts of people seeing images of Christ burned into their toast and other miraculous things. He had always passed these off as coincidence, overactive imagination, or perhaps . . . hallucination.

Was that it? Was that what was happening? Was the stress he had been under causing him to hallucinate? He looked down at his eggs again and saw a bird, perhaps a seagull. Why hadn't he ever noticed these shapes before? He stared across the room, catching his reflection in the window. He looked every bit as confused as he felt.

That was when he heard a voice whisper his name. The sound appeared to be coming from his plate. Don looked down and saw the dog image had gone, as was the seagull; apparently, both had been absorbed back into the mound of eggs. In its place was something Don couldn't believe he was seeing.

A pair of perfectly shaped life-sized human lips had formed in his scrambled eggs. As if this were not strange enough, the lips were moving. Don stared unbelievably at the silently moving lips as he heard words forming in his mind.

"Oh, Don. Oh, poor Don. What are we going to do about you?"

Don stared at the undulating lips; now certain something must have snapped in his already stressed mind. Was this what it was like to go mad? Had his mental train jumped the track? Don felt like he was still sane, yet his scrambled eggs were speaking to him, not just speaking, but apparently doing so to suggest they were disappointed with him.

"Whaah?" That was all Don could manage to squeak out. He was starting to realize he might truly be losing it.

"You, Don. We're wondering what we're supposed to do about you."

Don stammered, "Buh . . . buh . . . but you're jus . . . just my plate of eggs. You can't be . . . I mean . . . I can't be hearing . . ."

"Oh, we get it, Don. You think just because we're a plate of eggs, we can't be speaking. You probably think you must be suffering some sort of psychotic breakdown or something. Maybe you are, or maybe you're not. Who are we to say? After all, we're just a plate of eggs."

Don found he couldn't think of anything to say. He sat in awe of what was happening on his plate.

"Well, Don. Here's the thing. We may just be a plate of rapidly cooling scrambled eggs, but even we are smart enough to recognize the source of your anguish. It's your boss, Don. All of your problems lead back to the same point of origin. That point is Guy T. Littleton. He's the reason you've been so stressed for the past several years, Don. He's why your wife divorced you, took your house, and left you living alone in this dump of an apartment.

"The stress you allowed that idiot to put you under ruined your life, Don. He caused you to become withdrawn and incommunicative. But do you know what, Don? You let him do it. That's right, Donny boy. He may be a first-class bully and a-hole extraordinaire, but here's the thing. Idiots like Guy Littleton can only succeed at being jerks if people like you let them.

"No wonder your wife left you, Don. Remember how she called you a wimp for not standing up to him? She was right, Don. You are a wimp, a loser. And now you're stuck here alone in a crappie apartment, being chastised by a plate of scrambled eggs. What's wrong with this picture, Donny boy?"

Don tried to speak through trembling lips, "I . . . I don't know . . . I don't know what . . . to do."

"Of course you do, Don. You know exactly what you have to do. It's Saturday, and the office is practically empty. But you know your boss will be stopping in for a few hours to put in the appearance of working. But we both know he'll really be hiding out in his office watching porn on his tablet and probably pleasing himself with the five-knuckle shuffle, won't he, Don?"

"Yeah . . . that's probably right," he replied.

"No one else will be around, Don. This is your one chance to regain your manhood. This is your opportunity to show your ex-wife that she was wrong. You can prove you're no wimp, no loser, Don. You can do this. You have to do this."

In a monotone, hypnotic voice, Don said, "I have to do this," as he stood up from the table, walked across the kitchen, and took a butcher's knife from a drawer.

He walked barefoot in his pajamas toward his front door in a daze, picking up his car keys and office security badge. Behind him, the plate of uneaten scrambled eggs sat cooling. To anyone else, the breakfast would look uneventful. But not to Don.

He was a man on a mission. As he opened the door, he was smiling, all the while repeating, "I know what I have to do."

THE THING ABOUT BARBIE

Author's Note: Again, Twisted Pulp magazine approached me about writing a story to accompany their Barbie pinup feature. I figured I might as well give it a try, and this was the result.

"Brenda, this obsession of yours has gotten way out of control," Herbert Weinstock said to his wife. He was standing in his living room with his briefcase, ready to head out to work. He looked about the room with a combination of disgust and frustration.

"I don't know what you're talking about, Herb," she replied.

"Jesus, Brenda. You've gotta be kidding me! It's this obsession you have with collecting all this Barbie crap! For God's sake! You're fifty-seven years old. Why the hell are you still collecting these ridiculous dolls?"

Herbert pointed to the hundreds of boxed Barbie dolls that lined the shelves on almost every wall. He had known his wife collected everything Barbie-related when he married her thirty-five years earlier, but back then, her collection had been relegated to a small extra bedroom in a seldom-used area of the house. Now, Barbie paraphernalia was found in abundance in every room.

Brenda replied, "You just don't understand Herb. You never understood. The world of Barbie isn't simply about collecting dolls; it's so much more than that. The thing about Barbie is it's a . . . well, I suppose it's a lifestyle."

"Lifestyle?" Herb shouted, "More like a cult of mindless idol-worshiping minions. That's it! It's idolatry; that's what it is. Brenda, you've become an idol-worshipping pagan!"

"Don't be ridiculous, Herb. You just don't get it. Barbie is so much more. Did you know that Barbie's full name is Barbara Millicent Roberts, and she was brought to us in 1959? Her creator was a wonderful woman named Ruth Handler. Barbie grew up in the fictional town of Willows, Wisconsin, and she was named after Ruth Handler's daughter, Barbara. And did you know Ken was named after Ruth's son, Kenneth? But in Barbie's world, he is actually called Kenneth Sean Carson, or Ken for short. Did you know he was introduced to the world in 1961, just two years after Barbie came into our lives?"

"Did I know? Of course, I knew. After all, I've been hearing you spew this ridiculous Barbie history nonsense for more than three decades."

"Well then, Mr. Smarty Farty, did you know there were 176 different Barbie dolls produced with 9 body types, 35 different skin colors, and 94 different hairstyles?"

"No, Brenda, I didn't know that, and guess what? My life has gone on just fine without knowing that."

"Well, Herb, allow me to improve your knowledge. The Mattel company recently released a separate line of gender-neutral dolls called 'Creatable World.'"

"Gender-neutral? All those stupid Barbie World dolls are gender-neutral. Ken's got no equipment, neither does Barbie, and neither of them have nipples. If that ain't gender-neutral, I don't know what is."

Ignoring his comment, Brenda added, "And for your information, that new Barbie movie had made around 1.5 billion dollars, Herb; not million but billion."

"And I hate to think how much money came from you and your weirdo friends. I'll bet you saw that movie like ten times."

"Oh, I saw it way more times than that, Herb!"

"Like it's not bad enough, you're blowing all of our money on this doll garbage, but now the movie?"

"Think about it, Herb, Barbie's popularity is rising again. It's a rebirth of interest in Barbie's world. My collection will be worth even more now."

"First of all, your collection is worth nothing if you don't sell it, and if you did ever decide to sell it, the junk is only worth whatever some other idiots are willing to pay for it."

"Oh, Herb. You'll never understand. Barbie is for everyone. Barbie now covers every aspect of society. There are hearing-impaired Barbies, heavier curvy Barbies, Muslim Barbies, Mexican Barbies, even a Barbie with Down Syndrome."

"Wonderful! A retarded Barbie? I suppose that was made in honor of all you lifetime collectors."

"That's a horrible thing to say, Herb! It was a very kind thing for the Barbie folks to do. Now, truly everyone can find a place in Barbie world."

"Really, Brenda? What about crazy 57-year-old overweight women who insist on living a fantasy life vicariously by collecting and hoarding stupid dolls? Where do those women fit in, Brenda?"

Brenda was taken aback for a moment, then regained her calm and said, "I'll have you know, Herbert Weinstock, we Barbie enthusiasts are much more than collectors. We are the caretakers of the Barbie universe. That responsibility is a great and noble task. As you have so eloquently demonstrated by your juvenile comments, it can be a challenging duty, fraught with criticism and ridicule from those who are simply too ignorant to understand."

"Ignorant? Ignorant? Look, Brenda. I've had it! I'm going to work, and when I get home, these dolls better be gone, or I'm going to pile them up in the backyard and burn them."

Brenda screamed, "You . . . you wouldn't! You couldn't do something so horrible. You wouldn't dare!"

"I most certainly would and most definitely will! Mark my words, Brenda!"

With that final declaration, Herbert left for the office, slamming the front door behind him. The impact caused several boxed Barbie toys to fall from their shelves. When one of the boxes fell, it revealed a small opening that had been cut into the wall and which was hidden by one of the boxes. Brenda reached into the void and retrieved a very special Barbie character. She had created it by modifying a damaged Ken doll she had picked up at a flea market. It was one Herbert had never seen.

She looked around the room at her prize collection and said, "Well, girls, I suppose we always knew it would come down to this someday."

* * *

Herb sat at his office desk, still fuming over the morning's confrontation with his wife. He realized he shouldn't have lost his temper and given her the ultimatum. It wasn't that he didn't feel justified in doing so; it was just that now he was committed to acting. If he did nothing, any of his future threats would become impotent. If he did what he threatened to do, his wife would never forgive him. There would likely be no need for future threats, as she would probably divorce him and take half of everything they owned, if not more.

As he sat at his desk, staring at his clasped, sweaty hands, he suddenly felt a sharp pain at the back of his neck. The agony was incredible, worse than anything he had ever experienced before. It felt like his flesh had been flayed. He reflexively tried to reach his hand back to the painful spot, only to discover he couldn't move. Whatever malady had suddenly hit him, it had completely paralyzed him. He wondered if perhaps he was experiencing a stroke.

Herb believed he might be having a panic attack because he couldn't breathe. It was as if something was cutting off his airways. Then the pain shifted to the front of his neck, and as he dropped face-first onto his desk, a steady stream of blood-tinged drool leaked from the corner of his now-dead mouth.

* * *

"Well, that should take care of things. Don't you agree, ladies?" Brenda asked the silent Barbie figurines staring out from the clear plastic display windows of their coffin-like boxes.

She was looking down at the customized Barbie character he had made herself. It might have once been a Ken doll, but it no longer looked anything like one. Brenda had meticulously sanded off most of its hair, leaving only a semicircular fringe of hair around its head. What remained was hand-painted gray. She had also given the figure a gray mustache.

Brenda had hand-made a pair of plaid boxer shorts and a white wife-beater undershirt, complete with beer and pizza stains. She had made a round foam pot belly that filled out the shirt. It was no coincidence that the doll looked exactly like Herb. Nor was it surprising that the doll's clothing had been made from Herb's unwashed underwear or that the doll's belt had been made from a string woven from strands of Herb's hair Brenda had taken from his hairbrush over time. In fact, most people would probably say the doll could be Herb's doppelganger if it weren't for the fact that its head had just been sawed from its body.

LINCOLN PRESCOTT

/ 1 /

The dark can be strange and often two-timing mistress. She can be like a cocoon, surrounding and enfolding you in her arms, protecting you. She can also be a cloak of invisibility, shielding your enemy as he awaits to attack. I counted on her to do both that night, as I had a somewhat unpleasant task to take care of. Forgive me for waxing poetically or perhaps philosophically is a more accurate description, but sometimes that's just how my mind works.

Whatever the case, I had found myself hiding in the darkness, standing in the shadows, with my back resting against the rough surface of a brick building. The structure appeared abandoned, which was just how I wanted it to be. Hell, just about all of the buildings around that part of the city were abandoned. At that juncture, all that mattered was that the building provided me with sufficient cover and was located directly next to where I eventually needed to be.

I could feel the cold chill of the bricks pressing against my spine, but I refused to let that distract me. I was a man on a mission and didn't have the time for such distractions. I had done this many times before and knew that focus was essential. I had to do something I hadn't done in a long time, but I had no doubt I was up to the task. It was dirty work, illegal work, and some might say immoral work. Those in the know would call it what it was . . . wet work.

I had honestly thought I had left this part of my life behind me years earlier, but apparently, I had not. And if I were, to be honest, which I usually tend to be, I was ok with being back in the game; not happy, not sad, just resigned to what would soon happen. Some might argue that there were better ways to solve this problem, ways that might not result in my landing on death row. They would be correct, of course. Yet there I was, counting the seconds until go time. Could I have turned and walked away? Most certainly. Did I? Most certainly not.

I didn't become frustrated as I waited because I knew I wouldn't have much longer to wait. As always, I had done my due diligence, and in doing so, I had discovered that my quarry, like most people, was a creature of habit. Not all of those habits were good ones, but they were habits, nonetheless. And those sorts of repetitive patterns tend to make my job easier. It was Saturday night, so my target would be at the strip club, as he was every Saturday night.

My name is Lincoln Prescott, and I am Linc to my friends. That is to say, those few friends I have. Come to think of it, they probably aren't so much friends as simply acquaintances. You see, I can't afford to get too close to people or let them know too much about me. It's just how things must be. I've mastered the art of making people think they know me when all they truly know is the superficial external persona I choose to show them. They don't know the real me. The real Linc Prescott would most likely terrify them. Hell, I frighten myself sometimes.

On that night, as I took advantage of the dark mistress's ability to give me cover, I was dressed in black from head to toe, complete with a black balaclava. I trusted her to make me invisible as I waited in the shadows. Although I had checked and knew there were no security cameras in the area, I suspected they would be blind to me even if there had been. Besides, I knew the strip club didn't allow any cameras in the area as they needed to ensure there would never be any record of their patrons' visits.

That establishment of debauchery was known only as "The Joint" to its special clientele. It was as invisible to passersby as I was. There was no brightly illuminated tacky neon sign advertising the club's existence, no widows adorned with blinking beer signs, not even a small placard nailed to a door. It was the sort of private club that, if you didn't need to know about its existence, you simply didn't know. That was how it worked.

That area of the city is known by locals as Hell's Toilet and for a good reason. It's not just the land that time forgot, but the land that time had no idea ever existed. It's like the wild west was, a place void of laws and the moral compass that makes up the thin, fragile membrane separating us from animals. In Hell's Toilet, everyone is an animal; it's understood and expected. It's a Darwinian nightmare landscape the cops gladly ignore, and as a result, rarely can law enforcement officers be seen.

Like its nickname suggested, the alley where I waited was a toilet, a dung heap, and a dump with trash and waste scattered everywhere. It was strewn with empty food containers, beer cans, scraps of clothing, used condoms, and even soiled baby diapers. As I stared down at one of the diapers, I wondered, who in the Hell would bring a baby anywhere near this place? The stench in the alley was practically overwhelming, but I could and did tolerate it to do what had to be done.

/ 2 /

As I waited patiently, I recalled the events leading up to the inevitable confrontation that would occur in a few minutes. Several days earlier, I had been taking my evening stroll around my upscale suburban neighborhood. Yes, I still find it difficult to think of myself as not only being part of such a place but actually fitting in with these yuppie stereotypes. As I walked, I heard loud music from a home across the street and several doors down from mine.

I had yet to meet the new residents who had moved in several weeks earlier, but I knew their names. I had seen them coming and going and had a bad feeling about them. I learned from past experiences how important it was to know everything I could about potentially troublesome people. As a result, I managed to do a bit of investigation into these people, as was my way. The family went by the surname Domingo, although I decided it might be best not to put too much faith in that. Santos Domingo and his wife Carlotta - at least that's how the couple represented themselves in the sales agreement—were listed as the homeowners.

The subdivision I call home is a quiet, unpretentious, upscale neighborhood located behind a nearby town, which was likewise a calm and serene place. The demographic is upper-middle-class, two-income households. We have some younger couples with small kids and some older, retired empty nesters. Although many different races and nationalities can be found in my subdivision, white is the most predominant race. The bottom line is that it's a family-oriented neighborhood, which is why a single guy like me is considered something of an oddity. Regardless, blasting loud music is something out of the ordinary for our subdivision and attracts negative attention from my neighbors.

However, the only ordinance I could locate regarding noise violations stated there could be no loud noise after 11:00 pm. Since these new neighbors blasted their music earlier in the evening and promptly turned it off by 10:59, the police could do little about it. In the few short weeks that the Domingo family had lived there, I had observed police cruisers passing slowly by the house many times. Many neighbors called the police to complain. Hell, I even called several times myself. I had hoped that, because of the excessive volume, regardless of the time, the police might be willing to address it. But at least for the present, they had not.

That evening in our neighborhood, as I walked further along the sidewalk, I saw one of the neighborhood kids sitting on the curb in front of his home. He had his head down but occasionally looked up at the house from which all the loud music emanated. It was a little boy I knew, eight-year-old Reilly Melbourne. He was a good kid, and I had known his parents, Jill and Wallace. They were good folks, and it angered me to see him obviously upset. I needed to find out what was troubling him.

"What's the matter, Reilly?" I asked.

The boy looked up through red-rimmed eyes and, after wiping the tears away with the heels of his hands, sniffed, then said, "Oh, hi, Mr. Prescott. Um, sorry to be crying like a baby . . . it's just Skipper, my dog."

"I know Skipper, Reilly. He's a good pup, isn't he? So, what's wrong with old Skipper?"

"He's gone. He's missing," Reilly said as his voice broke and fresh tears fell.

I asked, "Missing? You mean he ran away."

"That's what my dad thinks, but I don't believe it. Skipper was a good boy and was scared to leave the backyard. Everything scared him, Mr. Prescott. That's why he barked so much. I think he always tried to sound brave when he was really scared. And he never left our backyard, even if the gate was open."

"Was the gate left open, Reilly?" I asked, trying my best to keep my tone non-accusatory, yet I wanted to help the kid figure out what might have happened. Sometimes, kids forget and leave the gates open. I was wondering if that was a possibility.

"No, it wasn't left open, Mr. Prescott. We have three gates in our yard, and all of them were closed. I even looked to see if there were any holes under our fence, and there weren't any."

"I'm sure you don't need to worry. I'll bet Skipper will find his way back home before you know it."

Reilly hesitated momentarily, trying to hold back a new flood of tears. "I don't think he'll ever be coming home again, Mr. Prescott. I think that guy who lives there took Skipper." Reilly pointed at the house I had just been watching, the one blasting loud music.

"The Domingo house? Do you think Mr. Domingo took your dog? Why do you think that, Reilly?"

"That Domingo guy is a bad man. I heard he takes drugs and sells them, too. Did you hear that, Mr. Prescott?"

"No, Reilly. I hadn't heard that. But you probably shouldn't tell stories about people if you can't prove they're true." The fact was, I had heard such stories before from other neighbors and was certain they were spot-on accurate. This Domingo character might as well have a neon sign over his head with the word "dealer" flashing.

"I know I shouldn't say, but I'm sure I'm right about him stealing Skipper."

"What makes you think he would want to take your dog?"

Reilly pointed at the noisy house, "Those people over there stay up really late having parties, and then they want to sleep all day. But Skipper likes to wake up early, and he barks a lot. Mr. Domingo hates how Skipper barks and has come over to our house yelling at my Mom and Dad about it."

"What did your parents say?"

"My Mom said she would call the cops if he ever came around again. My Dad told Mr. Domingo that if he set foot on our property again, he would take his shotgun and blow him back to Mexico, South America, or whatever toilet he crawled out of."

I had to suppress a chuckle. Don't get me wrong, I have no use for people like Domingo or his drug-taking ilk. I don't care where they come from; bad is bad. It's their lifestyle I have no tolerance for. All the families in my neighborhood work their butts off for their small slice of American pie. They wake up every day and drive to some mediocre job where they have to deal with some arrogant know-nothing boss for a paycheck that barely gets them to the next paycheck.

These are honest, law-abiding citizens who pay taxes and follow the rules. They deserve a nice neighborhood free of crime and disruption. Me, not so much. I've done many things in the past that were so far beyond the realm of law and order that it would be better if you didn't know. Plausible deniability is a good thing to have. Ignorance honestly can truly be blissful when it comes to me. So far, I have managed not to get caught crossing those legal lines. In fact, it had been several years since I had found any reason to do so, but I suspected this Domingo character would end up being a reason for me to return to my old ways. It's strange how sometimes you just know.

Men like Domingo blatantly thumbed their noses at the system and believed society's rules didn't apply to them. And honestly, that sort of thing really pisses me off. But Domingo's defiance was not my problem. That's a problem for the authorities. That might bother me; however, it wouldn't warrant me standing in the filthy mess outside the strip club, waiting to do what I planned. That would require something more serious. Most people would say stealing a dog might not be a capital crime, but in my books, breaking a young boy's heart was. And taking a young boy's dog was right up Domingo's alley.

/ 3 /

As far as my neighbors knew, Lincoln Prescott was a single, middle-aged factory worker with no kids. He kept his property in good condition and was friendly with everyone. I'm sure they've speculated in private about the details of my personal life, but they never asked me and respected my privacy.

I've gathered that some of my neighbors assume I'm an eligible bachelor; others suspect I'm divorced. I can tell who they are because the wives are a bit too friendly, and the husbands try to keep them away from me whenever possible. A few wondered if I was a widower, while others suspected I might be gay. However, no matter what they might think, no one ever feels close enough to me to inquire.

I always manage to keep my personal business to myself and keep people at arm's length. If some of my neighborhood friends learned about my past, the parts no one but I know about, they would stay as far away from me as possible. And who could blame them?

I should clarify that it's not that I'm a bad man, but I'm no choir boy, either. The game of life chose to deal me several less-than-desirable hands. The early years of my life were an unfortunately typical story told by more young men than I cared to think about. Most of those men told their stories from behind bars. I grew up a poor inner-city kid with an abusive drunk for a father and a drug-addled mother. I learned to lie, cheat, steal, and fight on the streets to survive. I'm not saying this to garner anyone's sympathy; I'm simply giving you a little history.

I wanted more out of life, so I steered clear of drugs and gangs. I became what some people call a loner. I just found I enjoyed my own company, and there's nothing wrong with that. I also worked my skinny little butt off in school, and I'm not ashamed to say I excelled academically. However, I kept those accomplishments as quiet as I could. My school was tough, and I knew if the other students thought of me as a brainiac, things wouldn't go easy for me.

As it was, I had to build some tough guy creds to survive in the place. I quickly became known as someone to not screw with. That happened after I put a bully twice my size in the hospital. If you go after the biggest and toughest character you can find and come out of it alive, even the most hardened criminals in the school will keep their distance.

When I turned 18, I graduated and joined the Marines. I saw the TV ads about the few and the proud. I figured I didn't have too much to be proud of so far. Yeah, I had good grades, but they were not good enough for a free ride to college. I never participated in athletics, so no scholarship there either. I figured maybe Uncle Sam might be able to do something with me. I spent some less-than-pleasant times in the middle east and saw more than my share of combat. When my time in the service was up, I had become a well-honed killing machine, thanks to Uncle Sam. Upon reentering the world, I quickly discovered that finding my place in society would be a significant challenge.

I was trained to kill and had discovered not only was I good at killing, but I seemed to be missing whatever gene or that crucial part of the brain that felt remorse. Maybe it was growing up the way I did- tough childhood and all. But for me, taking someone out was just something I did. It gave me no pleasure, nor did it give me any discomfort. Killing another human being was no different than switching off a light. Does that make me bent or broken? Perhaps it does, but that doesn't really concern me either. Life deals you a hand, and you do your best with it.

For a time, when I was having trouble finding employment, I contemplated becoming a paid assassin, you know, a hitman. All things considered, I was more than qualified. I had done the same job for the government for a lot less money. But I opted not to go that route as society tended to frown on such activities, and I had no desire to end up in prison or strapped to a table with a needle in my arm.

Fortune chose to shine down on me when I met a lovely young woman named Tanya, whose love helped make my journey into this new life much easier. I found a good-paying factory job that allowed me to buy us a small townhouse. It wasn't in the best part of the city, but it seemed like paradise compared to the Hell on Earth where I spent my youth. I felt I could finally start putting my violent life behind me for good.

Tanya and I eventually married and had a beautiful daughter we called Isabel. She was the most perfect child ever born. I was very lucky during those years. I was living a life I never imagined as a poor city kid, and it had all been possible thanks to Tanya and Isabel. Then, as seems to be how things always go for a slob like me, tragedy struck.

I was working overtime to make extra money. Isabelle was growing rapidly, and Tanya saw a perfect bedroom set for our little girl. I needed to find some legal way to pay for it, so when the overtime gravy train pulled into the station, I hopped on board. We often joked that the only men who volunteered for overtime were the needy and the greedy. I knew which one I was and was reminded every time I had to pay the bills.

One night, while I was working late, three local thugs broke into my house and killed Tanya and my beautiful little Isabel. The things they did to Tanya and my baby girl before shooting them both in the head were beyond description and something that will haunt me until the day I die. The guilt I felt from not being home to protect them was insurmountable. I wanted to die and had considered suicide on more than one occasion. However, I chose instead to embrace hatred and seek vengeance.

The police could never identify or catch the murderers, and I had begun to believe they would never face justice. But I was determined to find and deal my own version of justice to these scum-sucking pigs no matter what. I began frequenting some of the city's worst dive bars, hoping against hope that I might get a lead that I could use to find the killers. I had nothing left to lose as I had already lost everything.

Then, one night, while I was sitting at the bar of one of the city's most disreputable drinking establishments, I heard a group of men at a table behind me laughing drunkenly and carrying on as if no one else could hear their conversation. Not only could I hear them, but I could see them in the bar's well-worn mirror.

One of the men, a tough-looking, huge character with slicked-back greasy hair, a grimy tee shirt, and prison tats on his bulging arms, was bragging about how a few months earlier he and two of his buddies had "done a rudeness" to some uppity bitch and her little girl. He said he and his boys had "ended them but good."

Later, I followed the thug out of the bar, and after hitting him in the back of his neck, I dragged his unconscious body into a nearby alley. Let's just say after some unpleasant physical persuasion, I was able to determine this was one of the characters I was seeking. After beating the pig to within an inch of his life, I got the names of his buddies. Then I took care of that last inch of his life and "ended him but good."

Eventually, I tracked down the other two killers one at a time, and after spending many hours of quality time with each of them, I was confident they would never hurt anyone again. After all, it's extremely difficult for dismembered corpses to do too much damage to anyone.

That was the real me, the Lincoln Prescott, whom my suburban neighbors knew nothing about. And it was that version of me who now stood in the shadows of a filthy alley, waiting patiently for Santos Domingo to leave the strip club and face judgment for what he had done to hurt poor Reilly Melbourne by stealing and then killing his dog, Skipper.

/ 4 /

Yes, I realized that most people might say Skipper was just some kid's dog, hardly worth making a fuss about, let alone doing what I planned to do. But that wasn't the point as far as I was concerned. I conducted my investigation and discovered Domingo had lured the dog out of Melbourne's backyard with treats. Then he had put Skipper into a cage in the back of a van.

It would have been bad enough to learn that Domingo had taken Skipper out of town, into the woods, and shot him. But no such easy fate had awaited Reilly's poor, gentle pup. I learned that Domingo ran an illegal dogfighting and gambling ring in an abandoned warehouse in the city. These dogs were starved and then pitted against each other in a fight to the death.

Skipper was a timid, domesticated dog with no history of violence. Domingo had thrown Skipper into a ring with savage dogs bred to be strong and forced to fight and kill since birth. Within ten seconds of the fight, Skipper's throat had been torn out, and he lay dying on a concrete floor, blood spreading in a crimson pool. That was the sort of horrid creature Santos Domingo was. And I intended very soon for Domingo to meet the kind of person the real Linc Prescott was.

As I stood in the shadows, the door to the strip club opened, and a tall, muscular Hispanic man in an expensive suit walked out with his hand in front of his jacket. I recognized him as Domingo's right-hand man, Rocko.

"Shoulder holster," I thought to myself as I took inventory.

Rocko looked around to make sure no trouble waited in the shadows. He looked in my direction but never saw me because that's how I wanted things to be. When he was confident the coast was clear, Rocko turned, opened the door, and said, "All good out here, Boss."

A few seconds later, Santos Domingo walked out, looking every bit the smug, confident hood he was. Holding his own gun now, Domingo looked up at his bodyguard and said, "Bring the car around, Rocko. I'll wait here."

Before Rocko could reply, Domingo heard the barely audible yet familiar "pfft" sound of a silenced weapon. As Rocko's head exploded, Domingo's face was splattered with blood and gore. Then, the huge corpse crashed to the ground like a fallen oak tree. Domingo was half-blinded by the blood splatter in his eyes but raised his pistol. Before he could shoot, Domingo heard another muffled shot and felt his hand burn with searing pain as his gun clattered to the asphalt.

Clad in black, I walked out of the shadows and approached Domingo, who was bent over, cursing and clutching his injured right hand in his left. Domingo glared at me with hatred and said, "What the Hell is this? Who are you? You screwed up big time, boy. Do you have any idea who I am?"

I lifted my facemask to give him a good look and replied in a calm, steady voice, "You're Santos Domingo. Two-bit punk loser, dog killer, breaker of a little boy's heart . . . and annoying neighbor."

"You? Hey! I know you. You're that weird guy who lives alone in my neighborhood. Oh, man, did you mess up! I'm going to see you die slowly, Pal."

I shot Domingo in his left kneecap. He fell to the ground screaming in pain, crying like the baby he was, and unable to speak.

I said, "You know, Santos, everything would be fine in your miserable little world if you had only left Skipper alone."

"Skipper? Who . . . the Hell . . . is Skipper?" Domingo managed to squeak out.

Then I shot Domingo in his right ankle, and Domingo howled with new-found agony as he lay on the ground.

"Skipper was Reilly Melbourne's dog, the one you fed to your pit fighters." A look of sudden realization appeared on Domingo's pained face.

Domingo said with astonishment, "You mean . . . you're doing all this . . . over a stupid dog?"

I understood men like Domingo simply didn't get it and would never understand. I smiled and said, "All this and more."

Then I shot Domingo between the eyes. I looked around to ensure Domingo's screaming didn't attract unwanted attention. Then I walked over to the strip club's door, rang the doorbell, and turned to stroll back into the shadows, carefully stepping over both corpses.

I knew the club owners would ensure things got handled properly upon discovering the carnage. They couldn't afford to have the authorities snooping around their place, not with all the drugs, dog fights, underage heroin-addicted strippers, and prostitutes. I had learned the club had paid bribes for the cops and local politicians to look the other way regarding their illicit activities, but that wouldn't hold water when it came to murder. Such a thing would attract way too much bad attention. This little event would have to be swept under the rug, and they would do so nicely.

/ 5 /

Reilly Melbourne was out in his backyard, sitting on his patio with a look of unhappy acceptance on his young face. He had a well-chewed baseball that he gently tossed from hand to hand. Reilly had spent many hours playing fetch with Skipper using that ball. The boy never found out what had happened to his dog, but after several months he had now come to terms with the fact Skipper was never coming home again. The loneliness was still hard, but every day, things seemed to get a bit more tolerable for Reilly.

A lot had happened during those many weeks. Reilly had heard his parents talking about how the Domingo family had mysteriously packed up their belongings and fled their home under the dark cover of night. No one had seen Mr. Domingo in weeks and assumed the couple might be splitting up.

Reilly's Dad had said, "Good riddance to bad rubbish," whatever that meant.

The local bank had put a sign on the house that said, "Foreclosure Sale," and Reilly had seen several nice families with kids looking at the home. He hoped whoever bought the place had kids his age. The neighborhood didn't have many kids, and Reilly could use someone new to play with, especially now that Skipper was gone. His parents had told him he could get a new dog, but Reilly wasn't sure he was ready to do that yet. He really missed Skipper.

Reilly sat staring out into the yard, reminiscing about how he and Skipper used to play fetch with the ball. After a while, he felt something bump against his leg and heard a little whimpering sound. Reilly looked down to see a little black and white puppy nuzzling his ankle. He couldn't believe what he was seeing. The little dog looked just like Skipper had looked when he was a puppy.

Reilly reached down and picked up the dog, who promptly set to work, smothering Reilly's young face with doggy kisses.

He looked around the yard but saw no sign of anyone. Reilly asked, "Where did you come from, boy? You sure are a cute little guy."

Around the side of the house, I smiled unseen as I turned and headed back home.

TAIL GUNNER JOE

Authors note: In mid-2022, I was asked by friend and author Mark Slade of Screaming Eye Press if I was interested in writing a goofy and funny story about a character Mark made up named Tail Gunner Joe for their men's magazine called Rumble. *The premise was that during the Korean conflict, his plane was shot down, and a mad scientist put his brain into the body of a gorilla. The idea was that after the surgery, Joe would begin working with the black market to transport stolen goods. Yes, the idea was as goofy as it sounds, but I am always up for a challenge. So now, I give you Tail Gunner Joe.*

The man began to wake slowly, in a stupor, feeling like 200 lbs. of soggy elephant dung. He had far too many questions running through his mind, "Where am I? What happened to me? Who am I? If God and Superman fought, who would win? So, so many questions. All he knew was he seemed to be lying in a bed in a dimly lit room.

"Uh oh!" he thought, "Not again!" A faint memory began to form in his mind. The last time he felt like this was a few months earlier, in early 1950, when he awoke one morning, naked, on a straw mattress in a thatched hut. He was in bed with an equally naked, toothless sixty-some-year-old Korean grandmother, a very contented-looking female dog, two ducks, and a spilled plate of pork dumplings, complete with dipping sauce. He was glad he had no memory of the previous night but was sorry he couldn't recall eating the dumplings. He really loved dumplings.

Then, another memory relating to that one popped into his mind. He and his squadron of B-29 Superfortress flyers had landed in South Korea. His job was tail gunner, and his somewhat uncreative nickname was Tail Gunner, something or other. Tail Gunner Pete? Tail Gunner Frank? No, that didn't seem quite right. It would probably come back to him eventually. It was his name, after all. The only thing he could remember was that he and his buddies had decided to go out and have one last bout of hellraising before they had to begin their bombing runs, which were scheduled to take place later that week. He had no idea how much he had to drink or how he'd ended up in that bizarre situation with madam gum-flapper and her barnyard menagerie.

That was how he felt now: confused and disoriented, yet at the same time, he was surprisingly quite strong, perhaps stronger than he had ever felt. He tried to sit up but found himself strapped to the bed. Wherever it was he happened to be, the great strength he now felt wouldn't do him any good. He couldn't move his head and couldn't see anywhere but the ceiling directly in front of him. He was relieved that the roof was not thatched but appeared to be some sort of metal roof, perhaps a hospital or laboratory. A thatched roof and restraints might signify something much worse than that previous embarrassment.

"Whew. Dodged that bullet again," he thought, recalling the morning after the incident with the old woman. Much to his dismay, her dog had followed him back to the base, constantly rubbing against his leg. He obviously had made an impression. He had to chase her away and then felt a bit sorry that he didn't even get her name: the dog, not the old woman.

There was a bad smell in the room, like wild animals, like the stink of a zoo. Was he being held captive in a zoo somewhere? He felt the air in front of his face flutter as if a bird had flown close enough for him to feel the flapping of its wings. He heard a wild chittering sound made by a squirrel, and it was also frighteningly close to his face.

He realized he was hungry and was having strange cravings. It was not his typical need for cheesesteak sandwiches or pizza but for food and fruit, which he usually hated. He wanted a salad, a really big, really leafy salad. He also had an unexplainable craving for bananas, not just one, but an entire bunch.

Then, a soft voice came out of the darkness, saying. "Ah, so I see you're awake."

"Y . . . yeah . . . I'm awake," the confused man said slowly, intending to say more but shocked at the sound of his voice. It was deeper than normal and somewhat raspy, catching him by surprise. It sounded like a female impersonator making a bad impression of Cher. He also noticed that his head felt like John Bonham and Keith Moon had a drum-off inside his skull. "Where . . . where am I? What the Hell is wrong with my voice?"

"Oh yes. Questions, questions, so many questions, I'm sure," the other voice said, sounding surprisingly cheerful. "I assure you all your inquiries will be answered in due course. I, too, have plenty of questions, my new friend. For example, what's your name?"

The man thought briefly, trying to fight through the thick cotton candy fog clouding his mind. Then it came to him, "J . . . J . . . Joe. I think my name is Joe. That feels right. Yeah . . . they call me Tail Gunner Joe."

"Hum," The voice said, "I suppose that makes sense, all things considered. However, I would have pegged you for a Waldo or maybe a Wendel. Then again, I suppose Tail Gunner Waldo doesn't have a very good ring to it. Well, Tail Gunner Joe, do you happen to know your last name?"

Joe replied, "Of course. Sure, it's . . . it's . . . huh? Sorry, I got nothin'. Maybe it's Smith."

"Really? Smith? That's the best you can come up with, Smith? Not the most creative sort, are we?"

"Forgive me all to Hell and back, but I'm not feeling quite myself here. You know what I mean?"

"Oh yes. I most definitely know. More than you may realize. Well, I suppose we have to call you something; how about Simian? Joe Simian. That feels right to me. How do you like that name?"

"Simian? Why does that name sound familiar? Well, I suppose it's ok for now, but how about you tell me where I am and why I'm strapped down? Say . . . you're not some weirdo pervert who's been doing dirty sexual things to me while I was asleep, are you? Because I'm not into kinky crap, no matter what you might have heard. Well, there was that time with the dog and the ducks, but let's not bring that up."

The man sounded like he had been caught off guard, "Why . . . why no, of course not. I'm not that sort of . . . absolutely not. I'm a man of science."

Joe asked, "You mean, like a doctor or something?"

"Yes . . . a doctor . . . or something," the man replied vaguely.

"Well, how's about you get me off this table so I can get out of here."

"I'm afraid that's not quite possible at this time. You're strapped down for your own protection as well as mine," the doctor said.

"Protection. What are you talking about? I'm an American soldier; I'm one of the good guys. I can't see you; it's too dark in here. But you aren't Korean, are you? You sound American to me, and your voice has no trace of any accent. Look, I promise I won't hurt you."

"Don't be so quick to make promises when you have no idea whether or not you can keep them," the doctor said; then, he hesitated momentarily and reluctantly said, "Here's the deal, Joe. Several weeks ago, your plane came down as it was leaving a bombing raid over North Korea. I believe it might have been shot down or had some sort of mechanical malfunction. The bottom line is it crashed, and everyone on the plane was killed."

Joe was even more confused, "Um . . . excuse me. But I'm pretty sure I wasn't killed, or else I wouldn't be here talking to you. Right? I'm no doctor, but isn't that how those things usually work?"

Hesitantly, the doctor said, "Well, yes. But that's where things get tricky, or perhaps hairy would be a better word." He let loose an insane-sounding chuckle, "You see, you were barely alive when I came upon your downed plane. Your body was crushed beyond repair, and I managed to keep you alive just long enough to take a few significant corrective measures."

"Corrective measures? But how could my body be crushed? I feel very strong, like I have the strength of a gorilla."

"Interesting choice of words," the doctor said, once again giving that crazy chuckle. "Well, Joe. As things worked out, I had to make a choice. I had to decide whether to let your brain eventually die as your body had done or try something else, something risky but also revolutionary."

"Something else? Revolutionary?" Joe asked, beginning to get worried.

"Yes, I suppose there is no good way to say this. I had to take your brain and transplant it into the head of a gorilla."

Joe said calmly, "Oh, is that all . . . I was afraid . . ." Then he shouted, "Hey! Wait a minute . . . did you just say gorilla?"

"Why, yes. Specifically, a western lowland gorilla; scientific name, Gorilla gorilla gorilla; phylum, Chordata; class, Mammalia. It's a relatively small gorilla with dark brownish-black hair and a large skull. Its average size is about 200 to 600 pounds, with males being about twice the size of females. They tend to be herbivorous and have a lifespan of about 35 years. The one whose body your brain now occupies was about five years old, so you should be good for another thirty years, give or take."

"G . . . g . . . give or take?" Joe said in shock.

"Why, yes. No one can be sure of such things. Then again, without the operation, your lifespan would be zilch. You'd be el-dead-amundo."

"So, that's why you have me strapped down. You're afraid I might go, pardon the expression, ape, and tear you apart."

"Well, there is that," the doctor replied.

Joe shouted, "You sick and twisted bastard. Why didn't you just let me die? How am I going to survive inside the body of a gorilla?"

The doctor said, "Oh, Joe, I'm sure you'll adapt."

"Adapt? Adapt? Adapt to being in the body of an ape? How the Hell do I adapt to being a monkey?"

"Forgive me for correcting you, but a gorilla and a monkey differ. For example, monkeys are primates that belong to the *Haplorhini* suborder and *Simiiformes* infraorder, whereas Gorillas belong to the *Hominidae* family and *Gorilla* Genus. Gorillas are considered the largest primates by physical size. Monkeys have long tails that can be used to help them balance, while Gorillas are tailless. There is also a significant difference between monkeys and gorillas in terms of evolution when it comes to diet and posture as well. It is also interesting to note that gorillas are the closest taxonomical relatives of humans in the animal world, that is, after chimpanzees and bonobos."

"Bonobos? Bonobos? What the Hell is a Bonobo?" Joe asked.

The doctor started to speak, "A bonobo is . . .."

Joe shouted, "Never mind. I don't know and don't care. Look, Doc, give me a break here. Ok, look. You don't have to release me yet, but could you at least turn on the lights? I need to see what I'm dealing with here, you know?"

"Very well," the doctor said as he turned on the laboratory lights. Harsh fluorescent illumination seemed to scald Joe's overly sensitive eyes.

"Jeeze, Doc. You're killing me here," Joe shouted.

"Just relax, Joe. Close your eyes and slowly open them until they get used to the brightness."

Joe squinted his eyes, gradually opening them, and eventually, he could clearly see the ceiling and some of the area around. He was in a metal building like an airplane hangar or Quonset hut. He wanted to get a better idea of just how bad his situation was. If his brain really was inside a gorilla, what would his life be like from this day forward?

"Come closer, Doc, so I can see you, and please, explain to me how I'm supposed to live my life trapped in the body of a gorilla?"

An odd-looking little man in his sixties, bald, with just a fringe of wild, bushy white hair and equally bushy eyebrows, came into view. His eyes were large and showed an extraordinary level of intelligence, coupled with what looked to Joe like an equal amount of insanity. Then again, he realized it would take a combination like that to do what this man had done to him.

Something was sitting on the doctor's shoulder. It looked like a parrot or some other large bird, but its head resembled a squirrel's. Joe asked as calmly as he could manage, "Um, excuse me, Doc, but there's some kind of weird bird-squirrel thing perched on your shoulder. Care to tell me what that's all about?"

The doctor glanced over to his shoulder, then raised his hand, extending one finger, and said, "Oh, that. That's Carl. He was one of my first successful experiments." The bird-squirrel creature fluttered from the man's shoulder to his outstretched hand, preaching on his extended finger. "He's a sweet little thing and completely trained."

As he said those last words, the Carl creature took flight from the doctor's finger, leaving a runny blob of bird/squirrel crap in his wake.

The doctor explained to Joe about Carl while simultaneously flicking the errant turd off his finger and onto the floor. He. said, "Like yourself, Carl was one of my success stories. You wouldn't want to see my failures."

Joe realized what the doctor said was true. He was certain he didn't want to see himself in a mirror. Then he realized he never got an answer to his previous question, "Anyway, Doc, as I asked earlier, would you please explain to me how I'm supposed to live my life trapped in the body of a gorilla?"

The doctor stared down at him and then said, "Well, I hadn't really had much time to think about that. I was quite busy saving your life. I suppose you'll have to learn to make the best of it. I mean, you are still alive and have your human mind and intelligence, and as a gorilla, you'll have great strength."

Joe knew the doctor was right, as he was already feeling much stronger. Then he said, "I suppose that's true. Gorillas are strong, and that's probably a good thing. Right?"

Then his eyes grew wide as he suddenly had an epiphany, "Say, Doc, do gorillas have big schlongs? It would be awesome if this body had a foot-long kielbasa. Whoa, think about it! Wait till I get back to the States and my girlfriend gets a look at my tallywacker of terror. I'll be able to run a three-legged race by myself. It'll be awesome. Maybe I can get into making stag films. I could bill myself as the human tripod. Please tell me I got a monster dong, Doc."

"Well, about that . . ."

"Oh boy, more bad news is coming. I can feel it," Joe said with frustration.

The doctor sighed and said, "Unfortunately, you're right. You see, the only gorilla I had available was a female."

"What? Now, wait a cotton-pickin' minute there. Are you seriously telling me you put my brain into the body of a female gorilla?"

"Well, Yes, I suppose I am."

"Not a big, strapping savage chest-pounding, schwantz-swinging male gorilla, but a namby-pamby, no-nuts, frail, delicate little female gorilla."

The doctor said, "To be honest, she was not so frail or delicate. She was well over three hundred pounds of solid muscle. I'm sorry, but I don't see why it's all such a big deal."

"You don't, do you? So, not only do I not have a foot-long war wanger, but I have no wanger whatsoever. Is that what you're trying to tell me?"

"Yes, I suppose that's correct."

"You suppose? Well, I suppose you supposed correctly. What am I going to do now? I'm a pitcher, Doc, not a catcher. I like women, not men. What am I supposed to tell my girlfriend when I get home? Well, Honey, not only am I now a gorilla, but it seems I'm a lesbian gorilla."

The doctor thought for a moment, then said, "Perhaps your girl would not be opposed to a bit of girl-on-girl gorilla action. Do you suppose she ever tried, as they say, playing for the other team?"

"Of course not. My girl is 100% woman," he hesitated momentarily, then said, "Then again, there was that time she told me about when she was away at girl's summer camp, but I'm pretty sure that was just experimental. But what about my squadron? What the Hell am I supposed to tell my commander? Sorry, Captain, but now that I'm a gorilla, I'll be too big to sit in the tail gunner seat, so I'll have to be assigned to the motor pool with the rest of the grease monkeys."

"As far as the Air Force is concerned, you were killed in action."

"But they won't find my body, will they?"

The doctor hesitated, then said, "Well . . . yes, they will. It's just that it will be a mess, what with the accident and the removal of your brain. Messy business, all that. I'm sure they will chalk that up to scavengers having their way with the corpses. Lord knows, I barely beat the blighters to the bodies."

"Ok, so I can't go back to the military. And my girlfriend back home won't be an issue since if I'm dead, I can't go there either. So, to summarize, everyone thinks I'm dead. My brain and essence occupy the body of a chick gorilla, complete with gorilla gina. I can't go live in the jungle unless I'm prepared to be used as a love pin cushion being assaulted by every male silver-back gorilla within sniffing distance. I can't stay here with you since, for one thing, I have no idea who you are. And for another thing . . . there are probably a million other things. So, Doc. What do you recommend I do?"

The doctor seemed to ponder this question and then said, "I know some people who are active in the black market. It's how I get most of my lab supplies. I've heard that they always look for others to work with. I think if we shaved your face, arms, and hands, we might be able to pass you off as human. Not the most attractive human, but human nonetheless. After all, apes are our closest relatives in the animal kingdom."

"Man, oh, man! This is all so uncool. It's probably the least coolest thing I've ever heard of. But what choice do I have? I don't suppose you'd consider shooting me and ending it all."

The doctor said, "I would prefer not to. But if that's what you want, I'd be willing to euthanize you." He reached over to his metal worktable and picked up a syringe filled with a clear liquid. It was only water, but Joe had no way of knowing that.

"You mean, you'd really do that?"

"Yes, if that's what you really want."

Joe thought for a moment, then said, "Nah! Forget about it. I guess I'll have to make the best of this. Hey, Doc, how about you unstrap me and let me get up and get a feel for what it's like to have this new body?"

Reluctantly, the doctor said, "Ok, Joe. If you promise to behave yourself."

"I will. Look, Doc, I've been thinking about all this. And although I'm not thrilled with being a gorilla chick, you're right about one thing. At least I'm still alive and can think with my own brain."

"I'm glad to hear that," the doctor said as he released Joe from his straps.

Joe sat up and slowly got off the table, surprised at how quickly he was getting accustomed to this strange, new body. Looking around the room, he saw many wooden cages occupied by various animals. Then Joe realized that the animal stink he had been smelling was coming from himself; he'd have to do something about that. In fact, he had to do something about many things very soon.

"I've been thinking, Doc, maybe that job with your black-market pal is worth considering. Do you have his name handy?"

The doctor walked over to his desk and returned with a piece of paper covered in barely intelligible scrawl. Joe took the paper in his hairy black hand, read it, and then memorized the name, address, and phone number. He looked at the doctor and asked, "Say, Doc, don't you have an assistant, nurse, or somebody who works with you?"

"Heavens, no!" He said with great surprise. "My work is far too secret to risk having anyone steal my ideas. All my information, skills, and right here." The doctor pointed to his head.

"Sweet," Joe said, "that's exactly what I wanted to hear." With one quick swipe of his massive hand, Joe promptly removed the doctor's head from his body, leaving a bloody neck stump pumping blood for a few seconds before the corpse collapsed to the floor. The bird/squirrel thing tried a divebomb attack, and Joe plucked it out of the air, bit its head off Ozzy-style, and spit it onto the floor. Then he ambled over to the cages and released all the animals.

He looked into a nearby mirror, and although shocked, he gently rubbed his chin and said, "Well, it appears I have some serious shaving to do and have a date with my new career."

SWEET JANE

*"I'm on the path to being someone I'm equally terrified by
and obsessed with. My true self."*
—TROYE SIVAN

*"I was terrified to be my true self because I felt that it wasn't enough.
But I allowed myself to break down those walls."*
—HANNAH BROWN

"I yam what I am, and dat's all dat I yam."
—POPEYE THE SAILOR

/1/

The rain beat down on the roof of the new Lexus RX 500, sounding like the thundering hooves of a dozen stallions. The night was dark and miserable, with his county in the midst of one of the worst storms they had seen in a decade or more. The local weather service called for several inches of rainfall and warned of potential flash flooding. Paul Stoddard couldn't wait to get his new wheels out of the storm and into the safety of his garage.

Paul supposed he should be grateful there was no hale to accompany this storm. The last thing he wanted to deal with was hale damage on his new car's finish, especially since he had busted his butt for the past several years to be able to afford this baby. It had been a good financial year for him, and now this latest promotion from regional to national sales manager had been just the boost his bank account needed.

"Paul Stoddard, national sales manager," Paul said aloud to himself in the privacy of his new car. "Yeah, baby! You know it!" He shouted as he smacked his fist triumphantly against the steering wheel. He was still trying to wrap his head around this latest promotion. As confident as he sounded, Paul had been experiencing his typical mixed emotions about his new responsibilities. He was, of course, proud of his promotion and thrilled with the salary increase. However, he was also apprehensive and perhaps a bit insecure about his abilities to handle the job.

Fortunately, he recognized these emotions from the many other times he had to deal with them while climbing the corporate ladder. Now, at the ripe old age of fifty, his hard work was financially beginning to pay off in dividends. He knew, eventually, he'd find a way to work past these feelings of uncertainty. In the end, he would most certainly succeed as he always had. He was Paul Stoddard, dammit, and that meant he could do anything. Hell, he already had.

As the car traveled along the slick country two-lane, Paul made certain to avoid as many of the numerous water-filled potholes in the road as possible while simultaneously keeping alert for deer. Two things you could always count on along Central Pennsylvania highways were potholes and deer. He looked up ahead and could hardly believe his eyes. Someone stood by the roadside in the pouring rain with their thumb extended, looking for a ride. As he got closer, he saw a long, lean leg leading up to a short skirt and realized the hitchhiker was a young woman.

Despite the dismal weather, Paul was feeling good today, and as his momentary doubts about his abilities began to fade, he experienced a resurgence of confidence, although perhaps overconfidence would be a better description. He decided to play the knight in $65,000 worth of shining armor in the form of rolling steel and rescue this damsel in distress. Who knows? Maybe if she was impressed with him, it could lead to a little sumpin-sumpin, as they say. He assumed the woman might be a bit "loose" regarding the morals department. Why else would she be out here, thumbing a ride on a dark, miserable night such as this?

Suddenly, Paul imagined dozens of sexual fantasies ala Penthouse Magazine that flashed through his mind as he pulled the car over to the shoulder and opened the door for the woman.

/ 2 /

"Please, come in out of that horrible weather," Paul called over the noise of the storm.

The young woman ducked into the car, sat on the seat, and immediately apologized, "I'm so sorry for all the water I'm getting in your beautiful car."

"Don't worry about it," Paul said, "It'll dry."

She looked Paul in the eye and said, "That's so sweet and considerate of you. Thank you, by the way, for the ride."

Paul was taken aback by her eyes. Those eyes seemed incredible, radiating a light that appeared to cross the distance between them and wrap itself around his soul like a lasso. He realized how ridiculous that thought was, but it was how he felt.

"N . . . no . . . no problem," Paul stammered, "Happy to help. So, um . . . where are you heading?"

She smiled a million-dollar Hollywood smile and said, "Nowhere in particular. I suppose I'm heading wherever you're going." There was that mischievous look again, "I'll see what adventure awaits me at the end of the line."

Again, Paul found himself captivated by this mysterious and incredibly sensual young woman. To call her a young woman was a bit of a stretch; physically, she appeared more like a girl. Paul guessed she couldn't be much more than eighteen years old. "Legal or San Quentin quail?" He wondered, then mentally chastised himself for having such a thought.

"Sounds like you're something of a free spirit," Paul said, feeling like the fantasies he had been imagining might have a shot at becoming a reality. How did those stories in Penthouse Forum all seem to start? "You may not believe this happened to me. I can hardly believe it myself . . ."

She chuckled and agreed, "Oh yes, you could most definitely call me that."

"Oh, by the way, I'm Paul, Paul Stoddard," he said as he extended his right hand for a shake, not expecting what followed.

The woman took it, gave his hand a gentle caress that sent shock-waves of sensuality surging through his body, and said, "I'm Jane Sweetwater, but people just call me Sweet Jane."

Paul's throat felt dry, and he wasn't sure he could put together two sensible words to reply. To distract himself, Paul checked for oncoming traffic and, seeing none, pulled out onto the highway. Then he gulped, tried to find moisture in his mouth, and asked, "Sweet Jane? You mean . . . like the Lou Reed song?"

"Yeah, that old guy. My parents were big fans of his. I guess that's why they always called me Sweet Jane. Were you a Lou Reed fan?"

"No, not really. I knew who he was. I was something of an amateur musician back in the day, but I wasn't really into that whole New York and New Wave scene. You know, bands like Lou Reed and the Velvet Underground, The New York Dolls, the Ramones; not my thing."

"They were all before my time. I don't know any of those names except for Lou Reed. You know, because of my folks."

Paul remembered that at fifty years old, he was old enough to be this girl's father. He suddenly felt dirty for having the thoughts he had earlier. His own daughter was not much older than this girl, but unlike Sweet Jane, she was safely tucked away in her junior year of college.

He said, "Um . . . if you don't mind my asking . . . I mean . . . you seem kinda young to be . . . you know . . . out thumbing a ride . . . on a night like this, out here in the middle of nowhere."

She smiled and said, "I'm nineteen. And I've been doing this for a long time, so you don't have to worry about me. Although it's sweet of you to be concerned. Usually, no one is."

In a brief moment of moonlight breaking through the gloom, Paul noticed a dark expression cloud Sweet Jane's young face, momentarily cracking her easy-going facade, and he realized by that brief look this girl had experienced more than anyone so young should have. He thought again of his daughter, and a new wave of shame passed over him. If his ex-spouse knew what he had been thinking earlier, Paul would have been given an earful. Then again, he was always given an earful; that's part of the reason for the title "ex."

Paul asked, "You mentioned your parents earlier. How do they feel about you . . . you know, traveling about like this . . . alone?"

"They don't feel anything . . . they're dead."

Paul was stunned again. He hadn't expected that. He said, "Oh . . . I'm so sorry . . . I didn't . . . I mean, I never . . ."

"Don't sweat it, Paul. It was a long time ago, back when I was fourteen. I've had years to deal with it. I'm ok now." She put her hand on Paul's thigh, much closer to his crotch than his knee.

Again, his throat began to feel dry as electricity pulsed through him.

"So, um . . . if I may ask . . . what happened to your folks? Were they in a car accident or something like that?"

Sweet Jane's voice took on a more somber and monotone quality as she said, "No, Paul. Nothing like that. They were both murdered."

/ 3 /

Paul grabbed tighter to the steering wheel, shocked by Sweet Jane's revelation and certain he would lose control of his car. When he could think coherently again, he said, "Did you say . . . murdered?"

Still, in that same matter-of-fact monotone, she replied, "Yes, they were stabbed to death in their sleep with a butcher knife from our kitchen while I was in the bedroom down the hall from them. I heard their dying screams."

"Oh my god! That's terrible! What an awful thing to have to go through," Then he realized something and said, "You were lucky to have survived. Did you hide under your bed, in a closet, or climb out a window?"

"No, nothing like that. I just pulled the covers over my head and went back to sleep. That's where the police found me when they arrived. I'm told a neighbor called them after hearing my parents screaming."

Paul felt like a thousand worms were crawling under his skin. This was one of the most horrible stories he had ever heard, and hearing it from this young girl in that strange, detached tone only made it seem worse.

"So, what happened? Did they catch the killer?"

Jane sighed and said, "No, the police never found out who did it."

"I'm so sorry to hear that, Jane. Such an awful and traumatic thing to go through at such a young age."

"It was what it was, and I managed to move on."

"So, what happened to you after that? I mean, did you go into the foster care system?"

"No . . . well, not at that time. I was turned over to my dad's brother, Mark, my uncle, and his wife, Lenore. They lived in another state and had a young son, Bobby, who was a few years older than me."

"So, that was a good thing, right? I mean, you were with family. That's gotta be better than with strangers."

"You would think so, and in the beginning, everything worked out pretty good . . . until . . ."

Paul asked, "Until what?"

Jane's voice seemed to get even more distant when she said, "Well, I feel a bit funny sharing this with a stranger, but . . . things were ok until Uncle Mark and Cousin Bobby started making late-night visits to my bedroom."

Paul knew where this story was heading, "On no, Jane. Are you saying . . ."

"Yeah, they raped and sodomized me nightly. Aunt Lenore knew what was happening but did nothing about it. Some nights, she even sat on a chair watching them, you know, do sick stuff to me. She even got in on the fun twice and molested me while they watched."

"Oh my god! That's terrible. Did you go to the police or maybe a teacher or minister for help?"

"No, Paul, I couldn't. I was a stranger in their town; they were well-known and respected. Mark was even active in his church leadership. Aunt Lenore volunteered for school events, and Bobby was his class's president. I was just some discarded piece of trash dumped on them."

"I'm so sorry, Jane. How long did you have to deal with . . . with the abuse?"

"Luckily, not long. There was a tragic fire, and the house burned to the ground. Uncle Mark, Aunt Lenore, and Cousin Bobby all died in the fire. I was the only survivor."

"Sounds to me like they got what they deserved," Paul said, although he couldn't help but notice the strange coincidence that this unusual young woman had managed to avoid death twice.

Jane didn't reply.

"So, what happened after that?"

She said, "I was shipped off to my father's Aunt Sarah, my great Aunt."

/ 4 /

"She was really old, like in her eighties. She was half-crippled and bonkers in the head, you know?"

"You mean she was senile?"

"Big time. Aunt Sarah didn't know who I was most of the time. She thought I was her kid or something, which was weird since she was never married and had no kids. I guess it's strange how you get when your brain starts to go . . ."

Although it was mostly dark in the car, Paul could see Jane making circular motions with her finger around her ear, the universal sign for crazy. She said, "If I hadn't been able to care for myself, I probably would have starved to death. I ended up taking care of her most of the time. She often crapped herself too. Not a fun experience, I'm telling you."

Paul said, "That was nice of you to care for her. I assume she eventually passed away."

"Yep. She did a header down a flight of steps and broke her neck along with a bunch of other bones. And before you ask, I was not sent to live with any other relatives. I guess we ran out of takers. I was put into the system, which bounced me from one abusive home to another until I ran away when I was sixteen, and I've been on my own ever since."

"You poor thing," Paul said, "How tragic. It seems you've been through so much."

Jane said, "I have. Yet here I am, stronger than ever."

Paul sighed, then said, "Look, Jane, I'm going to suggest something . . . and I hope it doesn't sound weird or anything . . . and there's no catch . . . I expect nothing in return."

"What is it, Paul?" Jane asked, but she already knew what he was going to suggest. She always knew.

"You see, I'm divorced, and my daughter, Cindy, is away at college. I have a big house all to myself. If you would like, you could spend the night. You can get a nice shower, and I can cook you a delicious dinner. You are welcome to sleep in my daughter's room and borrow some of her clothes while I run those wet things through the washer and dryer."

Jane was quiet momentarily, then slipped her hand up toward Paul's crotch and said, "That all sounds fantastic, but I have to find some way to pay you for your kindness."

Paul gently pushed her hand aside and said, "I appreciate the offer, but there is no need. You have been through so much; I cannot, in good conscience, take advantage of you like that. Allow me to just help you tonight, and tomorrow, you can be on your way if that's your wish."

Jane slowly pulled her hand away, unsure of what to make of this stranger. She said, "Ok, Paul. I accept."

Paul thought he saw a strange expression cross Jane's face in the moonlight. It was one that momentarily sent chills racing down his spine.

/ 5 /

Later that night, after Jane had dinner, she was relaxing on the sofa dressed in a pair of Paul's daughter's pajamas. A crime drama was playing on the television; Jane was hardly paying attention to the show as she was a bit troubled. Paul had been so kind to her, much more considerate than she deserved, yet she knew who and what she was, and nothing could change that.

"So, what are we watching?" Paul asked as he walked into the family room carrying Jane's recently washed, dried, and folded clothes.

Jane said, "I don't know. Some cop show. Not sure which one, but it doesn't really matter anyway. They're all pretty much the same."

"Yeah, I get what you mean. Did you ever notice how on TV the cops always manage to catch the murderer in an hour, but in the real world, people get away with murder all the time?"

Jane hesitated momentarily, wondering what Paul was getting at, then said, "Yeah. I pretty sure everybody wonders about that, but that's just, you know, TV." Actually, she had never thought that and was a bit concerned why Paul would bother asking her such a thing. She now knew what she had to do.

"Well, Jane. It's late, I had a very busy, and I must say, interesting day. I'm going to bed now, and I'll see you in the morning. I think you'll sleep well in Cindy's bed tonight. Goodnight, Sweet Jane."

Again, Jane was caught off guard by the kindness this man offered her, and he expected nothing in return. She wished he had treated her badly or demanded sex or something to justify her actions. But then again, he did show signs of suspicion. Regardless, she had no choice, so later that night, she would murder Paul Stoddard in his sleep.

/ 6 /

Paul heard the door to his bedroom slowly opening as he sat upright in the darkness, waiting for Sweet Jane to come to him, not as the mysterious woman of his sexual fantasies but as the serial killer he knew she really was. And, as he suspected, Sweet Jane had not let him down.

She stood silhouetted in the now open doorway to Paul's bedroom, backlit by the nightlight in the hallway. He could see something long and pointed in her hand, and he knew it was a butcher's knife from the wood block in his kitchen.

In as calm a voice as he could manage, Paul asked, "So, Sweet Jane. This is how you repay my kindness, by killing me in my sleep like you murdered your parents so many years ago?"

"I never said I killed them, Paul. But yeah . . . you're right. I did stab them to death, and I burned Uncle Mark's house down, and I pushed that senile old bitch down the stairs."

"My guess is there have been others you have killed as well," Paul said from the darkness.

"Yes. Many others."

"And now you plan to kill me, someone whose only mistake was being kind to you. Care to explain why?"

Jane said, "I'm not sure I understand either. I suppose it's just who I am, just how I'm wired. I'm not doing this because it's fun or exciting or because I get some sort of thrill from it. I just do it because I have to."

"You may be surprised to know, I understand," Paul replied.

"You do?" Jane exclaimed, "But how can you understand?"

"I just do," Paul said, "It's not because of how your parents treated you or your subsequent abusive experiences. You see, Sweet Jane, you are truly an unusual commodity. Female serial killers are very rare. They are few and far between. However, I pegged you as one right from the start."

Jane was puzzled, "But how did you know?"

"I suppose it takes one to know one, as they say," Paul replied heartily.

Jane was confused, "Takes one to know one? That makes no sense. I don't understand. You're not a serial killer; even if you were, you're not a woman."

Although Jane could not see Paul in the darkness, she could tell by his voice he was smiling as he spoke the next shocking words. He said, "No, not a woman anymore."

/ 7 /

Jane was stunned to silence for a beat, eventually finding her voice, "What are you saying? You said you had a daughter and were divorced from . . . from your wife."

"Not true, sweet, Sweet Jane. I said spouse; I never used the word wife. If I had ever referred to my husband, I would have been careful to say spouse, not husband."

Jane gripped her knife more tightly and took a single step across the doorway's threshold. She was becoming more uncomfortable by the minute. This was not going at all as she had planned. Jane decided the best thing to do was to keep this freak distracted long enough to get within stabbing distance.

She said, "So you're telling me you were a woman once, as well as a wife and mother?" She took another small step forward and heard a clicking sound. She recognized it as a gun getting ready to fire.

"That's far enough, Sweet Janie," Paul said as he clicked on the reading light on the end table beside his bed. When her eyes adjusted, Jane saw Paul pointing a large caliber handgun directly at her. She didn't know enough about weapons to determine the gun's ability to inflict damage because she had never used firearms. However, based on the size of the hole in the barrel, she decided that the hand cannon most definitely could cause some major damage.

Paul said, "In answer to your question, yes, I was a woman, a wife, and a mother. In fact, I gave birth to our daughter, Cindy. I tried to be a good wife and do the whole family thing. But . . . well, unfortunately, I, too, was a female serial killer. I had over a dozen kills before transitioning to a male and another six after that. And you, Sweet Jane, will be my seventh."

SOUL SOUP

"I don't believe in any particular definition of the afterlife, but I do believe we're spiritual creatures and more than our biology and that energy cannot be destroyed but can change. I don't know what the afterlife is going to be, but I'm not afraid of it."
—ALAN BALL

"Everyone fears the cut of the blade. It doesn't matter after that. I know the spirit survives as there is so much evidence of the survival of the personality in the afterlife."
—DAN AYKROYD

"It's questionable whether I believe in God or Jesus, but I do believe in a spiritual world and some kind of afterlife."
—CARL FROCH

The man in the bed opened his eyes and tried to focus both his vision and his mind. Where was he, and how did he get there? He looked slowly around the dimly lit room. He seemed to be in a hospital, judging by the room's appearance and the place's antiseptic smell. Yet the space seemed less like a hospital and more like a home.

He didn't hear the beeping and humming of machinery nor the sounds of busy people rushing to and fro. The room seemed to be a place of rest and relaxation rather than a place for sick people. In the dim lighting, Norm saw walls tastefully decorated with attractive wallpaper in subdued yellow and brown striped colors. There was a nightstand next to the bed with a light of extremely low wattage, apparently designed to provide the minimum amount of illumination so as not to disturb the residents in the room.

Norm sat upright in bed and waited for the cobwebs to clear from his brain. "Ok, Broaden," Norm said to himself, "You've got to try and remember, pal. Yeah, you have to figure this thing out."

He thought hard about it but came up empty. In fact, Norm had no idea how he had ended up here. He moved to the edge of the bed and allowed his bare feet to dangle over the side as he thought. If he was in a hospital or a convalescent home, something must be wrong with him. But Norm felt fine; in fact, he felt better than fine. The typical pains he associated with being over sixty were gone. Nothing hurt, and he felt forty-five instead of sixty-five. However, Norm did notice that he was naked, which he found unusual since he had never previously slept in that state.

He said to the empty room, "Well, this is rather embarrassing. Good thing this is a private room, and it's not chilly; back to the business at hand. I've determined I'm not hurt and apparently in good shape. I may be wardrobe-challenged, but I can deal with that in due course. So, I may not know why I'm here, but I suppose it's time to find out where I am."

Then he heard what sounded like the hum of dozens of voices, all moaning or speaking unintelligibly from somewhere outside the wall behind him on the other side of the room. At first, he thought it might be a group of people outside talking. But he changed his mind when he realized the voices seemed to come from thousands of people mumbling at once, not just a few.

Then the sound reminded him less of people having a normal conversation and more like something else. He had a flashback to when he was an eight-year-old boy sitting next to his younger brother in church. Whenever the congregation participated in what was known as "the responsive reading," the minister would read a bible verse, and then the people would respond by reading the response line aloud from their bibles.

To young Norman Broaden and his brother, Brian, the murmuring of the congregation sounded unintelligible. The two brothers would look at each other, chuckle, then mumble in as deep a voice as they could manage each time the congregation would respond. It always seemed funny for them as kids, but Norm didn't feel this would be the case with the similar sounds he heard now.

He recalled how his Aunt Mabel, a religious zealot, had chastised him and his brother after church one Sunday for what she called "making a mockery" of the responsive reading. She said, "That sort of behavior is sinful. God is listening, Normie. God always listens, and he heard you and Brian carrying on. He may just decide to send you both to Hell someday when you die for what you've done."

After the dressing down from Aunt Mabel, Norm had many unpleasant nights filled with horrible dreams of burning in the fires of Hell, all because he joked with his brother in church. They never did the mumbling, giggling thing in church again. However, like all childhood fears, this one eventually passed, and Norm went on to live his life and commit many more sins, most of which were a thousand times more severe than clowning around during a church service.

Norm had decided if he was ever going to Hell, he wanted to make sure it was for good reasons, so he did his best to pile up those reasons. He had lived over sixty-five years and planned on committing many more sins before permanently checking out of the game of life.

He stood at the bottom of his bed and looked to the far end of his room, where he noticed several large windows through a small crack in heavy, room-darkening drapes. Norm walked over to the windows and, fumbling in the near-darkness, found a pull cord, which he assumed was used to open and close the drapes. Tugging carefully on the rope, Norm noticed the sliver of an opening begin to widen to an inch or so larger.

Bright light flooded the room, temporarily blinding him as he held his hands up to protect his eyes from the luminous assault. It was light more brilliant than any he had ever seen. The strange chorus of moaning voices seemed to grow louder, so loud Norm thought he couldn't stand it. When his eyes slowly adjusted to the change, Norm pulled hard on the cord and opened the drapes to their maximum capacity. Then voices suddenly stopped, leaving behind silence as quiet as a tomb.

At first, as his eyes adjusted further, he could see nothing but whiteness. Then Norm saw something he could scarcely comprehend. A brightly glowing mist filled the entire wide scope of his vision, but not like any fog Norm had ever seen. He had always understood that fog was essentially comprised of low-hanging clouds. But these clouds, if they were clouds, appeared to have a thick, gelatinous consistency.

Norm believed if he could reach out and touch one of the clouds, his fingers would come away sticky and covered with a disgusting white ooze coated with a transparent membrane of some viscous fluid.

Then, the massive wall of the strange gooey substance began to move and swirl around. It was rotating, revolving, and diving in on top of itself, resembling a taffy-making machine Norm had seen at a fair as a young boy. However, this taffy was glowing with a blinding whiteness and was visible as far as Norm looked in every direction. As impossible as it might be, the swimming visage had to be miles high and across, encompassing the entire sky before him.

As he stared hypnotically at the swirling mass, it solidified further and changed color from blinding white to what appeared to be hundreds of different shades of human skin. Then, the accumulation formed into shapes resembling human arms, legs, heads, and torsos. They were all hairless, coated in the same film of slime, with no decisive sexuality visible. There were millions of semi-solid beings of every hue, all sliding into then emerging out of this massive primordial stew of . . . of what? Norm wondered what this vision might be that he saw moving in and out of this giant cauldron of the sky.

Were they beings? Norm didn't think so, at least not living, breathing beings. They were obviously without skeletal structure, or else they couldn't move as fluidly as they did in this undulating mass. But if they weren't living creatures, then what were they? Then, two words suddenly popped into his mind, "Soul Soup."

He wondered what those two words meant. Then Norm realized he was looking at a swirling collection of souls; millions of former living beings joined in this churning stew. Norm had no idea where that realization came from, but he knew he was right. He couldn't comprehend, however, why he would be privy to such an incredible sight.

Stunned and confused by the impossible tableaux playing out before his eyes, Norm backed slowly away from the window, and the backs of his bare legs bumped into something. He turned to see he had backed against the bed. Then he noticed something he hadn't seen previously: someone occupied the bed.

Coming closer, Norm saw something his mind could barely understand. The body in the bed was his. But how could that be? Was he dreaming or having an out-of-body experience? Was he alive in that bed, or was he . . .? Norm stopped mid-thought because the strange moaning had begun anew behind him.

Norm sensed something very bad was about to happen and was terrified to turn around and look out at that mass of flowing former humanity again. Then, as Norm stood with his head down and back to the window, the moaning grew louder, sounding less like people talking and more like moans and cries of pain, as if a million souls were simultaneously weeping with agony.

Finally, he forced himself to turn around slowly and look up at the window again. The heavy drapes were gone. The hardware supporting the drapes was also gone. Then Norm saw that the windows separating himself from the mass of souls were gone.

He looked up at the constantly moving sky of writhing creatures and understood these poor souls were not only lost but also suffering in unimaginable pain. As they swam in and out of the fleshy soup, the faces he saw wore expressions of anguish like Norm had never seen before. Their eyes bulged out of their faces, and mouths hung wide open, emitting moans of incredible torment. The viscous fluid coating these creatures was no longer clear but had turned to a translucent crimson color.

These millions of lost souls flowed over and under each other on a slipstream of blood-infused gel. Norm realized these pitiful creatures were not just lost souls, but damned souls, destined to spend eternity swimming in this Hell-spawned stew of agony. His heart went out to them in their torment.

Then he looked again at the body in the bed behind him. Everything was suddenly certain. There was no doubt that the resident of the bed was him and was most certainly dead. But he wondered how he could be dead yet still standing beside the bed, looking down at himself. Then he felt something warm and slimy wrap itself around his ankles.

Norm kicked at whatever had touched him, and it released him. But as he turned back to the window, he saw a sight that caused his stomach to clench, and he felt as if his bowels would let loose. Some of the creatures, the gelatinous tortured souls, were oozing over the windowless sill, sliding onto the floor and crawling toward him.

His mind could scarcely comprehend the vision of semi-liquified humanity spilling into the room. The moaning increased in volume, and Norm could hear the screams of thousands of tortured souls as the crawling mass slid closer to him. The floor was coated with crimson fluid as the bodies of the damned seemed to pile over each other.

Then Norm felt two warm, slimy hands grab his left ankle while another slid high up his right leg. He felt his body losing all cohesion, becoming something other than what it had once been. Then, an aching, burning pain spread throughout him as he melted into the mass of undulating flesh.

Norm released an agonizing moan as his now semi-liquified soul became part of the soul soup. His last conscious and truly individual thought was that memory of him and Brian mumbling during the responsive reading in church. That sound had been so funny back then. Now, not so much.

BULLET POINTS

*"Stories are how we remember: we tend to forget lists
and bullet points"*
—Robert McKee

"Bullet points are not the point."
—Seth Godin

*"New research into cognitive functioning—how the brain works—
proves that bullet points are the least effective way to deliver important
information. Neuroscientists find that what passes as a typical
presentation is usually the worst way to engage your audience."*
—Carmine Gallo

*"It's important to remember the Gospel is a story:
not a set of bullet points"*
—Timothy Keller

/ 1 /

- Devon only thought in bullet points.

/ 2 /

- Devon also spoke, read, and listened exclusively in bullet
  points.
  - o Sometimes, he would accept a sub-bullet point.

- o But no more than two.
- o Or maybe three on a good day.
- He and his friends refused to read books; they wouldn't even read a long sentence.
  - o All information had to be broken down into concise bullet points.
  - o It was typical of many of his generation, especially young coworkers, and it drove the older workers mad.

/ 3 /

- Those millennial types expected immediate gratification and would not take the time for story or character development.
- Older coworkers nicknamed Devon "BP" for "Bullet Points."
- They hated Devon and all his "bullet point" friends.

/ 4 /

- The older workers decided to take matters into their own hands.
- They formulated a plan, a very deadly plan.
  - o For them, it was more of an evil game.
- They sent each troublesome employee an untraceable email document containing critical information.
- They were giving Devon and his cronies a way to save themselves if they were so inclined.

/ 5 /

- Devon really should have read his document.
- His young coworkers should have read their documents as well.
- Patience is a virtue, people say, but in this case, it meant so much more.
- It was a matter of life and death, but they wouldn't know until it was too late.
- Here is the document

/ 6 /

To: Everyone
From: Human Resources Department
Subject: Dress Code And Attendance Violations
Please take the time to read and understand the following information thoroughly.

It has come to the attention of the Human Resources department through management channels that there have been numerous violations regarding company dress code requirements and attendance policy. We have strict guidelines regarding these areas that must be adhered to.

As described in our employee manual, violations of these policies will be dealt with in the following manner. A first offense will result in a verbal warning. A second offense will result in a letter of reprimand being placed in your employee folder. Any additional violations will result in immediate and final termination of employment.

If there are any questions, please reference the following sections in the employee manual for further information: Section D-2.3.123, Section A-12-1-4, and Section T-3.2.7.

To whom this email really concerns, this is not a warning from our HR department. In fact, they know nothing about this, and with good reason. This extremely important document contains vital information pertinent to you and your young coworkers' longevity within this company. It also addresses another subject even more important than professional success. We'll get to that subject in a bit.

We, the creators of this document, represent the older generation of employees, those you refer to as "Boomers." We are the workers who have heard you say should "either retire, die, or both!" That's right, we know everything you say behind our backs. You people who insist on having all your information handed to you in the form of easily digestible bullet points. You make us sick. Do you all think you're Joe Friday or something? "Just the facts, ma'am, just the facts." Then again, you likely have no idea who Joe Friday was or, for that matter, have ever heard of Dragnet.

You seem to forget that we "old people" built this company from nothing to the major corporation it is today over the past forty years. We did it by explaining situations in full sentences and paragraphs, not bullet points. We made sure that everyone involved understood the role they had to play. And yes, that meant reading actual written paragraphs and pages. For your information, we still read detailed documentation at work as required, and believe it or not, we read novels at home just for the pleasure of doing so.

When did you and your friends last read a book for the simple joy of reading? Our guess is never. You all prefer to wait for the movie to spoon-feed you the book in simple, easy-to-digest segments of instant gratification. It doesn't matter to you that the film no longer resembles the story told in the book because you never read it in the first place. All you know is that the movie was chocked full of violence, action, car chases, exploding buildings, and naked women.

So, by now, I guess that you've stopped reading this little tale of ours, judging it to be nothing more than a bunch of old farts mouthing off and being afraid of all you up-and-coming young Turks. The truth is we do see you as a threat, but not to us. We have our pensions and 401k accounts, and soon, we'll collect our social security. Most of us are debt-free. We're working for insurance coverage and saving more money for retirement. But you are most definitely a threat to our company, the same company that provided us with a generous lifetime of employment.

We spent more waking hours at the office than home, building that company to what it is today, while you all were just twinkles in your mommy's eye. Yet here you are, with your silly ideas and pathetic work ethic. You come in late, take extended lunches, leave early, and spend your days unproductively. Yet you all demand high salaries. If that's not bad enough, you rarely stay with a company for more than five years anyway, then move on to the next opportunity. You're like a useless duck who lands in a pond, splashes around, disturbing everyone, and then flies away to wreak havoc at another pond.

Yes, we're quite certain that by now, you have most definitely stopped reading this dissertation and deleted it or just ignored it. That's fine with us. This is a completely secure document that can't be saved, duplicated, or copied. Once you start reading it, the document will time out in five minutes and destroy all traces of itself anyway. There is a reason for this.

We wrote this message to warn you, yet we knew you wouldn't make it this far. Regardless, here's the important part, the part you really needed to read. Unbeknownst to you, we have slipped a slow-acting deadly poison into your energy drinks. We've been doing this for several days now, and soon, one by one, each of you will die. Some will be in the next day or so, and the rest will be by the weekend. No one will know it was us, and no one will be able to trace anything back to us.

Our only hope is that the new people the company eventually hires to replace you upon your demise will be more receptive to getting the whole story. If they start chanting your "bullet points" mantra, they'll join you in the great bulleted document in the sky.

If, by some chance, you made it this far, then you're in luck. Here is what you need to do to stay alive. There is an antidote for the poison, located in the lunch room storage cabinet where they store paper products like paper towels, plates, and napkins. It is in a small bottle appropriately labeled "Bullet points." If you read this, you passed the test and will live, at least for now. You will have to change your ways and learn patience. Otherwise, you will die.

You can complain to anyone you want, but you will never find out who we are. Heed this warning.

/ 1 /

- Devon never read the note.
- His coworkers never read theirs, either.
- Devon died.
- His coworkers died.
- They were replaced.
    ◦ Will their replacements work out?
- Time will tell.
    ◦ We will be watching.

THE BOX

/ 1 /

The light from the living room lamp cast its soft amber glow about the place, projecting shadows across the minimal furnishings. That was how the man in the recliner liked his lighting, soft and subtle. None of that harsh LED lighting for Marvin Kellerman, no-siree. It would be incandescent lighting all the way or no lighting at all, as far as he was concerned. He recalled reading how the government hoped to eliminate incandescent light bulbs by the end of 2023 because they were considered less energy efficient.

The Department of Energy claimed that the average family could save about $100 annually if they switched to LED lighting. Marvin couldn't care less about a lousy $100. He wanted his lighting the way he liked it, and that was that. Besides, the new bulbs cost at least three times what his current light bulbs did. Yes, they also lasted three times as long, but so what? He had read somewhere that when Donald Trump was president, he shot down the idea of eliminating incandescent bulbs because they made him look orange. Marvin was not a fan of the former president, to say the least, but he was grateful for that decision, even if it was based on stupidity. He hated to be the one to burst Donald's bubble, but the man looked orange because he was orange, as in spray-tan orange.

Marvin didn't care what the government wanted to do or what they might decide to do. He was a self-sufficient individual. Marvin had gone to several home centers to satisfy his needs and bought himself all the incandescent light bulbs he could find. He suspected he had all the bulbs he would ever need for the rest of his life and then some. He stored them in boxes in his attic where they were ready and waiting to be used. That was how Marvin Kellerman did things: see a problem and solve it.

Some people thought Marvin was a bit fixated, obsessive, and perhaps anal-retentive. Those people would be right, even though he didn't think of himself that way. Marvin felt he was efficient and organized. Although it was true he planned things out to the smallest detail; it was only because he wanted things to be perfect. He liked his world to be exactly the way he wanted his world to be. There was no room for drama or upset. Smooth sailing was how Mr. Marvin Kellerman liked his ship to float. And now, after dealing with the problem that had caused him so much upset, Marvin was relaxing with a good book on his recliner under incandescent lighting. Ah, life was good again.

Still, he was a bit troubled about what he had recently done. He was certain he had dotted every "i" and crossed every "t," yet he couldn't help but review every detail about it, feeling he might have missed something. He needed to be certain because one slip-up and he would find himself on death row. And that would never do because he was sure all government facilities like offices and prisons were now using those damnable LED lights. Death row was bad, and lethal injection was worse, but team those up with no incandescent lighting, and it might be more than Marvin could take. Besides, reliving a project he was so proud of gave him great pleasure.

He set his book down, closed his eyes, and started at the beginning, recalling every detail he could remember, no matter how insignificant it might seem, to ensure he didn't miss anything. Marvin decided to start with designing and constructing what he called "The box," which was perhaps his most ingenious idea to date. If one wanted to get the greatest satisfaction from his vengeance and restore harmony to his personal universe, the box Marvin designed and built was a great way to accomplish this.

/ 2 /

From the outside, the box looked about as basic and simple as any rectangular crate might appear. It measured seven feet long, two feet wide, and twenty inches deep. It was made of one-and-one-quarter-inch thick construction-grade plywood. The wood was not weather resistant as there was no need for such precautions. The crate was designed for one-time use; what became of it after the deed was done was irrelevant.

The box was open at the top but had a lid that fit inside it rather than over the top. This lid was also about a foot or so shorter than the length of the box. This inside-fitting feature and the shorter length were essential for the box's functionality.

The bottom of the box was where the real action came into play. Sketched on the bottom of the box was a grid of lines and points. The grid was 10 points across and 35 along the length, creating 350 individual points spaced on 2-inch squares. Like the lid measurements, the rows of lines started a foot below what Marvin thought of as the head of the box. It took him quite a while to accurately sketch the intersecting grid of lines with a steel straight-edge and #3 drawing pencil. Next, Marvin placed a small "x" at each line intersection using a six-inch steel scale.

After the grid and the points were all plotted, Marvin used the 1/8-inch hole in a metal circle template to painstakingly trace a circle at each intersection point, all for use as a visual reference. Most people might think this step a waste of time, but Mrs. Kellerman's oldest son, Marvin, was a stickler for accuracy, and if taking the time for this step prevented problems or inaccuracies later in the process, then that is what he would do.

He constructed his box on the workbench in his woodworking shop in his garage, where the light was brighter yet still incandescent, not LED or fluorescent. Marvin's shop was a masterpiece of organization, where every tool, every screw, nail, washer, or any shop item had its own place, was organized logically, and was labeled with care. For example, if you needed a half-inch long 6-32 wood screw, you wouldn't have to spend time rooting through jars or boxes of random screws hoping to find what you needed. In Marvin's garage, you would simply go to the organizational chest of many small drawers and go to the plastic pull-out drawer with the label reading "Wood Screws 6-32 x .5," and you would have just what you wanted.

Japanese manufacturing experts used this sort of organization in their six-sigma programs, called "5-S," and would have been amazed at the level of organization Marvin had in his shop. For Marvin, however, it was just how he wanted and needed things to be.

Once the circles were drawn, Marvin went to the drawer in his tool chest labeled "Nail Sets and Countersinks" and retrieved his countersinking tool. It was a small hand tool made of tool steel, about five inches long, with a 3/8-inch knurled barrel. It resembled a small nail set tool ground to an approximately 90-degree point. Several years earlier, the tip had broken off of one of Marvin's nail set tools, and rather than throw it out, he ground the new point on the end and had an excellent countersinking tool. Waste not, want not was in practice at all times in Marvin's woodworking shop.

Using his countersinking tool and a hammer, Marvin carefully tapped a small indentation at the intersection points of his grid of lines, using the 1/8-inch circles he sketched previously as a guide to ensure he didn't go too deep. Three hundred and fifty points later, he had created an accurate grid of countersunk holes ready for drilling.

The next step in his process was to drill three hundred fifty 5/32-inch holes at each intersection, using the countersinks to locate his drill point accurately. As was true with the rest of his shop, Marvin went to the drill bit cabinet, opened the drawer marked ".125 - .1875 Drills," and selected the 5/32 drill, which had the equivalent decimal value of .1562 inch diameter.

Although Marvin could have used his corded drill motor and drill bit to drill the holes, he chose to take advantage of the flexibility offered by his Craftsman cordless V20 battery-powered drill. Because of the thickness of the wood and the large number of holes, the battery died halfway through the grid. This was no problem, however, because Marvin had a complete set of V20 series power tools and, as such, had a neatly organized rack he constructed himself, filled with nine fully charged batteries. He also had three chargers to recharge batteries while working and never had to wait. Marvin considered this just one more step toward maximum efficiency.

Soon, the entire grid was completely drilled through the rectangular box-bottom component, and it was time for the next critical step in the process. This would involve hammering three hundred fifty six-inch-long 60d spike nails through the pre-drilled holes. Marvin had chosen the hot-dipped galvanized ring pole barn framing nails that sold for twenty-eight cents each. He bought ten spares in case something went wrong during the next step in the process. This set him back about a hundred bucks, but he figured it would be worth it. Besides, he already accrued that much in plywood cost.

/ 3 /

When Marvin returned from the store with the spikes, he knew he would have much more work cut out for himself. The nails had a standard point on them, which, although quite sharp, might not be sufficiently piercing for the task Marvin expected them to perform. He could have taken the chance that the factory-supplied points would be good enough to do the job, but "good enough" was never good enough for him.

Marvin owned a Porter-Cable dual-wheel bench-mounted grinder, which he often used to resharpen dull drill bits. It had one wheel for rough grinding and a second for finishing. Wearing heat-resistant shop gloves, Marvin took one of the spikes and ground a long, thin point in place of the original one.

He timed the process and found it took him three and a half minutes to grind the desired point style. He believed his skill level would increase with practice, and he could get that time down to about one to two minutes per nail. With 359 more spikes to grind, Marvin realized he would be looking at 718 minutes or almost 12 hours of continuous grinding. Obviously, he would not want to do that non-stop, nor did he have the time to do it all at once if he chose to, especially since he still had a full-time job.

Marvin dedicated two hours after work each day to regrinding the points. If he started the next day, which was Monday, he should have them all completed by Saturday or Sunday at the latest. He had to allow a buffer for fatigue or other unforeseen circumstances.

Fortunately for Marvin, he was not up against any deadline other than those that were self-imposed. The truth was he could do what he needed to do when he was ready, and how long that took was irrelevant. So, it would be fine even if this task went into Monday or Tuesday. This knowledge reassured Marvin because grinding all those spikes would be a daunting task but one he could handle. Still, he was haunted by his own self-imposed deadlines.

By the following Friday evening, all of the spikes had new deadly sharp points, and Marvin had ten fingers and two hands that were aching with the strain of completing the job in record time. Sometimes he hated the way he was constantly in competition with himself. Marvin often felt he had to do something about that someday. He feared the need to excel, to not only be better than anyone else but constantly to be trying to beat himself might ultimately drive him insane. This was especially significant when you combined that drive with his need to be super-organized and efficient.

Marvin knew he was different from anyone else he encountered. He was extremely creative, capable of painting, drawing, and designing incredible art and music, all things requiring right-brained thinking. Yet he was also equally left-brained, making him logical, organized, and analytical. These two opposing personalities were constantly at war, sometimes making Marvin worry about how long he could hold his mind together. Then, as he thought of his latest project and the purpose for its creation, Marvin began to wonder if perhaps he had already lost the mental war his brain was waging. But that was a question for another day. Now, he had more work to do.

Marvin placed the rectangular bottom section of the box on top of a piece of 2 x 6 Styrofoam he had glued together from several smaller blocks he had purchased at a local hobby shop. These set him back about $50 and would likely be useless when he was finished. However, Marvin knew he would not throw the blocks out, despite the damage they would receive, because he couldn't admit there was no other use for the foam. Marvin prided himself on being able to find a use for everything, and he'd just have to wait until inspiration hit him. Until then, he'd tuck the assembled foam slab up on a shelf where it would remain for as long as necessary.

Once ready, Marvin began tapping the spikes one by one through the 5/32-inch pilot holes he had previously drilled. Again and again, his hammer struck spike after spike until all 350 holes were eventually filled. Marvin had created a grid of 350 nails spaced on two-inch centers, sticking four and three-quarter inches out of a piece of one-and-one-quarter plywood.

It comprised a bed of razor-sharp nails deadly enough to terrify even the most skilled mystic. Anyone attempting to walk on this bed of spikes would be in for a rude and painful awakening. Then again, that wasn't the purpose of this project.

/ 4 /

Marvin next sealed the underside of the nailed plywood with a waterproof liquid sealant, being sure to coat every nail head. He repeated this process five times, allowing each previous coat to sufficiently dry. This process would guarantee a leak-proof bottom to the finished box.

While the sealant was drying, Marvin cut one two-feet by four-feet piece of one-quarter-inch plywood, then a second two-feet by three feet part of the same thickness. Eventually, using his cordless drill motor with his Phillips screwdriver bit and #8 by one-inch wood screws, Marvin fastened these thin pieces of plywood to the nail head side of the part. Again, this might be considered an unnecessary step, but not Marvin.

He wanted to ensure that no downward force from the pointed end of any spike could jostle it out of its position. With the one-quarter-inch plywood screwed into the thicker base, it guaranteed none of the spikes would be able to push out. When this step was complete, Marvin flipped the part over and separated the foam backing material from the nails, storing the damaged Styrofoam neatly away, even though one side of it looked like Swiss cheese.

Next, using his Craftsman table saw, Marvin cut two pieces of one-and-one-quarter plywood into twenty-four-inch by twenty-inch rectangles. These would make up the two ends of the box. Then he cut two rectangular pieces twenty inches by seven feet, which would make up the sides of the box. Lastly, he cut the rectangle that would become the lid to six feet by nineteen and three-quarters inches, ensuring it would fit inside the box.

Marvin assembled the box sides to the bottom using one of his cordless drills with a 1/8" drill bit and a second one with the Phillips screwdriver head. He used #10 by two-inch wood screws to fasten the box together. Marvin ran a bead of extra-strength wood glue along mating surfaces before screwing them into place. He also used corner clamps and a small metal square tool to ensure the box was perfectly square. Again, in the scheme of things, squareness was irrelevant, but in Marvin's world, this, too, mattered.

Once the box was fully assembled, Marvin used silicon caulking and the same liquid sealant to apply multiple coats to the inside of the box, being careful to avoid getting any adhesive on the upper four inches of the spikes. Lastly, he sealed the entire outside of the box. It was now ready to serve its purpose.

/ 5 /

Jim Saunders was an idiot. As harsh and judgemental as that might sound, it was equally accurate. He was loud, crude, and vulgar, as many stupid people tend to be. That was something Marvin had trouble comprehending. Why did intelligent people tend to be more reserved, as if to suggest they lacked the confidence to expound on a subject aloud, lest someone prove them in error?

Stupid people didn't have such reservations. It always seemed to Marvin that stupid people had no problem saying whatever came into their mind, no matter how erroneous it might be, and doing so as loudly and crudely as possible. They also tended to repeat themselves if they didn't get the reaction they wanted the first, second, or third time. It is as if repeating the same incorrect information louder each time might suddenly make it miraculously true.

Marvin recalled something his father had told him. His father was not one to suffer fools and knew how to deal with them. He said, "Marvin, if you ever find yourself in an argument with a stupid person, the best thing to do is just punch him in the face. You'll probably end up having to do so eventually, so why waste time and energy arguing? Just cut to the chase and deck the idiot."

Unfortunately, Marvin was more passive-aggressive than his father and not one for confrontation or fighting. He supposed he got that from his mother's side of the family. Whatever the case, Marvin preferred to deal with things in his own way.

Jim Saunders was standing next to his car late Saturday night a week earlier, trying to find his car key. He was far beyond legally drunk and had no business even considering driving, let alone getting behind the wheel. But Jim had every intention of doing so. That was to say, until he felt a bee sting on the back of his neck. He quickly reached back to the place on his neck where he felt the sting.

Instead of finding an angry insect, he felt a needle with feathers embedded deep in the flesh of his neck. He shouted, "What the . . ." but before expressing a string of profanities and obscenities, Jim felt his eyes cross and fell face-first to the ground.

/ 6 /

Jim awoke slowly and with great confusion. It was nighttime, and he could smell a damp, earthy scent. He heard various sounds he associated with nature, such as crickets and night birds. From what little he could determine in his still-foggy state, he seemed to be in a forest or wooded area.

He felt like he was floating in the air. As Jim struggled to creep out of the darkness to consciousness, he realized, from the icy chill he felt from head to toe, that he was naked. A gag was in his mouth so that he couldn't cry out. His first confused thought of floating proved accurate as he could feel that he was being suspended in the air.

Jim could feel some sort of tape stuck to the back of his neck. If he tried to move his head to look from side to side, he couldn't. Perhaps the tape was also wrapped around his gag; he didn't know. When Jim tried to move his hands and arms, he discovered they were strapped tightly to his body with what was probably the same tape. He supposed it might be duct tape or perhaps package strapping tape. Then he realized his feet were likewise bound. As his vision began to clear, Jim saw that he was indeed in a forest. It was nighttime, and he could only see by the moonlight filtering through the thick canopy of tree branches and leaves overhead.

Then he saw something glistening in the moonlight that made his blood turn to ice. Long, thin wire cables led upward from his feet, his neck, and somewhere near the middle of his body. These wires ran up to and over a complex pulley system mounted to a wooden A-shaped framework resembling those used in backyard swing sets, but this one was only about four feet tall, not much taller than a saw horse. Then Jim realized, to his horror, what had happened to him.

Someone must have shot him with a dart full of drugs that knocked him out. Then the guy kidnapped Jim and brought him to this forest where he gagged, taped, and suspended him from this pulley and sawhorse contraption. But why? To what end?

What was this psycho's game plan? Did the kidnappers leave Jim for dead, figuring he couldn't escape and would eventually die of thirst, hunger, or exposure? Perhaps a bear or wolf or a pack of coyotes might attack him and have him for dinner. What was going on? He supposed he had some enemies; he was fairly certain everyone did. But he was sure he hadn't recently offended someone enough to merit this level of mistreatment. That meant his captor must be some type of stark-raving, mad lunatic.

Jim heard the crunching of leaves and the breaking of small sticks and realized something was coming, likely for him.

"Welcome, Jim," a soft-spoken male voice said, "So nice of you to join me."

/ 7 /

Marvin walked slowly toward the bound and suspended man, his knowing smile widened into a Cheshire cat grin. He had waited a long time for this particular adventure to become a reality, longer than most people might imagine.

He said, "Oh, Jim. We're going to have so much fun tonight. Then again, I'm certain I will have significantly more fun than you will. It's such a lovely night in the forest, under the stars. Don't you agree?"

Jim's gag prevented him from uttering more than a string of muffled grunts and groans. However, his eyes told a different story. They blazed with a hatred hot enough to melt steel. But there was something else in that piercing, murderous stare. There was confusion, uncertainty, and fear.

"Oh my. I just realized something, Jim. You don't recognize me, do you? I should have assumed that might happen. After all, people tend to change over time; fifty-three years is certainly a significant amount of time. Well, Jim, please allow me to reintroduce myself. I'm Marvin Kellerman. You probably remember me as Marvie Kellerman from your ninth-grade gym class."

Jim continued to stare angrily at his captor. He had no idea who this Kellerman guy was or why the crazy man was doing this to him.

"Still nothing? Wow, I can see you really don't remember me, do you? It's quite sad that you don't. How about the nickname Marvie Micro Weener, the American Bald Eagle? Does that ring any bells for you, Jim? After all, it was you who gave me that horrid name after you pulled down my gym shorts in front of everyone in the gymnasium that day, including the cheerleaders. Don't you recall? And there I stood, pitiful little Marvie Kellerman. My family was too poor to be able to afford a jock strap for me, and I was such a late bloomer. So those cheerleaders and all the boys in the class got a good look at my teenie little hairless package."

Jim's eyes finally showed recognition. He recalled how the Kellermans lived on the poor side of town and how he had bullied little, defenseless Marvie. Jim was never punished for his constant bullying since he knew little Marvin was too frightened to say anything. Jim also knew none of the other kids would report him because all the kids and more than a few teachers were afraid of him.

What Jim couldn't comprehend was that this lunatic, who had him at his mercy, was that same skinny little crying kid he had tortured so many years ago. He was a lot bigger now and apparently a lot crazier. If this really was Marvin Kellerman, why had he waited so long to get revenge? That incident happened decades ago. Jim was well into his late sixties, and although in fairly good health and still tough as nails, he was an old man now, the same age as this Kellerman character to the best of his recognition. So, why was Kellerman doing this now?

"Yes, that's right, Jim. It's me after all these years. So, I'll bet you're wondering why I've chosen to get my vengeance now. Well, it's like this, Jimmy boy. I'm alone in life and always have been. I never married and have no kids that I'm aware of. I recently retired and have all the time I need to do those things I have always wanted to do. But to be honest, Jim, I felt a bit bored by all this nothing time. I needed to find something to occupy the hours, a hobby. Then I started thinking of people who really had no business still breathing.

"No one had ever bullied me so mercilessly before you came along, so you became the first name on my list. I tried for years to put it all behind me and forgive you, but now that I'm getting older, I have to wonder why I didn't do this sooner. As I've said, I've waited a long time for this payback. You should be honored to be the first to enjoy a visit from me. By the way, there will be many more.

"You see, Jim, I have a list of everyone who has ever done me wrong. That list is quite long, but my time is short. You are my maiden voyage into the sea of revenge, so to speak. I'm looking forward to this and the others who will follow. I have a very special treat for you, Jimmy boy. It's a box painstakingly hand-crafted by yours truly over many long, hard evenings. It's in the ground, six feet below you. You'll also be happy to learn that none of the others on my list will get to enjoy this treat. I'll devise something unique for each of them.

"So, Jim, without any further ado, let's get this show on the road." Marvin unhooked the pulley line and slowly lowered Jim's bound body into the ground. Jim was certain he would be buried alive and could think of no more horrible way to die. But soon, his lack of creative foresight would be irrelevant. What awaited him was much worse than simply premature burial.

As Jim's body was lowered, he tried to struggle free but could not. After what seemed like an interminable amount of time, Jim saw the dirt sides of the rectangular hole appearing to rise around him. He smelled something he recognized but which sent chills of terror down his spine. It was gasoline.

Then Jim felt the first agonizing stab of pain. His back felt like dozens of needles were pressing against his exposed flesh. Then Jim tried to scream as the spines pierced his skin and began to travel deeper into his body. The pain was unbearable, and Jim was certain he would pass out at any minute, yet he remained conscious.

"How do you like my treat so far, Jimmy Boy? It's rather ingenious if I say so myself, and I must. You see, I'm using your own body and gravity against you. Your weight is pressing you further down onto the spikes, which, of course, are traveling up into your body. Eventually, they will pierce several vital organs and puncture one or both of your lungs."

Marvin grabbed the lid of the box, which he designed to fit inside the box while exposing the victim's face and head, and placed it on top of Jim's body. Then he grabbed a large rock from a nearby pike of boulders he had previously stacked for this purpose and dropped it down on the lid, causing Jim's body to move further down onto the spikes. Jim released muffled screams as every nerve ending in his body cried out in agony. Then Marvin dropped another boulder, another, and finally, the rest of the pile.

Looking down into what would become Jim's grave, Marvin saw the man was still alive, which was exactly what he had hoped to see. Despite his agony and weakness from blood loss, Jim's eyes still blazed with hatred for his captor. It became obvious to Marvin that Jim had no intention of letting Marvin see him beg for mercy.

"You certainly are a stubborn character, Jim. Then again, you always were. Dumb, ignorant, arrogant, and loud-mouthed was your claim to fame. That, and abusing those kids not as strong as you or those less fortunate. I had hoped you would have broken down and begged for mercy, but I suppose you realized there's no avoiding death with 350 six-inch-long spikes sunk into your body. I guess if you're not going to give me the satisfaction of seeing the terror in your dying eyes, I'll have to live with it.

"So, Jim, I think it's time we start to put this all to an end. Do you know what comes next, Jimmy boy? Would you care to make an educated guess? Oops, my bad. I keep forgetting how stupid you are. Would you prefer to make a moronic guess? Well, let me explain it all to you. I'm going to bury you alive, Jim. Although, in your case, I suppose it would be; I'm going to bury you almost alive. Oh yeah, and I'm going to burn you alive as well.

Jim's eyes suddenly seemed to get as large as half dollars, and Marvin smiled with great pleasure, knowing he had finally broken this arrogant fool. Then Marvin picked up his shovel, scooped a nice pile of dark, loose soil, and dropped it on Jim's face.

Jim went into full panic mode, his head thrashing as he moaned from the agony the embedded spikes inflicted. Marvin dropped several more shovels full of dirt onto Jim's exposed face, filling his mouth and nostrils. His ears likewise became clogged, and Jim could only faintly hear Marvin' muffled voice saying, "So long, Jim. It's been nice reminiscing." Then he felt heat all around him, and a new burning pain seemed to scorch every nerve in his body.

/ 8 /

Marvin lay in bed smiling with satisfaction, knowing that he had accomplished his deed successfully without any problems and without leaving any incriminating evidence.

What a great feeling it was to have completed such a noble task. What a great bonus that not only did his victim feel the pain of being impaled on 350 spikes, but he stayed alive long enough to feel the terror of being buried alive and to experience the agony of being burned alive. The utter joy brought a tear to Marvin's eye.

Marvin had remained at the scene, making sure nothing remained of his victim, the pulley system, and the box, except for some charred bones, a few burned screws, and the blackened spikes. Marvin had used his shovel to spread the remains before filling the six-foot-deep hole with loose dirt.

Marvin was happy that he thought to scrape off several inches of sod and topsoil, which he had set off to the side. When he added the sod to the top of the grave and scattered some leaves and twigs around, even he had trouble locating it. Marvin always believed that it paid to be thorough, and he most certainly was that.

He lay staring at the ceiling, waiting for sleep to come. Reviewing the details of this adventure into the realm of homicide made him feel comfortable that he had done a good and untraceable job and that he could and would do it again soon.

Marvin already knew who would be next; he had a list. Mr. Gordon Longmont, his boss on his first job, just made it to the number one position. Longmont had fired Marvin some 45 years earlier, stating that he, Marvin, was as useless as a fart in a windstorm, whatever that was supposed to mean. All Marvin needed to do was devise a suitable scenario for Longmont's demise.

When initially creating his list, Marvin had done his due diligence and learned that Longmont's wife had died a year earlier after losing a battle with cancer that she had been fighting for several years. Since her death, Longmont had sold their Pennsylvania home and moved to a swingers retirement village in Florida, where according to rumors, eighty-year-old Longmont was having the time of his life. The private community was said to be one non-stop drug, alcohol, and sex party. This wasn't a new thing for Longmont, as Marvin had learned that not only had Longmont cheated on his wife often, but he did so while she was lying in her hospice bed, dying.

Marvin wondered what Longmont's wife would think about how her husband was dancing on her grave. It would be great if she could rise from her coffin to confront him. Then, the creative wheels in Marvin's twisted brain began to turn at warp speed.

What if that scum-sucking Longmont awoke to find himself buried alive in a box with his dead wife's decomposing, maggot-infested, stinking remains? That sounded like the start of an exciting plan. Then Marvin recalled seeing the woman's obituary in the newspaper last year. Longmont's wife was buried in a local cemetery three miles from Marvin's house. But Longmont was all the way down in central Florida.

Marvin smiled with knowing pleasure as he turned off his bedside light, which was incandescent and never LED. As the room fell into blackness, Martin chuckled and said, "Road Trip."

IRON BEARD, SCOURGE OF DEAD MAN'S PASS

Author's note: In late 2022, South African author and publisher Christina Engela asked me if I would like to write a sci-fi story for an upcoming anthology about robotic space pirates. Although sci-fi isn't my typical genre for writing, I thought I was up for a challenge. Unfortunately, this was one of those projects that never came to fruition. However, this was my contribution.

/ 1 /

Interstellar travelers and long-haul freighters traveling through the Delta Quadrant, save for a few of the most foolhardy, knew to stay clear of the so-called shortcut vortex slicing perpendicularly through Subsector-37 and was known as Dead Man's Pass. Although it was true that taking that passage could save the traveler a significant amount of time - perhaps as much as thirty segments when compared with taking a long way around Subsector-37 - one had to ask himself, when considering taking the shortcut, was it worth the risk?

Dead Man's Pass had not been given its nickname and reputation frivolously but had earned it in blood and death. Although physically located within Subsector-37, a miscalculation in the galactic juris-dictional assignment map caused the passage to fall outside the law enforcement responsibility of either the Subsector-37 police or the larger Delta Quadrant troopers. The faux pas resulted in a jurisdictional battle tying up the Galactic Tribunal for the past decade and creating a lawless area.

It didn't take long for criminal types to take advantage of the lack of law enforcement in the passage. Initially, many criminals operated under the radar within the shortcut and managed to keep their real identities secret. One such mysterious character was a particularly ruthless individual named Doctor Na-tan VonSlag. He was a technological genius who secretly created an army of automatons he called the Scurvy Scoundrels.

VonSlag had been an expert in ancient Earth history, having been obsessed with the subject. He studied that era for decades and had derived the Scoundrels' name as a homage to the pirates of old. His army has driven off or killed all other pirates trying to claim their fortune in Dead Man's Pass. Although VonSlag was frail, sickly, and confined to a nuclear-powered ultra chair, he had always fantasized about being a swashbuckling space pirate, robbing and plundering the galaxy.

Now, through his robotic Scoundrels, VonSlag could vicariously live the murderous life he always dreamed of from the safety and anonymity of his Sector-10 laboratory. As far as the public knew, Dr. VonSlag was a harmless, handicapped, slightly eccentric, genius professor of automation at Sonatronix Institute of Advanced Technology.

What they never suspected, however, was that he owned a multi-storied factory building off campus or that he secretly controlled an entire army of deadly robot pirates through the use of the neurological cyber-interface technology he developed. The system worked because VonSlag's brain connected directly to the operating system of the leader of the Scurvy Scoundrels through a cerebral neural cyber link. This meant VonSlag essentially became one with this robotic leader. Then, once linked with the master machine, VonSlag could control the rest of the robotic pirates. This leader was a gigantic mecha-physical monstrosity feared throughout the galaxy and known as Iron Beard.

Although the nickname for the creature was a misnomer, the name stuck. In reality, Iron Beard was constructed of Naplomium steel.

Initially, VonSlag was unhappy with the name the public had given his robot, but after a while, he realized it was probably a more terrifying name than its actual designation of RX-37KB12. So eventually, VonSlag started referring to his murderous monster as Iron Beard.

The robotic unit stood over twenty feet tall and resembled a black and shining silver version of a seventeenth-century Earth pirate, complete with thigh-high boots, a puffy-sleeved shirt, vest, and wide-brimmed pirate hat. The robot even had a patch over one eye socket, although the monster was equipped with state-of-the-art optics in both eyes, unencumbered by the false eye covering.

The name Iron Beard came from the robot's long and full, 3D printed, then expertly-machined beard that looked as real as any living beard but whose edges and bristles were actually razor-sharp steel blades, which had been responsible for killing hundreds of unsuspecting victims. Although Iron Beard was equipped with various equally deadly weapons, such as knives and swords, VonSlag preferred to use the robot's beard to kill his prey. This was because after slitting their throats with his bearded blades, VonSlag could watch a video feed of his murderous exploits. He loved holding his victims with Iron Beard's massive hands and watching the light of life leave their eyes up close and personal. In VonSlag's sick and twisted brain, this brought him more pleasure than all the riches his robot pirates collected.

For the past decade, while the Galactic Tribunal argued and debated who had the right to police the passage, Iron Beard and his band of pirates terrorized Dead Man's Pass, and hundreds of people died while VonSlag laughed and got richer.

/ 2 /

"If I may be so bold, what in the name of all that's technical are you suggesting, Captain?" First Officer Bran Blaze asked incredulously, "Taking that shortcut through Dead Man's Pass is suicide!"

Deacon Shondo was captain of an independent interstellar freight hauling company operating under the name The Shondo-Go Transport Company. Captain Shondo was a big, muscular, good-natured, but no-nonsense boss who demanded and earned the respect of his crew. He ran his company like a well-honed military troupe. He was not one to turn away from any challenge, no matter how risky it might be. During the eighteen years since Shondo had first formed his company, he had never started a fight but had ended more than he or anyone else could remember.

Shondo had a long, thick, dark mane pulled back into a ponytail and sported a bushy mustache and full beard. He had charisma to spare with large, piercing blue eyes and a smile befitting any twenty-sixth-century vid-star. He wore two large platinum hoop earrings in each ear and could have passed for any swashbuckling pirate from ancient Earth history himself. The variety of Death's head tattoos adorning his bulging arms further enhanced that look.

Shondo gave his First Officer his special mischievous grin and said, "Honestly, Bran, suicide? Don't you think you might be exaggerating just a bit, my old friend?"

Although not as tall as his captain, the stocky first officer was every bit as muscular and then some. He kept his tattooed head shaved smooth and had a thick Fu Manchu mustache and goatee. He had three gold hoop earrings in each ear and, like his captain, might also be mistaken for a pirate.

Blaze replied, "Not even in the slightest, Captain. I've heard tales about bands of indestructible robot pirates, built to resemble 17th-century Earth pirates, that patrol the passage, capturing freight haulers and then torturing and slaughtering their crews. These vile creations are said to be led by a giant monster called Iron Beard. He is often referred to as the Scourge of Dead Man's Pass. People say he shows no mercy to his captors and takes pleasure in using his razor-sharp beard to slit his victims' throats and watch them slowly die."

Shondo smiled his killer smile and replied, "Well, now. This Iron Beard character doesn't sound like a very likable old dog, does he?"

Blaze said to his friend in a quiet, conspiratorial voice, "I know it's your nature to be a bit cavalier when it comes to danger, Deak. But you need to think about your crew. I'd wager that every one of them has heard similar tales about Iron Beard. I know they respect you and your decisions, but asking them to risk falling into the hands of a murderous maniac like Iron Beard and his mechanized minions might be more than they would be willing to do."

"Are you suggesting that you or my crew would go against me in this endeavor, Bran?"

"Of course not, Captain. You are both my captain and my long-time friend. I hope you know I would follow you right through the fiery gates of Mor-gor-on if that's what you needed of me."

"And the rest of my crew? What of them, my friend?"

Blaze hesitated for a moment, then said, "Some may question your decision, but in the end, I believe they will follow you as well. That's the reason I have expressed my concern. It's not just your life and my life hanging in the balance, but our entire crew."

"We have all faced death together many times before. Is that not true, First Officer Blaze?"

Blaze knew when Shondo addressed him as he had, calling him First Officer, his mind had been made up, and any further discussion was irrelevant. Blaze said, "Aye, aye, Captain. When shall I prepare the crew to enter the pass?"

"Have them ready to move by 13 hundred sectars and have them activate all battle stations. If we're lucky, we'll be through the pass before this Iron Beard character even knows we've entered. It's also possible he might not be interested in our little sub-class cargo hauler. But if he does, by Godd-Wonn, we'll give him and his walking tin cans a fight like they've never experienced before. Prepare thrusters and plot a course through the center of the pass at maximum speed."

"Aye, aye, Captain. By your command, we'll be ready to proceed by 13 hundred sectars."

/ 3 /

Na-tan VonSlag sat in his ultra chair, bored to tears, staring at a wall of more than a dozen large-screen computer monitors, hoping for some opportunity to send his army of pirates to battle. But each monitor showed nothing save for the vast emptiness of Dead Man's Pass. He supposed he should have expected as much by now. His robot pirates had been building quite the reputation over time, and VonSlag should have assumed the result would be much less traffic through the pass. Yet, he never expected it to dry up completely.

He realized it had been many segments, perhaps even several parcels since VonSlag had the opportunity to put his mechanized marauders to work. They presently remained in standby mode, hidden within the passage at two locations. The first vessel, which held several dozen robots, was located near the front of the pass and acted as the rear flank attack ship used to drive the unsuspecting travelers toward the second vessel situated at the opposite end of the passage. That ship was essentially a duplicate of the first with an equal complement of pirates. Both crafts were hidden in pockets on the sides of the pass, invisible to all ships until they attacked. Because they were identical, the two vessels changed responsibilities depending on which direction the transport ship traveled through the passage.

Both ships were well armed, sufficiently enough to stop any civilian transport vessels and disable them for boarding. During the time the Scurvy Scoundrels had been terrorizing Dead Man's Pass, Dr. VonSlag never lost a single robot. Even the biggest and best-equipped haulers found out too late they were no match for the pirates. As obvious as the cliche may sound, the Scoundrels operated like a well-oiled machine.

Once the target ship was immobilized, the robot pirates would board the vessel, kill anyone offering any resistance, no matter how small, and then capture those who gave up peacefully. These captures were transported to a third vessel, twice the size of the previous two, hidden at the center of the pass. Unfortunately, they didn't know this huge ship was home to the dreaded Iron Beard.

The captors believed by surrendering, they would be given mercy. They were not. In fact, they weren't even given the gift of a quick, peaceful death. Instead, many were thrown into cages like animals, where they either starved to death, died of thirst, or eventually turned on each other, fought, and died. Those who survived often fed on the flesh and drank the blood of their dead comrades rather than face such a death. Other even less fortunate fell victim to VonSlag's savage, brutal death games he played and carried out through the robotic mega-monster Iron Beard.

/ 4 /

"We're entering Dead Man's Pass, Captain," First Officer Bran Blaze announced, perhaps a bit too loudly and with more apprehension than he should have.

Captain Deacon Shondo admonished, "Perhaps, First Officer Blaze, we should call the passage by its true name. I think that might be more appropriate, don't you agree."

"Aye, aye, Captain. As you command. We are entering the Sub-sector-37 vortex. All battle stations have been made ready, and thrusters are set for maximum speed, Sir."

"Very good, Mr. Blaze. Have all battle stations been equipped with the new weapons I had loaded when we refueled at Rii-Jor 3?"

"Yes, Captain, they have been put in place and are ready to go," Then Blaze said quietly, "I've never seen weapons quite like those before. What in Godd-Wonn's name are those things?"

The captain smiled and said, "All in good time, Bran, my friend. All in good time."

"It's just that you know how I feel about bringing untested armaments onto a starship and placed into the hands of men who have never used them before. The crew has absolutely no idea what the weapons do. You have to admit, Captain, this sort of need-to-know may work fine when it comes to company secrets, but a little training goes a long way when it comes to defensive weaponry."

"Point taken, Mr. Blaze. However, fortunately for us, such extensive training will be unnecessary with these armaments. Here are all the instructions you will need to pass on to the crew. Tell them to point in the general vicinity of their target and pull the trigger."

Blaze questioned, "Begging the Captain's pardon, but isn't that being a bit flippant?"

"Perhaps so, Bran, my friend. But you know I tend to be a positive and confident sort of fellow. As such, I'm confident our crew will have no trouble using these weapons and feel positive about a successful outcome."

Blaze swallowed hard, released a sigh, and said, "I most certainly hope you're right about that, Captain."

Suddenly, a lookout at the rear of the spacecraft signaled a red alert and shouted over the monitor, "Enemy ship approaching from the rear."

/ 5 /

VonSlag donned the lightweight headset he used to interface with Iron Beard and the other robots. He linked with Iron Beard and began the neural connection process.

Once connected, he said, "Iron Beard, please give a status report."

A monotone computerized voice replied, "Good evening, Dr. Von-Slag. The Sub-sector-47 passage remains empty. No sign of any traffic."

"What do the border ships report, Iron Beard?"

The communication unit went silent for about 15 seconds, and then Iron Beard said, "Both spacecraft report no movement within Sub-sector-47 passage, Doctor."

VonSlag asked, "Doesn't that seem a bit strange to you, Iron Beard, that there is no traffic at all."

Iron Beard replied, "Although I am insufficiently programmed to understand feelings like 'strange,' I can logically assume that as our reputation spreads throughout the galaxy, fewer people will want to risk coming through the passage and falling into our hands."

"Too bad, my mechanized minion. I so love to hear them scream as you slice through their flesh."

"I am pleased you are satisfied with my design, and it is my responsibility to ensure that satisfaction."

VonSlag said, "Now if we could only find some trader vessels to rob and plunder, we'd be in business."

Suddenly, Iron Beard went silent for a few seconds. VonSlag was about to ask him to report when the robot said, "Dr. VonSlag. Our entry warship has spotted a small freighter entering Sub-sector-37, traveling at an extremely high speed."

"I see what's happening here," VonSlag said, "The captain of this ship obviously thinks himself cleverer than he really is. The inexperienced idiot assumes the speed he travels and the small size of his ship will allow him to pass unnoticed. Oh yes, Godd-Wonn does love a fool, and this captain most definitely qualifies."

Within a micro-sector, the first ship pursued the cargo vessel while the second blocked the vortex's exit. VonSlag believed this would be one of the easiest captures his robot pirates had ever made.

"Iron Beard, command my pirates to keep the number of kills to a minimum." VonSlag was starving for an opportunity to torture and kill as many victims as possible, as he had just come through a major murder dry spell. He especially enjoyed watching a hapless human soil himself and tremble with terror when brought before the colossal Iron Beard.

Although to any onlookers, VonSlag appeared to be resting in his recliner with his strange headset and bank of video monitors, not only was he linking with Iron Beard, but he was coordinating the robot's ability to send and receive data from more than two dozen robot pirates. This was no easy task, as it required incredible concentration and the ability to multitask to the extreme. Even though using the Iron Beard unit as a buffer helped to reduce these activities significantly, it was still a demanding challenge. Sweat beaded on VonSlag's forehead and trickled down his temples as he struggled to lead his pirates into battle.

/ 6 /

First Officer Blaze said, "More trouble, Captain. The ship at our stern is gaining on us. Within a few sectars, we will be within Magno-beam range. To make matters worse, a second vessel of equal size is approaching from our bow. They have us trapped, Sir. Shall I command a retaliatory strike?"

"Not just yet, First Officer Blaze. But have the men stand ready with their fingers on the trigger and await my command. Tell them it will be essential that everyone fires as simultaneously as is humanely possible, not before and certainly not after."

The space hauler suddenly felt a tug from the stern, and as the ship slowed, the crew was tossed about. Some crew members were knocked off their feet but regained their footing while maintaining most of their dignity.

Blaze shouted, "Captain! The stern spacecraft . . ."

"Yes, yes, I know, Mr. Blaze, the stern ship has locked onto us with his Magno-beam," Shondo interrupted.

"Shall I give the order to . . ."

Shondo smiled knowingly, then replied, "No, not just yet, my friend; we still haven't been locked onto by the vessel at our bow. Is that not correct?"

"Yes, Captain, that is absolutely correct. But do you think it's wise for us to wait?"

"Most assuredly, Mr. Blaze. In fact, it's not only wise but also necessary," Shondo said. "Do you trust me, Bran?"

"Of course, Deacon. I would trust you with my life."

"That's certainly good to hear since that's the exact situation we now find ourselves in. My life, your life, and our crew all rely on trusting me to make the right play. I promise you, Bran, that trust will not have been in vain."

Another jarring jolt knocked several crew members off their feet again as the spacecraft came to a screeching halt. An announcement came from the ship's bow: "Captain, the second enemy vessel on our bow has just engaged their Magno-beam. All motion has been suspended."

"Thank you, Mr. Blaze."

"Oh, and Captain, a third, much larger vessel has just approached on our port side."

"Very good, Mr. Blaze. I assume the pirates will be contacting us shortly. Maintain shields, but be ready for defensive maneuvers."

"Aye, aye, Captain."

/ 1 /

"All units prepare to board the transport vessel. Remember, use minimal force and capture as many living prisoners as possible," Iron Beard commanded.

VonSlag was anticipating the pleasure he would have when he tortured and murdered every crew member. Perhaps he would take the stupid captain first and make the crew watch while he had Iron Beard tear the man apart limb by limb. Iron Beard would systematically break each of the man's fingers first, then move on to his toes. Snap, snap, snap.

Then he'd cut off each digit, one by one, while VonSlag listened with ecstasy to each of the captain's screams. Then VonSlag would use Iron Beard's incredible robotic strength to pull both arms and legs out of their sockets and toss them aside like the biological trash they would become.

When the captain was reduced to nothing more than a bleeding torso with a head, Iron Beard would lift the dying man close to his face so VonSlag could watch the razor-sharp beard slit the man's throat and see the light of the man's life blinking out. After the other prisoners watched their captain slaughtered so mercilessly, they would be reduced to helpless, quivering mounds of space jelly, offering no more resistance than a cage of baby Gualafronds.

"Bring me my victims," VonSlag commanded, and the order to attack was passed down through Iron Beard to the robot pirate army. "Prepare to board the freighter."

VonSlag looked at his wall of large video screens, each divided into six smaller screens. Cameras with audio and video were mounted in the optical elements of each pirate and displayed on these smaller screens. As a result, the bank of eight large screens revealed forty-eight camera outputs simultaneously. VonSlag also had a large screen dedicated exclusively to the feed from Iron Beard, so he could watch the robot slaughter his victims on the big screen.

The screens displayed numerous views of the inside of VonSlag's two attack ships as the robot pirates prepared to leave their vessels and travel over to take the captured transport vessel. VonSlag's heart filled with excitement as he anxiously watched the video screens. This was going to be incredible, he was sure.

He turned to the big screen and said, "Iron Beard, hail the captain of the transport ship."

/ 8 /

"Captain, the robot pirates are hailing us," First Officer Blaze reported.

Not appearing the least concerned, Captain Shondo said, "Very good, Mr. Blaze. Let's see what they have to say, but be ready for the signal we discussed."

"Aye, Aye, Captain. Putting it on screen now."

Suddenly, the large monitor at the front of the Captain's bridge was filled with a terrifying sight. A giant robot was displayed sitting in a command chair, looking as menacing as the stories had portrayed him, if not more so. His shiny steel beard seemed to reflect light in every direction. The monster resembled a gigantic, metallic version of a 17th-century Earth pirate. When the robot spoke, it was not in the same computerized monotone voice it used when communicating with VonSlag, but it had a deep, booming, and menacing tone.

Iron Beard said, "Attention, captain on the freighter vessel. Your ship has been captured, and you are helpless. Please activate your communication screen so we can discuss the terms of your surrender face-to-face."

Shondo nodded to his communications officer, a young man of no more than twenty-five named Edmund Ron-Tar, and said, "Activate the video screen, Mr. Ron-Tar, and be sure the audio is activated as well."

Iron Beard leaned slightly forward on the large display as if to get a closer look at the humans on his own display screen and said, "I wish to communicate with the captain of your vessel. I order you to bring him before me."

Shondo stood, walked toward the display, and said, "My name is Deacon Shondo, and I am the captain of this vessel and owner of this transport company. With whom do I have the pleasure of speaking?"

The giant pirate robot boomed, "I am sure you know me, human. I am known as Iron Beard, the scourge of the Dead Man's Pass. Lower your shields and prepare to be boarded. If you do not resist, you will not be harmed. I give you my word."

Shondo slowly shook his head and replied, "Sorry, but the word of a talking soup can means less than nothing to me. However, since I am in a charitable mood today, I am prepared to discuss the terms of your surrender and permanent deactivation and that of your mechanical crew."

At his control chair, VonSlag couldn't believe the audacity of this Shondo character. Two large ships held his small freighter in Magnobeams, and dozens of robotic pirates were about to board his vessel, and the fool could do nothing about it. Yet he had the nerve to suggest the great Iron Beard should surrender? This meant he, Dr. Na-tan Von-Slag, would surrender, and he had no intention of giving in. VonSlag felt he had nothing to lose. It was bad enough that his body had failed him, and he was confined to his miserable ultra chair.

VonSlag would rather die than give up his control of his robot pirates. He couldn't wait to get Iron Beard's claws around Shondo's miserable neck. He had the freighter in his clutches and would make this captain and his crew suffer and die in ways never before imagined. VonSlag knew he would have a tough time holding back his rage to make this buffoon of a captain suffer for a very long time. But he would see it happen.

The giant Iron Beard looked directly at Shondo and bellowed, "You pathetic little worm. Do you think you have any chance of even coming close to stopping me? You have not only sealed your own fate but also forfeited the lives of your crew. I will take great pleasure in tearing you apart, Captain Deacon Shondo."

Shondo turned to his first officer and nodded, mouthing, "Now." Blaze sent a silent signal to every battle station on the ship, which displayed a digital counter. It started at five and counted down to zero when all the ship's protective shields momentarily dropped and all stations fired simultaneously.

/ 9 /

As VonSlag watched, every display screen went black, save for the occasional static crackle and a brief flash of the incredibly white light.

"Iron Beard report. What has happened?" VonSlag shouted. But he received no answer. "Iron Beard, respond; I command you." Still, there was no answer. The screens remained dark.

Suddenly, VonSlag heard a hissing in his headset, and a voice addressed him. It was a voice he recognized, although he had only heard it for the first time a few minutes earlier. It was that annoying and arrogant captain of the freighter. What was his name again? Was it Shindo or Sundo? It was Shondo, Deacon Shondo.

Shondo said, "Hello, Dr. VonSlag."

VonSlag was caught off guard. How could this buffoon know his name?

"It is Dr. Na-tan VonSlag, is it not? No matter. There's no need for you to either confirm or deny your identity. All that matters is that we are aware of who you are. More importantly, I know you control these mechanized pirates and have been all this time."

"B . . . but how? W . . . what?" VonSlag stammered.

Shondo said, "None of that is important now, Doctor. What does matter is that I have essentially fried the brains of your robot pirates, including that pile of scrap metal formerly known as Iron Beard. I used a newly developed electromagnetic pulse weapon to turn their circuits into garbage. It's a great weapon developed by one of your former students."

"A former student?"

"Oh yes. In fact, that same bright student figured out how your robotic neural network operated, then determined it was you who was the brains behind the Iron Beard robot."

VonSlag said, "Only one of my students has had the brains to do such a thing. It seems I have been betrayed by Ger-Don Cordell. Am I right about that, Captain Shondo? Don't bother answering, Captain. I know he was the one, and I'll deal with him in due course."

Shondo interrupted, "None of that matters now, VonSlag. Your pirate army is worthless. They'll eventually be towed to the interstellar recycling center in the Junq-Tar segment."

"So, you think," The Doctor replied, "You may be right about recycling, Captain, but they'll never go anywhere near Jung-Tar."

All the Magno beams suddenly disengaged, and the three ships returned to Dead Man's Pass entrance. VonSlag said, "Well, I suppose you thought you were pretty clever now, didn't you, Captain Deacon Shondo? You may have temporarily beaten my robot pirates, but their vessels are programmed to return to me on my command. Those programs are stored safe from the effects of your attack. When they arrive back here, I will begin the process of repairing them and making them even stronger than before."

Shondo said, "Good luck with that, Doctor. A brigade of Delta Quadrant troopers should be arriving at your secret lab immediately to take you into custody. And when your ships arrive, they'll be confiscated and turned into recycled scrap metal along with your robots. You see, Doctor, I've been working with the authorities from the start. This excursion was a trap to lure you and your robots out into the open so we could test the new weapons on them and end your reign of terror. So, Tell me, Doctor, have the troopers broken down your door yet?"

There was a brief silence, then VonSlag chuckled and said, "I don't know, Captain Shondo. Perhaps they have. You see, it's hard for me to know since I'm not there, and my ships are not heading to that location either. They are programmed to come to another secret laboratory you will never find. And your spineless informant, Ger-Don Cordell, my former student turned trader, knows nothing about its location. This is where I will rebuild my robot pirate army. When they are ready, and my Iron Beard is back operating at full capacity, the first people I'm coming for are you and your spy."

Shondo was stunned into silence. Neither he nor the Delta Quadrant officials had anticipated such an event occurring. Shondo was angry, frustrated, and a bit humiliated by the outcome of this carefully planned operation. How could they have been so arrogant and stupid as to think they could outwit such a criminal genius?

Trying to muster what little bravado he had left, Shondo said, "The Delta Quadrant troopers won't rest until they have you in captivity."

VonSlag said, "You're probably right about that, Shondo. But when they do, there will be a lot fewer of them. Goodbye, Captain Shondo, until we meet again."

The audio feed went dead. Shondo asked, "What did he mean by that? I have a bad feeling about this."

First Officer Blaze was speaking with someone over the subspace emergency communication channels. He looked like he might pass out, vomit, or both.

Shondo shouted, "What is it, Mr. Blaze?" Then, in a much more reassuring voice, he asked, "What's the matter, Bran? Tell me, my friend."

Blaze took a deep breath and delivered the worst news he ever had to convey, "That was Delta Quadrant command, Captain. They wanted me to tell you they stormed VonSlag's hideout, which was abandoned as he said it would be."

"Although that may be bad news, I suppose we'll have to deal with it."

"There's more, Deak. It's a lot worse. They sent in close to 100 troopers to take over the facility."

Shondo said, "Yes, that sounds about right."

"VonSlag blew the place to bits."

"What?" Shondo said disbelievingly.

"There were no survivors, Captain. All the troopers died in the explosion." Blaze's voice cracked when he said, "Almost 100 lives snuffed out in a millisecond. I can't believe it."

"That's what VonSlag meant. Godd-Wonn help us all. He said he'd rebuild his army and come for me. Fine, if that's what he wants, I'll have to be ready for him when he does."

THE TRAVELER

The sun was sinking low in the western sky, and a crescent moon was rising, washing the empty, forsaken roadway with its amber glow. Potholes large enough to destroy a car's suspension tattooed the highway, making driving more hazardous than walking, although walking offered its own special brand of danger.

The wind howled along the barren stretch, whispering like a barely audible voice as if warning listeners of eminent dangers. Perhaps that was a trick of nature or simply the result of wild imaginings. All along the way, occasional houses stood empty, looking like eyeless monsters, their windows long gone, leaving black voids. It seemed as if an all-encompassing gloom shrouded the roadway and permeated every crack, hole, and crevice like a fog of malaise sucking away the very essence of the place.

This realm of misery was a world where dark imaginations roamed free, nightmares lived and flourished like living sentient beings, and the thin vale separating the world of the living and the realm of the dead might be breached. It was where pockets of existence were pale enough to see into that other place, where dead souls wander aimlessly in search of forgotten truths. In some places, the ever-thining film keeping the dead in their eternal prison had ruptured, leaving portals where the damned might crossover, accidentally or otherwise.

A feeling of foreboding filled the lone traveler as he walked along the side of the highway. For all the traffic he had seen that night, the traveler could just as well have walked down the middle of the road. He wore a leather-fringed vest over a blue and white paisley print shirt. His bell-bottom jeans were tattered and worn and appeared to be held together in places by various sewn-on patches. On his bare feet, the traveler wore leather sandals, "Jesus sneakers," they were often called. His Brown hair was shoulder length, parted in the center, and sported a braided leather headband.

The traveler didn't appear to be walking with any plan or destination in mind, but he simply put one foot in front of the other, trudging onward along the desolate highway. The dead Autumn leaves crunching underfoot sounded like the cracking bones of a thousand tiny creatures, echoing through the emptiness of the quiet night, their cries long since silenced in death.

Up ahead, moon shadows frolicked on the crumbling walls of a dilapidated cottage, their contorted forms appearing ethereal yet simultaneously perverse and threatening. It apparently was late, and the traveler had no idea where he was. All he knew was he needed to find somewhere to spend the night. It felt like a storm was on the way, and when it arrived, the traveler wanted to be sheltered and out of harm's way. He couldn't recall why this was important, but he knew it was.

He approached the abandoned cottage and saw the door was standing wide open. He crossed over the threshold and stepped inside. The air was thick with the scent of decay within the battered, wooden structure, mingling with a vile stench of unrecognizable origin. The silence and stillness permeating the place was deafening, but the traveler didn't mind. He was comfortable with quiet as he had grown accustomed to being alone.

The cottage was a single-room structure with no electricity or plumbing. With the front door wide open, enough light filtered into the room for the traveler to examine the place. As he looked around, he saw a fireplace on the far wall, a sofa, a writing desk, and a wooden rocking chair. He suspected the well-worn sofa might have become wet and moldering, perhaps accounting for the foul smell in the place. If he chose to spend the night in this place, he would have to sleep in the wooden rocking chair. It might not be as comfortable as the sofa, but it would be dry. After all, beggars can't be choosers.

The traveler hesitated for a moment to contemplate a sudden revelation. Is that what he was, a beggar? He didn't believe so, yet he wasn't certain. In fact, the traveler suddenly realized he had no idea what his current employment status was or, for that matter, who he was. He was confused, wondering how he could have forgotten his name or what might have caused him to lose his memory. He supposed such things happened to people from time to time.

Perhaps he had fallen and bumped his head, or maybe some illness had resulted in the memory loss. Whatever the cause, the traveler found it all quite disturbing. He was alone in an unfamiliar rundown cottage off a podunk county two-lane in God-only-knows-where.

How did he get there? The traveler tried to recount what events had led him to this strange and foreign place. He found it to be an overwhelming task. He could recall walking somewhere in what seemed like endless blackness that had eventually led him to the desolate highway that brought him to this cottage. But where had he been going? At first, the traveler couldn't remember. Then he suddenly thought about music. Yes, music, that was it. Before he had found himself thrust into that dark place, the traveler had been walking along another road, thumbing his way to some sort of music festival.

Then, all he could recall was walking somewhere in the seemingly endless dark. At this place, in his recollection, he seemed to have a blank spot and was missing much, but from what little the traveler could recall, there had been a sudden and strange sensation that he had felt coursing through his body. He had first felt lightheaded as if he might pass out. Then he felt like his body was disassembling, breaking down into billions of particles, becoming unsolid, without substance until he finally seemed to pass through something.

The traveler awoke and found himself trudging along that lonesome, unfamiliar highway, unaware of who he was, where he was, or how he had gotten there. In the abandoned cottage, the traveler approached the fireplace and found several heavy, cylindrical decorative candles burning on the mantle. Who had lit the candles? He saw no matches anywhere, yet the candles burned brightly. He watched the flame shadows dance on the cottage walls, creating a spectral ballet.

He walked over to the desk and found a tablet and pencil resting on a mildew-stained desk blotter. In the dancing shadows, he saw a message printed across the top of the pad. It said, "2001 Memos." That felt wrong to the traveler. Despite his confusion and lack of memory, he felt certain of one thing: the year couldn't possibly be 2001. As far as the traveler could recall, it couldn't be any later than 1969. He didn't know why, but 1969 seemed right, but it did. And 2001 seemed very wrong. Judging by the condition of the notepad, it probably had been sitting on that desk for years, perhaps decades, which meant if the printed date had been accurate, the actual year could be 2010 or 2020.

The traveler thought for a moment, then remembered something else. Some dates and a name suddenly popped into his mind. The dates were August 15th through August 18th, 1969. The name he remembered was something called "The Aquarian Exposition." It was billed as three days of Peace and Music. But it also had another name; he just couldn't recall it. So, it was likely that he had not attended it. Perhaps as he was on his way there, he had somehow been transported first to the dark world and then to this bizarre place and equally strange time.

But that was too weird an idea for him to comprehend. It was the stuff of science fiction. The idea of him walking along a roadway in 1969 and now finding himself in 2001 or later was ridiculous. Besides, what purpose would such a transfer serve? As best as the traveler could recall, he was no one special, just a guy thumbing a ride to a rock concert. Rock concert? Yes, that was it! The musical event he was heading to was called . . . he almost had the name. He was so close, but as they say, "no cigar."

He stood silently, staring down at the desk calendar, hoping something would stimulate his memory and help him solve the mystery that had brought him to this strange place. He looked through the still-open front door and into the dark woods beyond.

"Woods," he thought. Then, a single word appeared in his mind, "Woodstock." That was it. That was the name of the music festival he had been trying to get to. It was to take place in upstate New York and was expected to attract thousands of music lovers. But that was where, once again, his memories ceased.

But why did the desk calendar say 2001? None of this made any sense. The traveler wondered if the year wasn't 1969 and was actually 2001 or later, then had he somehow been transported through time to this future year? That was ridiculous. Time travel was not only impossible, but the very idea created the opportunity for so many paradoxes that it wasn't worth considering.

Obviously, that desk calendar was someone's idea of a practical joke. Wasn't there a sci-fi movie called "2001, A Space Odyssey" released a year earlier, in 1968? Yeah, that was right. The traveler never got to see the movie, but he recalled all the hype and publicity surrounding the film. The calendar was probably some gag someone put here. It was more likely that it wasn't 2001 but still 1969.

The traveler tried to remember more about what had happened on his walk along the empty road to Woodstock. He suddenly remembered a significant difference between that road and the one he had just traveled. The road to Woodstock was not desolate and barren of people; quite the opposite. That concert was supposed to be a major event, and the road was packed with cars and pedestrians all working their way to a concert that would be like no other. Rumors said the event would be epic and history-making. The traveler recalled the traffic being so congested that it was a wonder someone like himself, walking along the side of the road, hadn't been struck and killed.

Then, the memories suddenly came flooding back to him like a tsunami. He had been walking along the side of the road, wearing the same clothes he now wore. He hadn't been paying attention to the traffic, as he felt the effects of some premo grass he had been smoking. Then he recalled something slamming into him and his flying through the air and falling to the ground. His head hit the ground, and for a moment, he felt excruciating pain in his head, then everything went black.

After that, he awoke and began walking somewhere in complete darkness. It wasn't like the road in this place but somewhere so dark he couldn't see a thing. The traveler remembered walking aimlessly with no recollection of time passing. He might have walked for hours, days, or years; he had no idea. He had even forgotten who he was and how he had found himself in such a horrible nothingness. Then, he had seen a faint light somewhere ahead in the blackness.

The traveler approached the dim light and saw it was a doorway through which he could see a roadway in the moonlight with no people or cars in sight. He pressed his hand against the space and felt a thin membrane that allowed his hand to pass through. Before he realized what he was doing, the traveler stepped through the doorway and began walking along the side of the desolate highway.

He now believed he knew what had happened. He must have been struck by some vehicle and died that day in 1969 and had ended up in the void existing somewhere between death and whatever comes afterward. Then, somehow, he passed into what appeared to be the world of the living, but many years later. How could that be? Was this his final destination? Was this his Heaven or his Hell? The traveler wasn't sure, but he didn't think so. This was some other place, some inadvertently accidental place.

If he was dead, the traveler was certain he didn't belong here. He realized he had no choice but to find a way to return to that black world, or he would never eventually get the opportunity to pass on to whatever his true and final destination was supposed to be. He believed he was right about his wrongly being in this place; it had to be a mistake, an accident.

The traveler fled the cottage and back out onto the highway. He had to retrace his steps and find where the fabric separating the living world from the dead would allow him to return to the void.

As he walked back in the direction he had come from, the traveler heard the sound of a large truck heading toward him. He didn't have time to get out of the way, and the vehicle bore down on him as if the driver hadn't even seen him.

The rig passed through the traveler as if he were as insubstantial as smoke. He stood on the roadway, staring down at himself in amazement. As the traveler pondered his situation, the moon became hidden by clouds, and the roadway was thrust into near darkness. The traveler saw the dim glow of a light ahead and ran toward it.

When he arrived at the source of the light, the traveler saw what he believed was a familiar glowing passageway. He hoped this was the same membrane he had passed through and the world of darkness he had come from lay just on the other side. For a moment, he was indecisive about whether to stay on this side of the passage and endure all the uncertainties this strange world presented him or pass through and return to the blackness of the world on the other side, which also had an uncertain outcome.

Then the traveler wondered, what if that doorway didn't lead to the previous world he thought of as his home base? What if it wasn't the doorway he originally passed through? What if it took him to another completely different world? What then? He didn't know what awaited him through that portal, but he knew he had no choice but to take the chance.

He pressed his hand against the thin film and felt it passing through. Then, before he realized it, he was on the other side of the portal. This was not the world of darkness but another world with another road. The traveler turned to look back at the passageway only to discover it was gone.

A crescent moon was rising, washing the empty roadway with its amber glow. As the doorway faded from sight, so did the traveler's memory. A feeling of foreboding filled the traveler's mind as he found himself trudging along a lonesome, unfamiliar highway, unaware of who he was, where he was, or how he had gotten there.

He was a traveler and eventually would recall and understand. Then, he would find another weak spot in the fabric of reality, and he would pass through because, unknown to him, he was the traveler and would be traveling for eternity.